MISS KOPP JUST WON'T QUIT

AMY STEWART is the *New York Times* bestselling author of the acclaimed Kopp Sisters series, which began with *Girl Waits with Gun*. Her six nonfiction books include *The Drunken Botanist* and *Wicked Plants*. She and her husband own a bookstore called Eureka Books. She lives in Portland, Oregon. For book club resources, Skype chats, and more, visit www.amystewart.com/bookclubs.

MISS KOPP
JUST WON'T QUIT

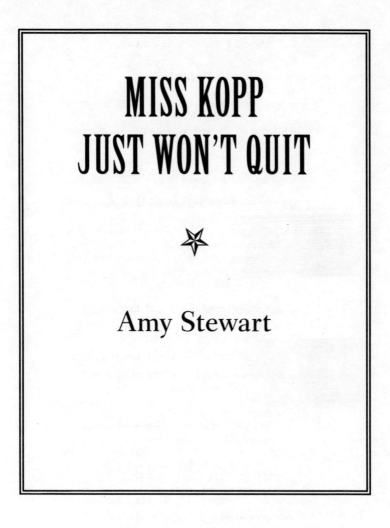

Amy Stewart

SCRIBE

Melbourne • London

Scribe Publications

2 John St, Clerkenwell, London, WC1N 2ES, United
Kingdom
18–20 Edward St, Brunswick, Victoria 3056, Australia

Published by Scribe 2018

Book design by Greta D. Sibley

Printed and bound in the UK by CPI Group (UK) Ltd,
Croydon CR0 4YY

Scribe Publications is committed to the sustainable use
of natural resources and the use of paper products made
responsibly from those resources.

9781911617570 (UK edition)
9781925713411 (Australian edition)
9781925693096 (e-book)

CiP data records for this title are available from the
National Library of Australia and the British Library.

scribepublications.co.uk
scribepublications.com.au

To Nicole Angeloro

❧ 1 ❧

ON THE DAY I took Anna Kayser to the insane asylum, I was first obliged to catch a thief.

I say "obliged" as if it were a hardship, but in fact I enjoy a good chase. A man fleeing a crime scene presents any sworn officer with the rare gift of an easy win. Nothing is more heartening than a solid arrest, made after a little gratifying physical exertion, particularly when the thief is caught in the act and there are no bothersome questions later about a lack of evidence or an unreliable witness.

My duties are hardly ever so straightforward, and my victories rarely so decisive, as Anna Kayser's case would demonstrate. Perhaps this is why the business with the thief lingers so clearly in my memory.

The scene of this particular crime was the Italian butcher where I liked to stop for my lunch. The proprietor, Mr. Giordano, put out a kind of Italian sausage called *salsicciotto* on Tuesdays that he seasoned with salt and peppercorns, then smothered in olive oil for two months, to extraordinary effect. He could sell every last one in an afternoon if he wanted to, but by doling them out on Tuesdays, he found that he could lure people into his shop once a week and make sure they left with all manner of goods imported from Italy: soap, perfume, hard cheese, enameled plates, lemon candy. The profits from those trinkets helped compensate for the cost of shipping over the extravagantly priced olive oil in which he aged the *salsicciotto*. I was but one of many willing participants in his scheme. Along with the sausage I took a bag of lemon candy weekly, finding it useful to dispense during interrogations.

The man ran out of the shop just as I rounded the corner onto Passaic Avenue. Mr. Giordano gave chase, but the thief had the advantage: he was young and trim, while the butcher was a rotund gentleman of advanced age who could do little more than stump along, huffing and shaking his fist.

He would've been out of luck, but there I happened to be, in my uniform, equipped with a gun, handcuffs, and a badge. I did what any officer of the law would do: I tucked my handbag under my arm, gathered my skirts in my hands, and ran him down.

Mr. Giordano heard my boots pounding along behind him on the wooden sidewalk and jumped out of the way. I must've given him a start, because he launched into a coughing fit when he saw who had come to his rescue.

In giving chase, I flew past a livery driver watering his horses, a druggist sweeping out his shop, and a boy of about twelve staring idly into a bookstore window. The boy was too engrossed or slow-witted to step out of the way. I'm sorry to say I shoved him down to the ground, rather roughly. I hated to do it, but children are sturdy and quick to heal. I raced on.

The thief himself hadn't looked back and had no idea who was in pursuit, which was a shame, as men often stumble and lose their resolve when confronted by a lady deputy. I was always happy to use the element of surprise to my advantage. But this one ducked down a side street, deft as you please, no doubt believing that if he stayed on bustling Passaic Avenue, more passers-by would join the chase and he'd soon be caught.

The detour didn't bother me, though. I preferred to go after him on a quiet tree-lined lane, with no more danger of loiterers stumbling into my path. I rounded the corner effortlessly and picked up speed.

He chose for his escape a neighborhood of large and graceful homes that offered very few places to hide. I closed the distance between us and was already looking for a soft patch of grass ahead on which to toss him down, but he saw an opportunity ahead. He'd done this before—I had to credit him that. He hurled himself over a low fence and into a backyard.

Here is where an agile man of slight build has the advantage. I was forced to abandon my handbag and to heft myself over the fence in the most undignified manner. Hems caught on nails, seams split, and stockings were shredded into ribbons. I landed on one knee and knew right away I'd be limping for a week. It occurred to me, at last, to wonder what, exactly, the man had stolen, and if he was really worth catching. If I'd abandoned the chase at that moment, no one—not even Mr. Giordano—would've blamed me.

But no matter, I had to have him. The man stumbled into a backyard populated by placid hens under the supervision of an overworked bantam rooster. He (the man, not the rooster) turned his head just long enough to cast a wistful glance at the chicken coop, which might've offered him a hiding place, a chicken dinner, or both, had I not been thumping along behind him.

The next hurdle was only a low stone wall. He cleared it with a nimble leap, as if he did that sort of thing every day, and he probably did. I tossed one leg over and knocked a few stones loose with the other, but by then I was only five feet behind and saw victory ahead.

It was my great good fortune that the next garden held no chickens or any other sort of hindrance, only a generous expanse of lawn fringed by an inviting bed of chrysanthemums that gave me the soft landing spot I required.

"Oooof" was all he could say when I took him by the collar and tossed him down. I landed on top of him, which was just as well, because his shirt tore when I grabbed him and he might've slipped right out of it and vanished, had I not thrown myself on him.

I didn't say a thing at first, because I'd given that last sprint all I had and wouldn't have lasted a minute more. It took us both a short while to recover ourselves. No one was at home in the house whose garden we'd just trampled: otherwise, the sight of a rather substantially sized woman sprawled atop a slender shop-thief certainly would've brought the entire family out.

Once we were sitting upright, and I had a firm grip on the thief's arm, we sized each other up for the first time. I found myself in possession of a tired-looking factory man, with the blood-shot eyes and glazed aspect of a drunkard.

The thief, for his part, didn't seem particularly surprised to have been caught by a tall lady in a battered gray hat. The business of thievery leads to all sorts of surprises: one must be prepared for novelties. He tried half-heartedly to shrug me off and muttered something in what I took to be Polish. When I refused to let go, he allowed himself to be dragged to his feet. The papery orange petals of the chrysanthemums adhered to us, making us look as though we'd been showered in confetti. I didn't bother to brush them off. The man hadn't yet been handcuffed and was likely to be slippery.

"Let's see what you stole," I proposed. When he only looked at me dejectedly, I yanked open his jacket and found within it a long and slender salami (not the *salsicciotto,* mind you—those were kept behind the counter under Mr. Giordano's watchful eye—but the cheap type that hung in the window and were easy to snatch). He'd also lifted a loaf of bread, now flattened, and a bottle of the yellow Italian spirits that Mr. Giordano sold as a curative.

It wasn't much of a haul, considering the trouble he put me through. I hated to throw a man in jail for stealing his lunch and bore some faint hope that I might return him to the shopkeeper and negotiate a truce.

"What's your name?" I asked (sternly, one had to be stern).

He spat on the ground, which was every habitual criminal's idea of how to ignore a question put to him by the law.

"Well, you made an awful lot of trouble." I slipped the handcuffs from my belt and bound his wrists behind his back. "Try to work up a convincing apology before we get there."

The man seemed to take my meaning and perhaps had some idea that I might be trying to help him, as much as any officer could. He had a resignation about him that suggested he'd done all this before. He walked limply alongside me, with his head down. For a man who gave such a spirited chase, he was as soft as a bundle of rags under my grip.

I retrieved my handbag at the edge of the fence and in a few minutes we were back at the shop. Mr. Giordano was sitting outside on an overturned barrel with the anticipation of a man waiting along a parade route. When we rounded the corner, he jumped up, beaming, and clapped his hands together. He was very pleasant-looking: old Italian men always are. His eyes gleamed, his cheeks were ruddy, and he grinned with unabashed delight at the prospect of a good story to tell over the dinner table that night.

Then came the words I'd been hoping not to hear.

"He took from me before! He steal anything I have. Egg, butter, shoe, soap, tin plate, button." Mr. Giordano ticked the items off with his stubby fingers.

It made for quite a list, but I didn't doubt it. The shop was overfull of small merchandise, easy to pocket.

"He stole needful things, then," I offered, hoping to play to his sympathies.

"Needful! I only sell needful things! Look down his pants. Black shoes for little girl."

It hardly need be said that I had no wish to look down his pants and was grateful to the thief for sparing us both the indignity. He appeared well-versed in the universal language of accusative shopkeepers, and shook his trousers as vigorously as he could considering that both his wrists were cuffed together. It was enough to make the shoes—tiny darling shoes of a sort rarely seen in Hackensack—fall from his trousers.

The shopkeeper snatched them up triumphantly, and rummaged through the man's pockets for the rest of his stolen goods. He looked disgusted over the condition of the loaf of bread, but set the salami carefully aside for resale and tucked the bottle of liquor into his apron.

Then he poked at my badge, which happens more often than one might think. People seem to feel they have a right to put their fingers all over a deputy's star, as if they own it.

"Sheriff?" he asked. "Sheriff Heath? Go tell him. He knows this one." Then he pushed his finger into the thief's chest. I had to step between them before all this poking escalated to fisticuffs.

With the likelihood of a peaceful settlement ever more remote, I said, "Mr. Giordano, are you quite sure this is the man who stole from you before? Couldn't it have been someone else? These thieves move awfully fast and it's hard to get a good look at them."

Mr. Giordano stuck his chin out defiantly. "No. It is him. Go to his house. Look for tin plates with painted roses. Look for sewing box with Giordano label. My wife!"

The effrontery of the theft of Mrs. Giordano's sewing kit was too much for even the man who did it, for he, too, turned shamefacedly away.

"He take money, too, but you won't find that," the shopkeeper said. "All gone."

That changed things. Money made it a more serious crime.

"Have you reported him to the police?" I asked.

Mr. Giordano nodded vigorously. "I report, I report, I report. Ask the sheriff."

What could I do, then, but to take him to jail? I turned out the man's shirt pockets for good measure and found a package of handkerchiefs with the Giordano ribbon still attached. If he had anything else tucked away, it would fall to the male guards to find it.

"I'm sorry, Mr. Giordano, and this man is sorry too," I offered. The thief didn't respond to a firm shake of the arm, so I tapped him under the chin and made him raise his eyes.

"Zorry," the thief said.

Mr. Giordano spat on the sidewalk. "Poles."

⊰ 2 ⊱

THE COUNTY JAIL sat alongside the courthouse, which meant that I was obliged to march my thief past the gaggle of reporters who congregated on the steps when court wasn't in session. It was an intemperate afternoon for late September, so the men huddled in a tight circle, shivering in their summer-weight suits, hands clamped on top of their hats against a frolicsome wind. Upon seeing that I had a man in my custody, they chased after me, waving their notebooks, shouting some version of my name in a newsmen's chorus.

"Miss Kopp!"

"Miss Deputy!"

"Police-lady!"

No one knew what to call me. Only one of them addressed me as Deputy Kopp, but he spoiled it right away with his inane questions.

"What'd this poor gent do, Deputy Kopp? Ask you to marry him? Did he get down on one knee?"

I wheeled around to face them, but I allowed the man in my custody to keep his back turned. "You know better. The man hasn't even been booked."

8

"Did you make that arrest all by yourself?" called a squat older man in the rumpled tweed characteristic of his profession.

"Do they allow lady officers to arrest a man?" shouted another.

"How'd you manage to catch a fellow?" asked a third, but he was laughed down by the others. Anyone could see that I towered over the man in my custody.

"If I failed to catch a man in the act of committing a crime, then you'd have a story to write," I told them. "The story would be that I wasn't capable of doing the job. I'm sorry to have deprived you of your column inches, but if you're in need of wrongdoing to write up for the evening edition, go sniff around the prosecutor's office."

That won me a round of laughter and a good-natured farewell. The prosecutor's office, housed in the courthouse next to the jail, maintained a long-standing feud with Sheriff Heath, made worse by the fact that Detective Courter of that office was running for sheriff. I was feeling just bold enough to remind them of it.

Only one reporter stayed behind. I recognized him from the *Hackensack Republican* pass tucked in the brim of his bowler. "I don't give a hill of beans about what the old sheriff thinks," he said. "What I want to know is what the new sheriff's going to say when a girl cop goes around dragging men off to jail."

I was at least able to take a little satisfaction from closing the door in his face.

The campaign season of 1916 had only just begun in earnest. Sheriff Heath was running, somewhat reluctantly, for a seat in Congress. It hadn't been his choice to step down as sheriff. The law in New Jersey prevented a sheriff from succeeding himself in office, which meant that he couldn't run for his office again until someone else had occupied it for at least one term. The local party officials had put him up for the legislature instead.

If Sheriff Heath had an appetite for serving in Congress, he didn't show it. He was a born lawman, happiest when he had a house robber to chase through the woods or a jewel-theft ring to break up. He ran the jail with efficiency, fairness, compassion, and even, believe it or not, conviviality. He appreciated the company of criminals, as long as they were behind bars. As such, he seemed to genuinely enjoy running a county jail.

His wife, Cordelia, was another matter. Any woman would hate living in the cramped sheriff's apartment on the ground floor of the jail: she couldn't be faulted for that. But it was also painfully obvious that her ambitions exceeded those of her husband's, and always had. She aspired to a wallpapered parlor in Washington and a dinner table set for ambassadors and judges. Mrs. Heath longed to be a legislator's wife, and considered it a deficiency in her husband's character that he was not yet elected to the office that she expected of him. As such, she'd taken a far greater interest in the election than he had, and ran his campaign with spirit and vigor.

I should explain who, exactly, was to become the next sheriff of Bergen County. I hadn't yet met the man, so at that moment I was wondering about him myself. His name was William Conklin. He'd served as sheriff before, and in fact had hired Sheriff Heath as a deputy in 1910. I'd been told to expect someone older and more experienced (Sheriff Heath and I were both nearing forty, while Mr. Conklin was of our fathers' generation), but I also believed he would share, more or less, in Sheriff Heath's ideas about the running of the jail. They were both of the Democratic Party, and one had trained and taught the other.

William Conklin was not running unopposed. As I have said, the Republican candidate for sheriff was John Courter, a detective in the county prosecutor's office, where he made it his business to oppose Sheriff Heath's programs generally and to thwart my efforts to carry out my duties in particular.

His campaign was something of a farce. He had little to say about how he thought the jail ought to be run or how the business of the sheriff's office ought to be conducted, and instead went around raising false flags and making inflammatory speeches on subjects that had little to do with the actual obligations of the office he sought.

There was no real contest between the two. A sheriff must show restraint and dignity, keep a cool head, and avoid rushing to judgment. Sheriff Heath won his election because he demonstrated those very qualities, and everyone, even the editors of the local papers who were so quick to stir up controversy, agreed that William Conklin would succeed Sheriff Heath in office quietly and capably. The *Hackensack Republican* stood alone in its support of John Courter.

I'd never had much of a reason to follow local elections before. My sister Norma had an opinion about every single man running for office—even the tax assessor could not escape her scrutiny—but I'd always found the whole business dull, and the names and faces interchangeable. What did it matter to me, back in the days when I was merely the eldest of three unmarried women living in the countryside?

Now, though, I was a deputy sheriff, and it mattered a great deal.

I COULD'VE TAKEN my fellow directly to a booking room, but I stopped instead to present him to Sheriff Heath personally, like a cat dropping a mouse at the doorstep. It is irregular to take an inmate to the sheriff's office, but he looked up with interest when he saw us lingering in the corridor.

"What did this one do?" he called from behind his desk. He wore a wide mustache that tended to hide his smile, but I couldn't miss a certain fondness in his expression. He liked to see any deputy make an arrest, but I think he took particular pride in seeing what his lady deputy could do.

"Stole his lunch and quite a bit more from Mr. Giordano."

Sheriff Heath gave a whistle. "And he waited until the Tuesday lunch hour to rob the place? Nobody told him how fond my deputies are of those Italian sausages."

"I'll get him booked," I said, and started to lead him away.

"Hand him off to a guard," Sheriff Heath called. "You're taking a lady to the asylum this afternoon."

That stopped me.

"One of mine?"

He shuffled the papers on his desk. "It's a lady in Rutherford. The judge gave the order this morning. Anna . . ." He found the notice and read it over. "Anna Kayser. Go on upstairs and make your rounds. You're leaving at five."

⊰ 3 ⊱

IT WOULD'VE BEEN improper to ask about Anna Kayser in front of my inmate, so I did as Sheriff Heath instructed and turned my man over to a guard so I could make my rounds. I had charge of the female section at the Hackensack Jail, where at that moment we had in custody a dozen female inmates, if one didn't count Providencia Monafo, an old Italian woman jailed for murder who'd contentedly serving her sentence for over a year and seemed more like a permanent resident than an inmate.

I was a resident of the jail myself: I slept among them, in a cell just like theirs, on most nights of the week, it being too long a journey from Hackensack to our farmhouse in Wyckoff for me to go back and forth every day. I'd made the cell quite comfortable, with a blanket from home, a stack of books, and a comb, brush, and whatever toiletries I might require to keep myself presentable.

I admit, with a certain pride, that I enjoyed a better night's sleep in my jail cell than I ever had at home, in spite of the groans, coughs, murmurs, and occasional tears from the inmates all around me. Here I was in command. I was rewarded not only by my salary, but by the camaraderie of my inmates, who made for lively company and whose fortunes, I hoped, would take a turn for the better under my influence.

Some of my inmates were, in fact, habitual criminals, which meant that they had enjoyed something in the way of an outlaw's career prior to their arrest. Lady criminals tended to possess an independence of spirit that I appreciated, even if I objected to the ways they had put their talents to use. But some were victims of circumstance, forced to act through poverty or desperation.

A grandmother, Harriet Janney, was of the latter type. She came from a prominent family in Newark and was only stirred to criminal action to save her granddaughter, who'd been living with her father in Hackensack. Mrs. Janney sought to return the girl to her daughter (the child's mother), who had run off to Portland, Oregon, under circumstances that remained somewhat murky.

Mrs. Janney fled with her granddaughter to the train station, but that's where they were caught. The father had spotted the pair leaving his house and followed them to the station, picking up a constable along the way and ordering Mrs. Janney arrested. I felt sure she'd be discharged from our jail with little more than a warning, but there had been some delay in putting her before a judge, so she sat in her cell, at the opposite end of the same block occupied by Providencia Monafo.

I put the two of them together because I knew there would be no bickering between them over the light housekeeping duty shared by cell-block mates: daily sweeping and mopping, dusting of the windows and cell bars, and a weekly airing of the bedding. My younger inmates saw it as an indignity that domestic work was to be part of their jail sentence, but older women tended to be resigned to housekeeping and to take it up without a great deal of complaint. When I walked down Mrs. Monafo and Mrs. Janney's cell block, I was pleased to see it mopped and dusted.

"Am I permitted to write a letter to my granddaughter?" Mrs. Janney asked when I stopped at her cell.

"You may write to the girl's father, and hope that he'll pass your message along," I said, "but you should know that the sheriff reads the letters."

Mrs. Janney laughed at that. She was one of those stout and sturdy women who couldn't be intimidated, even by her jailer. She'd lived too long, and seen too much. "I'm not going to plot a conspiracy with her. I only want to wish her a happy birthday. I promised her she'd be in Portland when she turned eight. She must think I've let her down."

"I'm sure her father's explained it in whatever manner he believes best," I said, "but I'll bring you some letter paper tonight."

From her cell, Providencia Monafo made a little snort and said, "Letter from jail? You frighten the girl. Give her nightmares of her grandmother in a jail cell."

Providencia had a way of sounding as if she knew things she couldn't possibly know, including the feverish dreams of an eight-year-old girl.

"Let's give Mrs. Janney time to decide for herself," I proposed, although the poor woman had almost certainly been frightened away from her plan by Providencia's dark prognostications.

I leaned into Providencia's cell and saw that she was content, as always. In her time behind bars she'd accumulated a few decorations, including a bundle of silk flowers and a small painting of a Roman church left behind by another inmate. She didn't read (she couldn't, as far as I knew, and when I offered to teach her, she feigned disinterest) and instead passed her days muttering over solitary games of cards. She didn't bother to make friends, as the other inmates came and went more frequently, but the weeks rolled quietly by and she seemed to appreciate the serenity.

She did have a way of seeing right through me, and it still un-settled me, after all this time. "You polished your buttons," she said when she saw my uniform, which I had labored over that morning. "You're going to be inspected."

I'd been told that the candidate for sheriff on our side, William Conklin, would be dropping by to meet the deputies any day now, but how did Mrs. Monafo know that?

"Maybe I'm the one who's going to make an inspection," I offered.

Providencia eyed me sharply from under her tangle of black hair. "Do the bottom one again."

I looked down and saw it covered in mud from my wrestling match with the Polish thief. I nodded distractedly to Providencia and went on to the next block, where I'd housed three inmates who were all serving time for their association with the men who actually committed the crimes. It is a poor defense for a woman to claim that she was simply caught up in the criminal affairs of her husband or (even worse) some other man. As a result, there wasn't much that I could do for them except to encourage them to find a better path for themselves once they were released.

Their crimes were remarkably similar, which was why I kept them together: they were less likely to inspire in one another fresh ideas.

The first was Grace Faletti. Her husband had taken up with five other men who made their living by holding up pay buggies. Such robberies generally went quite smoothly: the bandits would wait at a crossroads where buggies were forced to roll slowly by. This made it a simple matter to step on board uninvited. One man might hold the gun on the driver while another ransacked his pockets, but generally the gun wasn't even necessary. Drivers of open buggies who carried their fares around in their pockets understood that occasionally they'd be relieved of a day's earnings. They tended to turn the money over with little fanfare.

But a robbery just outside Teaneck had gone wrong, and the driver was shot. The bandits, being none too clever, left the man for dead and ran to their boarding-house, only a mile away, where Grace Faletti waited for them. The men set to quarreling, which delayed their departure, and a pack of bloodhounds led the constables to the boarding-house.

"I tried to tell them" had been Grace's only attempt at a defense. She didn't bother to explain which part of their foolhardy plan she tried to warn them about, but it didn't matter. This was a murder case, and she was to be held as an accessory and witness for the duration. She might not testify against her husband, but she'd certainly be expected to tell what she knew about the others.

Next to her was Ida Smith, and next to Ida was Louise Wilson. The two girls, both eighteen, had gone with two boys in a hired car to New York. The boys (one of whom was Louise's brother) had been drinking all day and were in such a violent temper that they argued with the chauffeur over the charges until all three men were in a fistfight while the automobile careened down the road. The machine ran into a ditch. Its occupants suffered only bruises and scratches, but the boys took it into their heads to rob the chauffeur and run off, dragging the girls, complaining, behind them. The police were convinced that this wasn't the first time the boys had tried a scheme like that, and expected the girls to help build a case against them. So far, Ida and Louise were standing pat.

"Any news of the trial?" Ida asked when she saw me.

"No, but I wouldn't necessarily be told. I thought you were to see a lawyer yesterday."

"My parents were here! I saw them from the window. They

17

spoke to my brother, but they didn't want to talk to me or Ida," Louise said mournfully. "I waited all day to be called down. Finally the guard told me they'd left hours ago. If they had a lawyer with them, I never saw him."

This was why I didn't like to have family members in the same jail together. Although they were kept on different floors and weren't allowed to see each other, matters between them could get complicated quickly. But I didn't want Louise to be overlooked, and felt it incumbent upon her brother to make sure that she was taken care of.

"I'll go to see your brother and find out if there's an attorney on the case," I said.

"What about me?" called Ida.

"You have a letter from your father," I said. "Answer it."

The younger the inmate, the less likely she might be to correspond with her family and own up to her mistakes. I thought it a valuable character-building exercise, and kept a close eye on the letters coming in and going out to make sure that my girls weren't hiding from their relations. They would need them someday— they just didn't know it.

The next two inmates in the female section had each acted alone. An urbane young woman named Nancy Fyfe had been arrested for driving an automobile recklessly while wearing apparel that, in the opinion of the police officer, would distract her attention from driving: a floppy hat, a veil, and a scarf. She shouldn't have been in jail for long over such a minor infraction, but there was some delay in persuading a friend to wire her the money for the fine, so there she sat.

Next to her on the cell block was an actress named Ruth Williams. She'd been arrested for breaking into homes in Fort Lee to steal jewelry and silver. She was found in possession of a diamond bracelet worth fifty dollars that had been reported as stolen to the police, so her conviction was almost certain. She claimed that she was out of work and only broke into houses so that she might have enough to eat, but no judge would be sympathetic to that story. All robbers needed the money.

I had been encouraging Ruth Williams to look into stenography as a more respectable line of work than actress turned house-robber. Ruth was no girl of eighteen with aspirations for the stage: she'd put in her time behind the footlights and looked a bit worn around the edges after so many years in pursuit of success. When she first came in, I praised her for sidestepping the usual traps that a woman in her situation might fall into, namely, that of allowing men to set her up in an apartment or to favor her with just enough jewelry, trinkets, and free dinners to keep her going.

"Oh!" she said, laughing, the first time I ventured into that line of discussion. "I did plenty of that, too, until there were younger and prettier girls to take my place. I might as well try my hand at stenography. I'm starting to look the part."

Since then, she'd applied herself to the courses, and was in fact working her way through a little booklet when I walked into her cell block.

"If I were anywhere but a jail cell," she said, without looking up from her book, "this would be too dull to bother with. But in here, it helps to pass the time. I might learn a little French, if you have a phrase-book."

"Je vous en ramènerai un," I told her, *"et je vous aiderai à pratiquer."*

"You speak so beautifully," called Nancy from the next cell over. "Ruthie only needs enough French to allow her to run off with a Frenchman. Have you a special course for that?"

"We could start with greetings and pleasantries," I offered.

"How do you say, 'Have you a large apartment in Paris, or a small one?'" Ruth asked.

She was one of those women who was graced with bold and beautiful features: enormous eyes, a wide expressive mouth, and high cheekbones. Even in a plain jail uniform, she was beguiling. Ruth was the kind of woman who could make charming inquiries into the nature of a man's real estate holdings and get away with it.

"I believe the custom is to wait for the gentleman to offer that information," I suggested, to the laughter of both of them.

"I've been waiting fifteen years!" Ruth cried. "I'm going to have to ask the questions myself before I rot away."

"You're not rotting," I said, and moved on to the next block, which was occupied entirely by strikers from a shirtwaist factory. I'd been sent to watch over the strike, ostensibly to protect the girls from harassment, but found myself obliged to arrest them instead, for throwing rotten eggs at replacement workers. It was the first time I'd seen anything resembling violence at a labor strike, but I'd been warned by the sheriff to make arrests quickly to send a message. The last thing he wanted was a union riot on his hands.

The girls had only been charged with disturbing the peace, and could've been released if they'd paid their fines. They refused to do so in hopes that public sentiment would turn in their favor if they were kept in jail long enough. I could see no evidence that their tactics were working and expected them to serve out the month.

"Miss Kopp!" one of them called when she saw me.

"Have you any news of the strike? We asked the guard who looked in on us this morning, but he told us to buy a newspaper if we wanted to know."

"But we can't buy a newspaper, because we're locked up in here," said another.

"He was having fun at our expense, you see," said a third.

"Yes, it appears he was," I said. "The strike is over, and I believe your friends have gone back to work."

"Without us?" they cried in a chorus.

"I don't suppose the factory agreed to our demands," said Marie, the eldest and most experienced of the group.

"They did not," I told her. "I'm sorry it went that way for your cause. Are you entirely sure you wouldn't rather pay your fines and be released? Couldn't you do more good out there than in here?"

"Oh, we have work to do right here in this jail. We decided that you should form a union," Marie said, "and we'll help you to organize it."

There was a policemen's union in Hackensack, but the deputies didn't belong to it. "I don't believe anyone has ever seen the need for a union," I said. "Sheriff Heath looks after us."

"There won't always be a Sheriff Heath," said another, ominously.

The girls were a quick study on the inner workings of the jail. I would have to remind the guards to keep their voices down.

"We do just fine," I said.

⇥ 4 ⇤

THE JOURNEY TO deliver Anna Kayser to the insane asylum was delayed by a couple of hours owing to the late arrival of Deputy Morris, who was to drive us.

"It's already dark out," I said to Sheriff Heath that evening. "Couldn't we go tomorrow?"

"It has to be tonight. One of the fellows upstairs was committed this morning, and Judge Stevens ordered him taken away before nightfall. He heard Mrs. Kayser's case right after that. In his wisdom, he ordered them transported together so as to save the taxpayers the cost of running the automobile twice."

"Well, that couldn't be more inconvenient. We'll have to go all the way south to Rutherford, then turn around and drive right past Hackensack on our way up to Morris Plains. All of this with your poor fellow riding along as if he's on some sort of sightseeing tour. What do we know about Mrs. Kayser?"

"Not a thing," the sheriff said. "She's a housewife. I suppose it's the usual trouble. Nervous prostration or the like."

Deputy Morris came around the corner just then, looking a bit ragged. He'd been ill for a week and still had watery eyes and a cough. It was unseasonably cold out, and with the wind came the threat of a storm. His nose was red from having been out in it.

"Ready, Sheriff," he said.

"Go on, then, both of you," Sheriff Heath said. "Morris has the particulars on the woman down in Rutherford. Our fellow won't give you any trouble. He's a lunatic, but he's good company."

"Drive him yourself, then," Deputy Morris said from behind his handkerchief, but the sheriff only waved us away good-naturedly. In the time I'd known him, Sheriff Heath had been shot through the shoulder chasing a robber through the woods, had an elderly inmate die in his arms, and had seen his wife and children threatened by a deranged inmate. A drive to the asylum with a cheerful lunatic and a housewife in custody was, in his opinion, light duty. I could hardly disagree.

Outside, the wind had picked up and a few raindrops splattered down. A guard was waiting alongside the sheriff's wagon. Our cheerful lunatic sat in the back, looking around with the bright expectation of a child about to go on an excursion.

"If you don't mind, I'll have you ride in back with him, miss," Deputy Morris said.

He never could get used to calling me Deputy. Morris was the most senior of Sheriff Heath's men, and my closest friend at the jail. When my family was under attack two years earlier, it was Deputy Morris who most often volunteered to spend the night in our barn waiting for the thugs to return. He'd become a good friend of the family since then. He and his wife even served as surrogate grandparents for Fleurette, as they lived near the music academy where she had, until recently, been a student. Sheriff Heath sent the two of us out whenever he could, and as a result we worked more than our share of cases together.

"I think that's best," I said. "Who is he?"

The deputy bent down and peered at him through the window. "Tony Hajnacka. Nice fellow, but he tried to slash his neck with a broken spoon. That earns him a trip to Morris Plains."

I bent down to get a look at him and saw the bandage around his neck. "Do you mean to say he did that in our custody?"

"Afraid so. I've never seen an inmate do a thing like that with a spoon. He might be a lunatic, but he's no imbecile. He's coming off the drink, too. Look how he twitches."

"I can manage a little twitching." I slid into the back seat alongside Tony.

He jumped and stared at me in surprise. "Are you the queen of this castle?"

Sheriff Heath was right: he'd make for lively company.

"I'm a deputy sheriff just like Morris here, but you can call me whatever you like."

"What I'd like," he mused, "is a nice quiet place in the country and five acres."

"That's just about what you're getting," Morris said.

I didn't like to make light of the lunatic asylum, but Morris had been at this job for a few decades. He knew when to indulge an inmate in his delusions.

It was clear right away that Morris was right: the effects of his craving for drink had not yet left Tony. He had a habit of scratching at his face whenever the idea of liquor came back to him, which it did often. His hands trembled, but he didn't like to see them shaking, so he tended to wring them together or to punch a fist into his palm, which rattled the handcuffs and bothered Deputy Morris.

"Don't let me hear the sound of your fist." Deputy Morris turned around to look at us. "Keep still back there," he told Tony.

"I've done nothing but keep still since I took up with you fellows," Tony said. "I'm a man who likes to roam about. I took a coal train all the way to Denver once."

"Why didn't you stay out there?" I asked.

"They didn't take to me," he said, with a note of wonder in his voice that such a thing might be possible.

I thought it best to keep him happy and distracted, so we carried on in that fashion for some time. It was dark by then, and slow-going into Rutherford on account of the deep ruts in the macadam roads and the intermittent rain. Deputy Morris groaned and muttered to himself as he drove. From time to time a gust of wind hit us broadside, and the wagon's top lifted like a sail. I could tell Morris was having to fight it.

When we rolled into Rutherford and found the street where the woman lived, Deputy Morris brought the automobile to a stop and nodded for me to step out with him.

"I'm going to stay here with Tony," he said when we were standing in the street. He kept a gloved hand over his mouth to fight his cough. "I don't like to think about what he'd get up to if I left him by himself. Mr. Kayser is supposed to be at home, and he can help you if there's any trouble."

I bent down to look at Tony, who was staring at his new surroundings with evident interest.

"That's fine. I've never had trouble arresting a woman. She'll probably go more easily if I'm alone anyway. But are you sure we have the right place?"

Anna Kayser's house was a snug and perfectly groomed cottage, with a neatly trimmed boxwood under the window and freshly painted shutters. Women bound for the lunatic asylum didn't usually live in cheerful, inviting homes.

Deputy Morris looked at the paper Sheriff Heath had given him. "This is the place. Says Kayser right here on the mailbox. They don't all live in shacks."

"I suppose not. Does she know where she's going?"

"She was committed this morning. We should've just kept her

at the jail today, but there was some mix-up at the courthouse and her husband must've taken her home. It's always harder when we have to go get them like this."

"And you don't know what might be the matter with her?"

He shrugged. "Only what the sheriff said. Housewife with a case of nerves."

I wished very much that I'd been told more about this case, but it was too late by then. There was nothing for me to do but to walk up to the porch and rap at the door. It opened right away and I faced a pleasant-looking older man whom I took to be her husband.

"Are you Mr. Kayser? I'm Deputy Kopp, from the sheriff's—"

He put a finger to his lips to silence me, then waved me inside. I didn't like the idea of sneaking up on the woman, but I followed him in.

He led me into a parlor furnished in the most ordinary manner imaginable. There was a green divan and two side chairs to match, a bookcase with a little writing desk built in, and a fire blazing cheerfully in a potbellied stove in the corner. The evening paper was folded neatly on a tray table alongside an ash-tray, and three magazines were arranged in a perfect fan shape on a round table. Atop the mantle was a lamp of pale blue glass painted with leaves and bunches of grapes, alongside photographs in frames that were dusted more often than anything in my house had ever been. From the kitchen came the odor of a steak in a pan, and the familiar sound of a potato peeler in an experienced hand.

How could anyone who kept a house like that belong at Morris Plains? I couldn't help but try to concoct a scenario that might explain it. Perhaps the wife was bedridden, and it was a housekeeper I heard in the kitchen.

But I could tell from the way the man closed a door that led

26

down the hall to the kitchen—silently, stealthily—that my idea was wrong. The lunatic that I was to take away to the asylum was at that moment cooking her husband's dinner.

In a low voice he said, "I'm Charles Kayser. It's my wife you're here to see." He was a perfectly ordinary-looking man, with sandy hair that thinned above his forehead but didn't disappear entirely, and an industrious air about him that suggested that he was in charge of something all day: an office or a shop.

"Is that her in the kitchen?" I asked, trying to sound indifferent about it.

He nodded and pulled a pipe from his pocket.

"She must be remarkably calm about going, if she's cooking dinner first."

He kept his eyes on the pipe, nonchalant. "She doesn't know she's going."

"But I thought she was committed this morning!"

"She didn't see the judge. It was just me and the doctor. She was . . . too unwell to travel." He said it with considerable care, the way one speaks of an invalid.

"She's well enough to run a kitchen."

He just shrugged. I saw no point in arguing with him. "If she doesn't know she's to be sent away, have you made any provision for her going?" I asked. "Has she a suitcase packed?"

"She won't need any of that. The doctor said to let her keep her routine until you folks came for her. Don't give her any time to get worked into a state."

There might've been some logic to that, depending on the circumstances, which at that moment had me entirely mystified. Was I to simply barge into Mrs. Kayser's kitchen and wrestle her away from her potato peeler?

The answer came to me, as it were, in the form of the lunatic herself, swinging the door open, no doubt to tell her husband something about dinner.

There she was: thin, pinched Anna Kayser, with strands of graying hair plastered to her cheeks from the steam, a checkered apron hung round her neck, and a look of horror rising from her pale lips to her colorless eyes.

She took in my uniform, which, apart from the skirt, was nearly identical to that worn by every police officer and deputy in New Jersey. Her eyes stopped on my badge.

I've never seen such terror come over a woman. She put her hands out in front of her as if she couldn't see the way, and turned to run down the hall, back to her kitchen, but her husband was too fast for her. In an instant he had her round the waist, the pipe still upright between his teeth. I could only watch them in astonishment, the backs of them, the form of her dress collapsing under his grasp as if she weren't inside it at all. His legs were anchored around her like fence posts.

"I'm not going! You can't do this!" Her voice rose to a high and nervous pitch.

"Now, Anna." He muttered something in her ear that made her jab him in the gut with an elbow. He must have been expecting that, because he held fast.

He kept whispering. Whatever he said had the effect of draining all the defiance out of her. "Don't send me back there. Don't do it, Charlie. They can't do a thing for me. They never could." She was choking on her words, heaving them out of her throat between sobs.

He said something into the hair at the back of her neck, but it only wound her up again.

"Then what's the matter with me this time? Tell me, tell me to my face, Charlie. Let me hear you say it."

She wrenched herself around to face him, and took another look at me over his shoulder. "Did you think I'd go quietly if you sent a lady to take me? Did you think it would make one damn bit of difference?" Her eyes stayed fixed on me but she jabbed him in the chest.

Mr. Kayser sounded like a father trying to coax a child into taking medicine. "Now, listen to me, dear. Dr. Lipsky agrees. Don't you think he knows what's best for you?"

She wasn't having any of it. "Dr. Lipsky works for you! He says whatever you pay him to say. I won't go."

"Of course you'll go. The sheriff's come for you."

"You carry me out, Charlie. Carry me out into the street, in front of everyone, and show them what kind of a man you are. Go ahead!" She slumped over after that speech, still crying a little, so that her husband was obliged to hold her up.

He turned around to look at me. I like to think I've earned my reputation as a woman of action, but I confess that I was frozen to my spot in the doorway and hadn't any inkling what I ought to do. Mr. Kayser, of course, had a very clear idea about that.

"I won't have to carry you out, Anna," he said. "That's why Miss Kopp is here."

But I wasn't ready to do any such thing. I stood there, perfectly still and hardly breathing, for far longer than I should have. Both Mr. and Mrs. Kayser watched me the way one watches a wild bird or a deer, in absolute silence, waiting to see what it does next.

Our tableau was interrupted when Deputy Morris banged the front door open and came through the sitting room into the little hall. There was a look of weary impatience about him. He brushed right past me and said, with a sort of booming authority that he summoned up in moments like this, "Mrs. Kayser, Deputy

Kopp and I are here to bring you to Morris Plains, for the treatment your doctor ordered."

He obviously thought that I should've been able to utter such words myself, but he hadn't witnessed the scene that just took place. Something was plainly wrong. I just hadn't yet worked out what it was.

I thought that if only I could get Deputy Morris outside, I could tell him what I'd seen. But I couldn't leave the Kaysers alone. Instead, I did my duty and took Anna Kayser firmly by the elbow. Finding herself outnumbered, she went along with me, through the sitting room and to the front door.

Deputy Morris glanced at me over the top of Mrs. Kayser's head. "Haven't you any handcuffs?" He was clearly astonished that I'd failed to drag her out of the house myself. Hadn't I just nabbed a thief that very morning under far more difficult circumstances?

I hated to drag her out in chains in full view of the neighbors. To make it less noticeable, I locked her wrists together in front rather than behind. Mrs. Kayser wore a knobby green sweater that frayed at the wrists. It gave me no pleasure to put metal shackles on her. She looked up at me, sniffing, but I couldn't meet her eyes.

There was a coat rack by the door. I took the sturdiest coat I saw and draped it over her shoulders. From a hat stand I selected a gray narrow-brimmed wool hat better suited to going to church than to a lunatic asylum, and set it on her head.

Mr. Kayser had been hanging back, watching all of this, his pipe between two fingers, just a man waiting for some sort of ordinary business to be concluded before he got on with his evening. When Deputy Morris opened the door, Mr. Kayser turned and went back to the kitchen without saying a word. The sound of plates rattling suggested that he was, in fact, going to sit down to his dinner, before we had even left.

Anna and I exchanged a look of shock and understanding. What man could eat at a time like this?

"You don't have to do this," Anna whispered.

Deputy Morris heard her and said, "Of course she does, ma'am. She's a sworn deputy and she carries out the law. You wouldn't want deputies changing their minds about the law on a whim."

He didn't phrase it like a question, and he didn't wait for an answer. It was a mess outside, with the wind picking up strength and the rain pelting down. There was nothing for us to do but to run out into it. The full and terrible truth of her situation must have come over Mrs. Kayser, because she sobbed as we ran. When she slipped on the brick walkway, she didn't try to get up (nor could she have, with the handcuffs) and I had to yank her to her feet.

I hadn't thought to look at her shoes. She wore a pair of felt slippers with a little wooden heel, suited for working in the kitchen but not for a storm like this one.

"She needs another pair of shoes," I called out to Deputy Morris, who had run ahead to pull Tony Hajnacka out of the back seat so that Anna and I could sit by ourselves.

"It won't matter at the asylum," he said as he hauled a jumpy and confused Tony around and put him in the front seat. He squatted down, groaning over his creaky knees, and wrestled with Tony's handcuffs to get them locked around the front door handle.

I settled Anna into the back seat, but stayed outside to speak to Deputy Morris.

"Something's not right here. She's no lunatic."

He put up a hand to shield the water running off his hat. "Are you telling me she didn't want to go?"

31

"Why, yes, and she also said—"

He opened the back door and gestured for me to get in. "None of them want to go. This isn't for us to decide."

It was impossible to stay out in the rain any longer. I looked back toward the house and saw Charles Kayser watching us from the wide front window, just the silhouette of him with the yellow lamplight behind him. He held a coffee cup in his hand and seemed entirely at ease.

⊰ 5 ⊱

INSIDE THE AUTO, Anna and I were shivering in our wet coats. Morris turned around and said, "Get her under the rug and she'll be warm enough." He sounded a little softer now, but I could see that he was overly tired and anxious about the storm.

I dropped a rug over Anna's lap. She kept her face turned to the window. It was just as well: there was nothing I could say to her with Tony Hajnacka listening. I wasn't about to suggest that an inmate didn't belong at Morris Plains, or that it was within my power to do anything about it. Tony would only insist that he didn't belong there either, and we'd be mired in an argument about it all the way to the asylum.

Instead I sat and brooded over what I'd done. I felt ashamed that I'd dithered so long that Deputy Morris had to come and take charge. I should've seized Mrs. Kayser at once and removed her to some private room to hear her side of things if I felt an explanation was warranted. But Deputy Morris was right: it wasn't our place to question the judge's orders.

Still, I knew perfectly well that lunatics didn't keep clean and comfortable homes and cook regular meals. Sometimes an otherwise sane woman went away for nervous exhaustion, but Mrs.

Kayser didn't seem any more nervous or exhausted than any other housewife—only furious over being committed to the asylum again.

Again? That bothered me the most. How many times had Mrs. Kayser been sent away? I knew that some people stayed at Morris Plains for years, and that some never left at all, but rarely did a person go in and out like a guest at a hotel.

We faced a long and impossibly slow drive north to the asylum. The roads were so dark that Deputy Morris was obliged to lean forward and squint through the glass. The automobile's top was soaked through and dripping. Every few minutes we would hit such a deep rut that a wheel would spin uselessly, making a terrifying sort of whine, and Morris would grunt and mutter something under his breath until he managed to sputter out of it and bounce on down the road. It was a wonder we didn't puncture a tire.

Between the noise and the cold—not to mention whatever torment might've been visited upon Anna Kayser and Tony Hajnacka as they drew ever nearer to Morris Plains—none of us spoke. We rode along in silence for nearly twenty minutes before the automobile ran through a particularly deep puddle that bounced all of us right out of our seats. Tony got knocked to the side and hit his head against the glass. He yelled something incoherent and jerked around, staring wide-eyed at Deputy Morris and then back at me and Anna.

"If you want to throw me out, just do it." He tried to raise his arms but remembered that he couldn't, because they were chained to the door handle, and bent over instead to rub his forehead on his sleeve.

"Nobody's throwing you out. Just be quiet." Deputy Morris coughed and wiped his eyes with a handkerchief. The motor car was barely moving. My harness mare could've carried us to the asylum faster.

"I heard they tie you to the bed at night and you can't so much as scratch your nose," Tony said. There was an agitated rattle in his voice. Whatever good cheer he'd possessed earlier was fast draining away.

"Oh, they do," Anna Kayser volunteered. "You get so stiff, being flat on your back all night."

Tony jerked around in surprise. I put my hand on Anna's shoulder and made what I hoped was a soothing *Shhhhhh*.

"You needn't talk about it," I said.

But Tony couldn't contain himself. He was bouncing up and down in his seat and straining to turn around and see the woman behind him.

"You've been in there already! You know about it! What about the copper baths and the rubber masks, and what about the syrup of mercury and the lighting-wires they put into your ears, and—"

"Yes, they have all of that," Anna said, in the manner of someone describing the furnishings at a dismal boarding-house. "And if you misbehave, there's a room with no windows and nothing but wool batting on the floor, and you'll stay there for days in the dark."

"Oh, I'm likely to misbehave." Tony rocked from side to side. Deputy Morris reached a hand out to throw him back against the seat, and the wheels skidded around on the road and threw us all to one side and then another.

"Damnit!" Morris roared. "Get him under control!"

I leaned forward and grabbed at Tony's coat from behind. I pulled him back against the seat and hissed into his ear. "Mr. Hajnacka, you're to keep very still and let Deputy Morris drive us safely."

But Tony was trembling, and I could tell that he was working himself up to an outburst. He might have done it, except that a gust of wind flew at us broadside. Morris cursed and clutched at the wheel.

Just ahead of us sounded an enormous crack and a tree branch crashed down on the road, the bare sticks screeching against the glass. The tree had the otherworldly presence of a person grasping at us from the darkness. We all shrieked at once as Morris brought the auto to a halt.

It was oddly serene for a moment. The four of us sat in perfect stillness with the wind whistling around and the rain hammering down. In the dark we all turned and looked at one another, then out at the long fingers of the fallen tree before us.

Deputy Morris coughed into a handkerchief and lifted his hat to wipe his forehead. "I'll go see if I can move it."

"Let me help," I said.

"Stay with the inmates." With that he was gone.

Staying with the inmates is never a terrible idea, so I didn't argue over it. The wound around Tony's neck had started to bleed again, with all the jerking back and forth. I leaned across the front seat and dabbed at it with a handkerchief. He didn't fight me.

Deputy Morris vanished into the dark. We could see nothing but a few branches in the glow of the yellow headlamps. I could faintly hear him coughing and swearing, and his boots sliding against the gravel. Finally the branches jerked out of view, a little at a time, and his bent form appeared across the glass. Then he was back inside, shuddering and wheezing.

He sat with his head down in his coat for a minute, and then he said, "These roads are washing out from under us. We're only just now outside of Hackensack. I don't think we'll make it to Morris Plains tonight."

"Do you mean to take me home?" Anna cried, suddenly hopeful.

He coughed again and dabbed at his eyes with his sleeve. "No, ma'am. I mean to take you back to the jail with us. We'll stay the night and try again tomorrow."

"Jail!" Her voice came in a high wail that agitated Tony and set him to rocking back and forth again. "You can't lock me in a jail. I've done nothing wrong."

Morris got the auto moving, and I slid over and put a hand on Anna's arm. "Mrs. Kayser. You're in the sheriff's custody, that's all. No one is accusing you of a crime. But we have to stop somewhere for the night."

"I can't go to jail," she cried. "Couldn't you send for my husband?"

"I'm going to make you very comfortable. We have a ward for the women and I'm in charge of it. It'll be clean and quiet, and there's good steam heat. I'll have a change of clothes for you, and I'll see to it that you get a cup of tea and a sandwich. I'll be in a cell right next to you all night long. You can call out to me and I'll come, no matter the hour."

Anna went a little limp, and I thought I might've settled her down, but Tony only wound himself up further. "Don't believe her! She won't come when you call. They never do. They lock you in a room with a bunk and a toilet and you can pound the bars all you like but no one"—here he rocked back and forth again and hit his head against the window rhythmically with each syllable—"no—one—ev—er—comes."

⇥ 6 ⇤

WE MADE QUITE a fretful and anxious party as we rolled into Hackensack. I suppose all four of us were, by then, suffering from nervous exhaustion in one form or another.

To Anna Kayser, the jail must have looked menacing against the night sky: it had been built to look like a medieval prison, complete with turrets and the kind of narrow windows through which one might lob a cannonball. It could appear rather nightmarish in the dark.

Of course, I was tremendously comforted when the jail's silhouette came into view, because it meant the end of a tiresome day and the prospect of a comfortable night's sleep for me. But I watched Mrs. Kayser wring her hands together, and I knew I'd have quite a job getting her into the jail and settled for the night.

The auto came to a stop in the long driveway that ran between the jail and the river. If the guards had known we were returning with inmates, they would've been watching for us and rushed outside to help. But we weren't expected back until after we'd delivered them to Morris Plains, so no one was waiting.

That wouldn't pose a problem ordinarily, because I could handle my inmate and Deputy Morris his. But here's what people don't understand about our job: unexpected circumstances and small deviations to our normal operations can throw us off course. We try to be prepared for anything, but in our line of work, that's nearly impossible.

Deputy Morris stepped around to open the door for Tony Hajnacka and unchain him from the door handle. I did the same, going around from the back seat to escort Anna Kayser out. For a moment, the four of us were right next to each other in the dark: Deputy Morris fumbling with Tony's chains, and me helping Mrs. Kayser to find her footing on the uneven gravel.

I don't know if Tony saw an opportunity and took it, or if he merely jerked away from Deputy Morris in a spasm of terror and found himself unexpectedly free, but either way, in the middle of that murky and muddy night, the unthinkable happened and our inmate ran off.

I didn't realize in that instant that he'd gone. All I knew was that Morris had slipped or was shoved. When he fell on the slick gravel, he shrieked in pain and somehow managed to pull Mrs. Kayser down with him. I would've gone over, too, as she grabbed at the sleeve of my coat to steady herself, but by then I had spotted Tony running for the river bank. I slithered out of my coat and ran.

As the jail was equipped with so few windows, there was very little light streaming down on us. I could make out just enough of Tony's figure to see that he moved with the uneven, loping gait of someone who hadn't the use of his arms. At least Morris had managed to chain his wrists together before he ran.

He was obviously heading for the river, although I couldn't say for certain whether he did it deliberately, intending to drown himself, or whether he simply couldn't see what was in front of him. Regardless, I shouted for him to stop and he lurched over the embankment anyway.

There was nothing to do but to go in after him. I tried to tear a few buttons off my heavy outer skirt, but they were so carefully stitched, owing to Fleurette's handiwork, that I couldn't rip a single one loose. I plunged right into the water, wrapped in far too much wool and tweed.

This was no gentle river with mossy banks. It served a commercial purpose and, as such, dropped off sharply and moved swiftly. The shock of all that cold water made it impossible to take a breath, but I forged ahead with the water up to my shoulders and rising. Now and again my feet struck a stone or a buried log, so that I could more or less propel myself along without engaging in anything that resembled swimming. In my youth girls did not swim: we bathed. As such I hardly knew how to keep myself alive in a river.

Tony was ahead of me, his head bobbing just above the black water. He was drifting toward one of the great sewer pipes that discharged into the river and made a frothy whirlpool where the water surged in. I'm sure I don't have to describe how foul it smelled, but in truth the odor didn't make any impression on me at the time. (I was only later able to recall the stench of the river because of the way it lingered on my clothes, no matter how many times I washed them.)

Tony coughed and gasped for air. At terrifyingly frequent intervals he disappeared for a few seconds and then came up again, retching and groaning. With his wrists chained together, I don't know how he survived for even a minute. His feet must've hit bottom once or twice too, which was all that kept him alive until I reached him.

It felt like I was in that river for an hour, but it must've taken only a few minutes for me to grab hold of him and wrap an arm across his chest. He didn't fight me, but he didn't help, either. I'd never had cause to haul a sack of potatoes across a river, but that was Tony Hajnacka, limp and weighty.

I dragged him to shore with only my feet to propel me. We went underwater together a few times, and even then he didn't kick or fight for air. He was heavy enough to pull me underwater with him, and might have succeeded, except that I had more to lose than he did at that moment. No inmate was going to escape or die on my watch.

I couldn't lift him out of the river. The best I could do was to heft him up against the embankment and to hold him there. My feet were braced against a slippery submerged boulder that threatened to give way, and because I had my hands under Tony's arms, I couldn't do a thing to keep myself steady without letting go of him.

Shoes and trouser legs gathered around us, but I couldn't see to whom they belonged. Four arms reached down to slide Tony out of the mud, and then someone took my elbow and hoisted me up. I couldn't get to my feet and was forced to lie there like a beached whale, gasping and sputtering in the mud.

Now the cold really set in. I'd lost all sensation in my feet and my heart hammered alarmingly in my chest. I pushed myself up out of the mud and there was Tony, right next to me, having been hoisted up on all fours so that someone could pound him on the back and force him to cough up all the water he'd swallowed. That had the desired effect, except that he vomited too, and gasped and coughed and choked some more.

Nonetheless, he was back on his feet before I was. He looked monstrous, standing over me in the light of a single lantern, covered in river mud and shaking, the bandage around his neck now gone entirely and the blood coming down in rivulets. His wrists were still in handcuffs and he was too weak to walk, so the guards had no choice but to drag him back to the jail, his feet scraping the gravel as he went. He had lost a shoe.

I managed to get myself sitting upright and accepted a blanket that was being handed to me. Sheriff Heath knelt down and put his face right in front of mine. "Is anything broken? Can you walk?"

"I suppose I'd better. You're not going to carry me."

He took my hands and forced me to stand, which was no easy feat because of the way the mud sucked at my wet clothes. My hat was gone, and it wasn't until I tried to take a step that I realized that I, too, was missing a shoe, only mine was a very sturdy boot that was nearly impossible to take off after a walk in the rain. I couldn't imagine how it had worked loose. The mud must've demanded a sacrifice from each of us.

At the sight of my stockinged foot, I laughed with a kind of nervous relief and said, "Nothing's broken. I'm fine."

"Then let's get you inside."

Everyone else had gone in. Only a guard waited at the door for us.

"What happened to Anna? I should get her settled. She was so nervous about coming to the jail."

"She'd be even more nervous if she saw you in this state. The guards have her. Let Cordelia look after you."

"Let's not bother Mrs. Heath."

"It's no bother."

I had no choice but to hobble across the drive, where the door to Sheriff Heath's living quarters was half-open. Mrs. Heath waited just inside, swaddled in a bathrobe, with a stack of blankets and towels in her arms. I hated to step in: my outer skirt had come loose and was dragging on the ground, with a mess of gravel, mud, and leaves at its hem. I stayed in the doorway and kicked it off, then tried to wring out my petticoats, but Sheriff Heath pulled me inside. Before I knew it, I'd been swaddled in clean blankets and deposited in a chair, with a towel at my feet and another one over my hair.

The sheriff closed the door behind him and, all at once, it was over. The rain, the river, the inmate bent on running away or drowning himself—all of that was suddenly far away, and I was in the Heath family's warm and quiet sitting room. For a moment I just sat there, shedding river water and mud, and giving off the odor of moss and the unmentionable filth of the sewer pipe.

It took a few deep and shaky breaths for my heart to reach any kind of normal rhythm and for the water to clear from my ears. When at last I was able to take hold of myself, I looked up at Cordelia Heath, who was at that moment holding a pair of towels out at arm's length with the expression of a woman who didn't like to have her towels soiled.

"Thank you, but it's not necessary." My voice came out gravelly from all the river water I'd inhaled.

"Apparently it is necessary," Cordelia said.

Sheriff Heath stepped in between us, took the towels, and dumped them on my lap to do with as I wished. Then he sat down across from me. He was drenched, too, from the rain, and splattered in mud.

"You saved a man's life tonight," he said.

"I only wish it hadn't been necessary. What about Morris?"

"His knee gave out. He can't stand on it. We'll take him home."

"Well, it was sloppy of us to try to move both of them at once in this storm."

"That's exactly what the papers will say," Cordelia put in. She was hovering around me, attempting to look busy, although there was nothing more for her to do but watch the river water seep into her good upholstery. "The last thing we need is another escaped inmate in the news."

I was the one who allowed an inmate to escape the year previous. I also caught the fugitive some weeks later, but that didn't matter: in his campaign, Detective Courter was already making speeches about how the sheriff was too weak to keep a criminal in jail. Nonetheless, Sheriff Heath protected me: he never told anyone that it was I who allowed the man to flee.

Cordelia must've known she'd gone too far. Sheriff Heath fixed her with a look that I could only describe as disappointed and said, "Deputy Kopp has only just finished crawling out of the Hackensack River with a half-drowned man under her arm. Do you suppose we could offer her something hot to drink?"

That was enough to send her out of the room, which was his intent.

"You're the first deputy to jump in the river on my watch," he said when she was gone.

"I didn't have time to think. He would've drowned."

"You could have too, in those skirts."

For the first time I noticed that he'd run outside in a suit of striped pajamas with a coat thrown over his shoulders. It embarrassed me to see him like that, but I must've looked even more shameful, in my sodden petticoats. I pulled another towel around myself for good measure.

From over his shoulder I saw his little boy standing in the hallway, staring at us through his father's deep brown eyes. Sheriff Heath turned and saw him, too.

"Go on back to bed," he said. "Deputy Kopp just had a fall in the mud."

The boy backed away slowly, but I had the distinct impression that he was still standing in the shadows.

"Something's not quite right about the situation with Anna Kayser," I said. "She doesn't belong in an asylum."

"The judge seemed to think she did."

By then, Cordelia had returned with a tray, looking like she could've boiled me in a kettle. The tea was too hot to drink, but I

44

wrapped my hands around the cup and lifted it to my face, breathing in the steam.

"I'm sorry," I said. "I'm afraid we woke the children."

She spun around to look down the hall and Sheriff Heath said, "I sent him back to bed. Cordelia, I wonder if we can't make Miss Kopp comfortable for the night."

"Oh!" Cordelia said. "I hadn't realized . . ." She glanced down at the little divan, which was altogether too dainty for my frame.

I wasn't about to be forced upon Cordelia. I jumped to my feet before she was obliged to invent an excuse. "That's kind of you, but no. I have a dress upstairs, and a comb and things. I need to look in on my inmates anyway."

I kept the blanket clutched around me with one hand. I didn't like to admit it, but a shaky kind of terror had come over me, as if all the fear I should have felt when I jumped in the river had only just now caught up with me. I also had an uneasy sense that Mrs. Heath was right: I'd been involved in yet another escape attempt. Even though the inmate was Morris's and not mine, and even though I'd caught the man, none of that would matter. It would be turned against me, and against Sheriff Heath. I wanted desperately to be alone, under a blanket, in the dark. A jail cell with a good lock on it sounded like the safest and most comfortable place in the world.

Both of the Heaths looked exhausted, too. "Go on, then," the sheriff said. "We could all use some rest. I'm going to look in on Tony Hajnacka, and make sure Morris got home." Turning to his wife, he said, "Send her up with a hot-water bottle."

"You needn't go to any more trouble for me." In fact, I didn't want to wait while Mrs. Heath got a bottle ready. But it was too late—she was already going back to the kitchen.

"It's no trouble," she said. "There's still hot water in the kettle."

45

I gathered up my things. My coat and outer skirt sat in the corner in a wet bundle. I wrapped them in a towel and put it under my arm. Mrs. Heath brought me the water bottle, covered in flannel, and there was nothing to do but to take it in the crook of my other arm, the way one holds a baby. We both recognized the gesture, and she smiled in spite of herself as she put it there.

The bottle was excessively warm, too, the way a baby was. I went out of their apartment with it clutched against my chest. Upstairs, Anna Kayser was already asleep in her cell. When I slipped the hot-water bottle under her blanket, she stirred and curled herself around it but didn't emerge from whatever dream had taken her away from here.

7

THE JAIL KITCHEN was the recipient, three or four times in the autumn, of a few bushels of misshapen apples from a farmer whose scruples forbade the brewing of even mildly intoxicating cider. I was pleased to find two good Winesaps in the kitchen the next morning, which I carried upstairs along with hot rolls and an entire pot of coffee. This was a luxury never accorded to an inmate. In fact, I endeavored to slip very quietly past the other cell blocks so that the unionists, reckless drivers, and light-fingered actresses under my watch wouldn't see me going by with a breakfast tray and come to expect the same.

But none of the treats I had on offer brought any cheer to the defeated figure of Anna Kayser, who wasn't accustomed to a jailhouse breakfast and didn't know she was receiving anything in the way of special treatment.

She sat at the head of her bunk, up against the wall, with her hair down around her shoulders and a blanket folded carefully across her lap. The guard who'd brought her inside the night before had issued her one of the inmates' plain house dresses, but it was flimsy and inferior to her own clothing, so she had merely folded it and set it carefully on the floor, along with the hot-water bottle.

The fact that she'd been allowed to keep her clothes was another kind of special treatment that she didn't know to appreciate: on an ordinary night, she would've been sent into the shower with tar soap for a de-lousing regimen, and every stitch of her own clothing would've been taken away. She was, in a sense, lucky that the jail's protocol had been abandoned owing to the chaotic scene the night before—but she didn't look like a woman who'd stumbled into any kind of luck at all.

I set the tray down and poured a cup of coffee for her. She sniffed it dubiously.

"It's the very same coffee they serve at the train station," I said, by way of making conversation.

"That does nothing to recommend it."

"I'm awfully sorry about last night. I promised to make you comfortable and instead—"

"You needn't apologize. You're the one who had to jump into the river." Mrs. Kayser's voice was weak and thin, but she managed a half-hearted laugh.

I polished an apple and held one out to her. "They're quite good if you don't mind the spots."

"Oh, I never mind the spots. There's an orchard out at Morris Plains, and we used to eat them right off the tree. It was the only good thing about the place."

She looked at me expectantly after she said it, having given me an opening.

"I wasn't told a thing about your situation, Mrs. Kayser. But you said something last night that didn't sound right. You said that you didn't want to be sent back."

She picked at one of the rolls, pulling off a bit of crust and tasting it. "You wouldn't want to go back, either."

"But isn't it unusual for someone to go twice to Morris Plains?"

What I meant to say was that it was unusual for anyone to ever be released from Morris Plains at all, but I thought better than to put it that way. Mrs. Kayser took my meaning regardless.

"When Charlie comes for me, they let me go." She said it in the most matter-of-fact way, as if it were perfectly ordinary for a husband to come and collect his wife at the lunatic asylum.

"But . . . what do the doctors have to say about it?"

Mrs. Kayser shrugged. "They don't say a thing to me. They might talk to Charlie."

"How many times have you been to Morris Plains, Mrs. Kayser?"

She leaned back and put her head against the wall, looking off into the distance and counting to herself. "Three. Four. This might make the fifth time."

"Do you mind if I ask why? If the doctors think you're well enough to go home, what happens to send you back?"

Something hardened in Mrs. Kayser's expression and I worried that I'd lost my opportunity. "I don't mean to cause offense," I said quickly. "But you said quite plainly last night that it was wrong of Charlie to have you sent away. I'm only trying to find out the truth in case there's something I can do for you. You don't have to talk about it if you don't want to. But the sheriff does have orders to take you to the asylum without delay. Now is the time to tell me."

She nodded, a bit dreamily, as if she were weighing her risks. Finally she said, "It started just after Charlotte was born. My youngest. She's fifteen now."

"I didn't see her last night."

"Charlie sent her to the pictures with her friends and now I know why."

"And it was after her birth that you were sentenced to Morris Plains?"

"I was ill during my pregnancy and confined for so long. But after Charlotte was born and the doctor finally released me from bed rest, I just . . . I just couldn't."

"Couldn't?"

"Couldn't get out of bed."

Anna Kayser looked to be about fifty-five, almost old enough to be my mother. But we sat together as equals, sipping our coffee and thinking about the kind of malaise that could come over a woman at a time like that.

"I couldn't get up," she said. "I couldn't dress, or look after the children, or go back into the kitchen and face another dinner. I just couldn't bear to do any of it. Charlie took me to Dr. Lipsky and made me tell him about it. Don't ever tell a doctor about anything unless it's something he can fix, like a boil or a broken bone. They don't know what to do about you otherwise."

I agreed entirely with that. "But you told him the truth."

"I told him I felt like I was drowning. I didn't know who I was. Nothing mattered to me, not even my baby. For that he sent me away for a year."

"A year!"

She nodded. "When I came home, little Charlotte didn't even know me."

"Who took care of her? And your other children—how many are there?"

"Four. The others are all grown now. Charlie hired a cook who lived in while I was gone. She looked after the whole brood."

"And was it any help to you at all, being at Morris Plains?"

"I couldn't say. Who knows what would've happened if I'd been allowed to stay at home and just soldier on? At the asylum they give you no choice but to get out of bed and do some kind of work. There's a chair-caning workshop and a little sewing operation, but I asked to be put on the inmate farm. I don't suppose handling a pitchfork and a plow did me any harm. I wasn't happy there, of course, but I did get up and work. After a year of that, Charlie brought me home."

"But not for long?"

"He sent me back two or three more times, for six months or a year, whenever I had my troubles again. Dr. Lipsky called it nervous hysteria. I was just so tired sometimes. Four children, you can't imagine. Have you any of your own?"

"No, but . . ." I paused, uncertain how to explain. "I did help to raise my sister. She was enough. She still is."

"Well, it was the same every time. Dr. Lipsky would order me to Morris Plains, and Charlie would hire a cook to take my place, until one day, without any warning whatsoever, he'd appear at the gates and announce that he'd come to fetch me."

"And what about this time?" I asked. "Why is Dr. Lipsky sending you away now? Are you feeling unwell?"

"No! I've been a little tired and forgetful, and sometimes in the night I wake up in a terrible sweat with my heart pounding and I don't know why. I get up and pace around and drink a glass of water, and Charlie says it bothers his sleep. But I haven't even spoken to Dr. Lipsky about that. I refuse to. You can see why."

"Do you mean to say that you were sentenced to Morris Plains without ever having been seen by the doctor?"

She sniffed. "Unless he's been peeking in the windows."

⇥ 8 ⇤

"I THOUGHT YOU'D gone home," Sheriff Heath said when I appeared in the doorway to his office. "I expect you'll want a change of clothes."

"And a bit more than that," I admitted. There was still the odor of the river in my hair. I wouldn't feel human again until I commandeered some of Fleurette's perfumed salts and soaps in a hot bath.

The sun had come out following the previous night's storm, and there was no sign of the scuffle that had taken place. Nevertheless, the sheriff and I both stood at his window and looked over at the river, and at the muddy embankment where Tony Hajnacka and I had collapsed the night before.

The sheriff turned and scrutinized me for a minute. "I told Mrs. Heath that very few of my deputies would have gone into the river after an inmate." He had a way of looking at me as if I surprised him, even after all this time.

"I didn't know I had a choice. What else was I to do?"

"I could imagine a fellow running alongside the river but not going so far as to jump in."

"And let him drown? Besides, I couldn't let another inmate escape. You'd have no choice but to dismiss me if I did."

Sheriff Heath shrugged as though he might have to agree with that, but he said, "As I explained to a reporter this morning, he didn't escape, and that's all that matters."

"So the papers have it."

"Of course they do. I had to go over to the courthouse to explain why the inmates weren't delivered to Morris Plains as ordered, and the reporters all followed me in. It was quite a dramatic story in the retelling."

"Mrs. Heath isn't going to like that."

"I won't hide the truth. You did a fine job. It reflects well on the entire department. I'm going to have the Freeholders give you a medal for it."

Sheriff Heath rarely made a joke, but I laughed anyway. "I'm almost as popular with the Freeholders as you are."

"They're accustomed to handing out medals. Morris collared a fellow in the woods a few years ago and held him half the night until we caught up with him. The Freeholders gave him one. You should have yours, too."

"I thought we were to keep me out of the papers until the election." This was Cordelia's idea, one she repeated to me at every opportunity. I had no objection to that idea: every fresh round of stories brought resentment from the other deputies, whose arrests were never seen as newsworthy, and stacks of letters from all over the country, mostly marriage proposals from lonely men. I could do without all of that.

"If anything, a sensational write-up in the papers will be good for our side," Sheriff Heath said. "I want the voters to remember that a reform program isn't meant to coddle the inmates. We're still handling dangerous criminals, and our deputies put their lives at risk."

"Well, I wish you wouldn't bother," I said. "I'm far more interested in Anna Kayser than the fellow in the river. Did you know this is to be her fourth time at Morris Plains?"

"Did she tell you that?"

"Yes, and I believe her. She suffered a nervous collapse after her youngest child was born and was kept there for a year. Now anytime she gets a case of the nerves, her husband calls in the doctor and off she goes."

"Then it's good of him to want her back and to try again. Most men wouldn't."

"She doesn't seem the least bit insane to me. I saw her house. This is a woman who keeps everything in order and has dinner on the table—why, she was in the kitchen when I came to get her. She's no degenerate."

"I suppose her doctor would disagree."

"But the doctor never examined her. He took her husband's word for it."

"Why would any husband want his wife in an insane asylum if there was nothing wrong with her? Didn't you say they have children?"

"They do," I said. "He hires a cook when she's away."

"She must not like being so easily replaced. But we have to carry out the judge's orders. We're just the chauffeur in this case."

"Couldn't I go speak to the judge who committed her?"

"If Judge Stevens wanted to hear from you, he would've said so. I saw him this morning and he's not pleased that we didn't deliver her to Morris Plains last night as promised."

"But what if I'm right, and there's some sort of fraud at work here? Is she to lose her liberty because we don't want to disturb the judge?"

This was the way to win a round with Sheriff Heath. He was a man of principles, and principles came before politics. "All right. Go and speak to the doctor if you feel so strongly about it. You can say that Mrs. Kayser made some puzzling statements while under your custody and that you only wish to make him aware of them.

But do it quickly, because there's an auto arranged for noon to-morrow. We can't keep her here. I've no authority to do so."

"Then I'm going now, before you change your mind."

"And home after. I don't want to see you here tonight."

WHEN I SLEPT at the jail, I wore an ordinary corduroy dress, which was warm and comfortable enough for sleeping but more presentable than a nightgown should I be called unexpectedly to duty. I'd changed into it the night before so that I could get out of my wet things, and was still wearing it, lacking any other clean uniform. I would've preferred to look crisp and buttoned up at Dr. Lipsky's office, but there was nothing to be done about that.

It was a chilly morning in spite of the sun. I walked as quickly as I could, marching past the shoppers and tradesmen on Main Street. Although I was out of my uniform, I did wear my badge, which caused people to take notice of me. One little boy stopped in his tracks and asked his mother if I was the sheriff. The woman laughed, a little too loudly, and told him no. Under any other circumstances I liked to stop and speak to curious children about the subject of lady deputies and to let them hold my badge, but I hurried on.

At the street corner three young men stepped apart from each other to make way for me. One of them whistled and called, "Lady cop! Am I under arrest?" The other two whistled just like the first one did, but once again, I didn't stop. If I took the time to scold every masher on the street, I wouldn't get anything done.

I found Dr. Lipsky's office easily enough, in a little white building occupied primarily by lawyers. There was only one other doctor on the door plate, and I recognized his name. Dr. Lipsky and Dr. Ogden, the county physician, were next-door neighbors.

I wish I could say that the doctor was a friend to the sheriff's department, but it was dawning on me that Sheriff Heath had few friends among the local officials. William Ogden was the county physician, the coroner, and the only man the sheriff was supposed to call if an inmate fell ill. The difficulty was that Dr. Ogden's idea of caring for a convicted criminal was to give him a dose of cod-liver oil and send him to bed. He stood up at every meeting of the Board of Freeholders and protested the invoices the sheriff submitted for the inmates' care. If we sent someone to the hospital, or called for a dentist or any other physician besides him, Sheriff Heath was held to account.

It was the belief of Dr. Ogden, and of many on the Board of Freeholders, that the promise of free visits from the county physician would only encourage the criminal element. A man need only to rob a bank, the thinking went, and he could have a boil lanced, a tooth pulled, and a remedy for gout prescribed, courtesy of the Bergen County taxpayers. Dr. Ogden even disapproved of supplying inmates with a shower, shave, and haircut.

It was nonsense, of course. We simply tried to make sure the inmates didn't live in filth, and we quite sensibly did what we could to rid them of vermin and disease before the others were infected. But there were too many, Dr. Ogden among them, who believed that filth and disease were fitting punishments for criminals.

I saw immediately what my difficulty would be. The courts relied on Dr. Ogden's testimony before they committed anyone to Morris Plains. He and Dr. Lipsky obviously worked closely together and, I suspected, shared many of the same views about their patients.

The lobby was unencumbered by any sort of receptionist. I followed the chevrons in the carpet down a somber corridor to Dr. Lipsky's office. From behind his closed door came a rumble of conversation between two men. The one who answered my knock was tall and bald, with a bow tie and a heavy mustache. He had a way of smiling that bared his teeth and pulled the corners of his mouth down rather than up. Clamped between those teeth was the stub of a cigar. The room, naturally, was filled with smoke.

"What's this?" the man said when he saw my badge. "Have I gotten myself crossways with the girl police? What did I do, stir my tea with the wrong spoon?"

He laughed and tried to shut the door, but I pushed my way inside. This brought his companion—Dr. Ogden, as I'd suspected —to his feet.

"This lady's looking for me. I suppose I'm needed at the jail. They keep handing out knives to the inmates, and expect me to come and stitch them up."

Dr. Ogden spoke in a deep and cultivated baritone, each word carefully enunciated as if he'd rehearsed his lines ahead of time. He was rumored to have a wife, but I couldn't imagine how any woman could tolerate a man speaking in such a pompous manner around the house. He was very refined-looking, trim and neatly dressed, just a hair shorter than me, with an unwavering upright posture that seemed to be intended as a reminder to the others that one ought to take more care in the alignment of one's spine.

It gave me some pleasure to tell Dr. Ogden that he was mistaken. "In fact, I've come for Dr. Lipsky. One of his patients is in custody at the Hackensack Jail and some questions have arisen. The sheriff sent me to speak to him about it."

Dr. Lipsky waved his cigar in the air, as if it were a flag of surrender. "I suppose our business can wait, Bill. Have a seat, Miss . . ."

"Kopp," said Dr. Ogden, before I could. He pulled the chair out for me, and then went and stood against the wall. Dr. Lipsky took his seat, planted his elbows on the desk, and looked at me expectantly.

"I charge by the hour, Miss Kopp."

I was trying not to look at Dr. Ogden, but I didn't like the way he was watching me. "It's a delicate matter concerning a patient," I said pointedly.

"Yes," Dr. Lipsky said, and raised his eyebrows to indicate that I should go on.

"Perhaps you wouldn't want it discussed in the presence of others."

Still his eyebrows were raised expectantly. He looked around, playing at being confused, until his glance lighted on Dr. Ogden. "Oh! Do you refer to the county physician? I can't think of a thing he doesn't know about my patients, or shouldn't know."

This wasn't going as I'd planned, but what choice did I have? "It concerns Anna Kayser."

He put his cigar on a little tray and leaned back in his chair. "Yes, the housewife in Rutherford. Poor creature. She's back at Morris Plains or, at least, she was supposed to be. What's she doing in jail?"

Before I could answer, Dr. Ogden stepped in. "The sheriff insists on handling all the asylum transportation, although I have recommended that the hospital take it over. You know that he allowed an inmate to escape from the hospital last year. Just last night another fellow ran off before they could get to Morris Plains. It only demonstrates that if they aren't locked behind bars, he can't keep track of them. The responsibility is too much for him. I've told the Freeholders so."

He might have been speaking to Dr. Lipsky, but he was looking directly at me. I tried to do the dignified thing and ignore him.

"Mrs. Kayser is only at the jail temporarily on account of the storm last night," I said. "We went to collect her in Rutherford, but the roads washed away and we never got past Hackensack. Owing to the late hour, we stopped for the night. The reason I'm here is that Mrs. Kayser tells a troubling story, and we want to make sure there hasn't been a mix-up before we take her away."

Dr. Ogden gave a light little laugh and walked around to stand behind Dr. Lipsky. "Miss Kopp, I have the most wonderful news for you. You need never concern yourself with the strange stories told by lunatics and hysterics who have been committed to the asylum. It is our obligation to listen to them, but not yours. You need only put them into the wagon and cart them off. Doesn't that sound wonderfully simple? I'm sorry the sheriff never took the time to explain your duties to you, but they are so much lighter than you've been led to believe."

Anyone who thinks that dealing with criminals makes for demanding work has never tried to keep a civil tongue when speaking to a man like Dr. Ogden. Nonetheless, it was my duty to do so.

Addressing myself to Dr. Lipsky, I said, "Mrs. Kayser has been committed four times. Her husband seems to have the power to send her away and then to come and fetch her again anytime he pleases. She doesn't feel that she's receiving any helpful treatment and says she has no need of it now. How can she be committed to Morris Plains if no doctor has examined her?"

Dr. Ogden started to work himself up into another speech, but Dr. Lipsky gestured for him to be quiet. "Miss Kopp, I've been treating Mrs. Kayser for over fifteen years, and I've known her husband even longer. When did you meet her for the first time?"

"Yesterday, but—"

"And from what university did you receive your training?"

I wasn't about to listen to insults from this man. I stood up, forcing him to do the same, and said, "You may call me Deputy Kopp. I'm here under the authority of the sheriff of Bergen County. There is a woman in our custody whose situation raises troubling questions."

"All manner of questions were asked and answered at her commitment hearing, which is why we hold them."

He had an infuriating way of making me sound like I didn't know my business. "If you can't give an explanation as to the cause of her commitment to the asylum," I said, "then I will speak to Judge Stevens myself and ask to have the case re-examined by a physician of her choosing."

Dr. Lipsky gave an insincere chuckle and said, "Cause? Nervous hysteria, of course. It was brought on by a case of puerperal insanity, which happens to some women after childbirth, but which may recur at any time and with very little warning. Mrs. Kayser's case is well known to me, and to her unfortunate husband, who has suffered under this burden longer than any man should. It takes only a word from him for me to know what the trouble is. A year or two at Morris Plains will be the best thing for her."

"A year? Have you been to her home? Mrs. Kayser keeps her place immaculate, puts dinner on the table every night, and is entirely modest and neat in appearance. What form of hysteria would you call that?"

"I believe I've answered those questions to the judge's satisfaction, Deputy." He spoke in a quiet and even tone, with his hands folded calmly on his desk. I realized, with a note of alarm, that he must've considered himself an expert in nervous women, and that he no doubt believed he was showing Dr. Ogden how skilled he was in dealing with one. Could they send anyone away, the two of them? Would they send me away, if I bothered them long enough?

It didn't matter: I was getting nowhere with them. "Thank you, gentlemen. I'll recommend to the sheriff that Mrs. Kayser be examined by her own doctor."

Again came the insincere smile from Dr. Lipsky. "My dear, you seem not to have understood any of this. I am her doctor."

I had nothing to say to that. Both men were looking at me with the kind of pity that made me want to scream, but if I did, I was by then entirely convinced that I might end up in the bed next to Anna Kayser at the asylum.

To think that I was her only defender, and I had so little power to help her!

Dr. Lipsky walked over to the door and held it open. "My dear, if you find it too disturbing to have involvement with the insane and feeble-minded, perhaps you'll find another line of work for yourself. It isn't for everyone, is it, Dr. Ogden?"

I marched out before Dr. Ogden could serve up a response.

≈ 9 ≈

A TELEPHONE WIRE carries news faster than any train or trolley-car, which means that word of my disagreeable encounter with Dr. Lipsky reached the jail before I did. I have no personal opposition to the use of telephones to conduct everyday business—although others in my family do, namely, my sister Norma—but I do consider it unsportsmanlike to telephone ahead with grievances more properly delivered in person.

I returned to the courthouse (rather than go on home for that desperately needed bath) because I was more certain than ever that Anna Kayser hadn't been given a fair hearing and must not, under any circumstances, be carted off to the lunatic asylum before I had a chance to investigate. I anticipated Sheriff Heath's reluctance—she wasn't our inmate, and it wouldn't do to pick an unnecessary battle with the county physician during an election season—but what I didn't anticipate was that John Courter would've arrived at the sheriff's office before I did, fuming over my conduct.

Both men were on their feet, both in their long black coats, as if poised for a duel. Mr. Courter must've only just walked in with whatever version of events Dr. Ogden had delivered by telephone.

"Sheriff, I—" I stopped short when they both turned to me.

"I don't mean to interrupt," I said, and tried to duck out, although it was already too plain what had happened.

"Oh, you do mean to interrupt, and to interfere in cases in which you have no jurisdiction," Mr. Courter said, "although I don't suppose you're to blame, as the sheriff tells me he's the one who ordered you to go." He wore a heavy mustache that sloped down at the corners of his mouth, giving him the appearance of a perpetual frown. It was one of many of his unpleasant characteristics, another being a kind of sanctimonious drawl that he employed whenever he wished to pass judgment on others.

"I was in possession of information that might have bearing on her case," I said. "Any citizen could've done what I did. It has nothing to do with jurisdiction."

"Nonetheless—" Sheriff Heath began to defend me, but I stopped him. I hated to see him take the responsibility, but that was how he protected all of his deputies.

"What matters now," I continued, "is that a woman has been deprived of her liberty, and sentenced to an indefinite stay at Morris Plains, without ever having been examined by a physician. I take it Dr. Ogden telephoned ahead and told you all about it. I can only assume that he asked, in light of new information, that she be given a fair hearing."

Mr. Courter grew quite red. The color traveled up from his neck and covered his bald head. "This woman," he roared to Sheriff Heath, pointing to me but refusing to look at me, "was employed as a ladies' matron at your insistence. She is neither detective nor investigator nor officer of the court. She has no education beyond a finishing school, and demonstrates a child's sentimentality that renders her unfit for anything more than passing out handkerchiefs to the ladies sobbing upstairs over the damage they've done to their reputations. Every day in which she remains under your employ is further evidence of your own poor judgment. But the voters will make up their minds about you soon enough."

He'd obviously been accustomed to giving speeches lately and considered this a fine one. He turned on his heel to go, but I was still blocking the door. He was forced to either look up at me to beg my leave, or to stare mulishly at the buttons on my collar.

I bent down so he had no choice but to look at me directly. "That woman upstairs has done nothing wrong." I was hardly able to contain my fury. "We won't release her until she's had a fair hearing."

Sheriff Heath cleared his throat behind us. "I'm sure Mr. Courter would like to be on his way."

Something in his voice told me I'd gone too far. I stepped aside and Mr. Courter ducked away like a cat who'd been too long underfoot.

When he was gone I dropped into a chair. Sheriff Heath paced around in front of the window.

"There goes another one of Ramsey's barges," he said as he looked out over the river.

John Ramsey was Sheriff Heath's opponent in his congressional race. He ran a brickworks that sat just downriver of the jail. The smoke from his kilns was ever-present, and at times so sulfuric that we were obliged to close the windows, even on a hot afternoon. But his was one of many such factories along the river, and on most days the odor was merely that of baked earth, and far more pleasant than what came from the mills and tanneries.

Because the jail was situated right on the river, we were accustomed to seeing his bricks float past on barges, bound for the rail yard. One of his men (Mr. Ramsey swore he didn't know who) liked to fly a "Ramsey for Congress" flag from the barge as it passed by the jail. It was obviously intended for Sheriff Heath's eyes, but that was nothing but a prank, and the sheriff rarely even saw it. ("Does he think I gaze out my window at his barges all day long?" had been his only comment.)

Ramsey was a man of some importance around town, having served as county clerk for many years, and wore good crisp suits and stiff collars as befitted a man of his standing. I guessed him to be fifty-five or so, with the gray hair and heft of middle age to show for it. His eyes were of some indistinguishable light color, his mustache of the wiry salt-and-pepper variety, and he wore a club pin on his tie.

He was, in every way, a gentleman with a temperament very unlike that of John Courter. He tended not to speak about Sheriff Heath at his campaign rallies, believing it unsportsmanlike to rail against an opponent, and preferring to tout his own accomplishments. In fact, Mr. Ramsey's unwillingness to criticize his opponent publicly was whole-heartedly reciprocated by the sheriff, which meant that they carried out entirely separate campaigns and rarely had cause to respond to the other's statements.

Only Cordelia worried about Mr. Ramsey's campaign. She kept a copy of his speaking schedule, made note of the groups that had endorsed him, and clipped every newspaper advertisement he ran, to make sure that her husband did more and better. This was proving to be a perfect occupation for her: it kept her busy and distracted, which meant that she had less time to fret over the insults and accusations that John Courter was throwing our way. There were more of those coming at us every day—and now I'd brought on the latest round.

"I don't know what Dr. Ogden said when he telephoned, but I doubt it was a reliable account," I ventured. Sheriff Heath kept his back turned. He was obviously troubled. "He shouldn't have even been in the room. I asked Dr. Lipsky for a private audience, but he refused."

"You did nothing wrong," Sheriff Heath said, turning around at last, "but there's nothing more I can do for Anna Kayser. I'm sorry, Deputy, but I run the jail, not the asylum. I can't meddle in every commitment hearing they conduct next door. We were only the chauffeur this time."

"But don't you agree that Mrs. Kayser has a case? Isn't there anyone to whom she might make an appeal? It can't be lawful for a person to be deprived of her liberty without even the most cursory examination by a physician."

Sheriff Heath looked genuinely pained over the situation. He was far from indifferent to the suffering of others. "You've done what you can for her. If she believes she's been treated unfairly, it's a matter for her attorney now."

"Her attorney? What housewife has an attorney of her own? If she knows anyone at all in the legal field, it would no doubt be a friend of her husband's, and she'd need her husband's bank-book to pay for it."

"You don't know that. Go on upstairs, and tell Mrs. Kayser what she can do to help herself if she wants to. Then I'm ordering you home."

I rose to go. "Once she's taken to the asylum, she's lost. They won't even let her write a letter. How long can we keep her here?"

He coughed and went back around to his desk. "It isn't for me to decide. The courts have ordered Dr. Ogden to carry both Mrs. Kayser and Tony Hajnacka to the asylum, with the assistance of a trained nurse. This one is out of our hands. You understand that, don't you?"

I allowed that I did understand, but I was not prepared to go along with it.

ANNA KAYSER SAT in her cell with the weary patience of the condemned. I'd kept her apart from the others, and conscripted a friendly guard to carry a hot lunch to her while I was away. She'd tasted a little of the soup and left the tray on the floor.

I let myself into her cell and sat alongside her so I could speak as quietly as possible. "I've been to see Dr. Lipsky."

She gave a little half-laugh and said, "I can only imagine what he made of the likes of you barging into his office."

"He wasn't terribly pleased. But he did admit that he never examined you. I think you have a case, Mrs. Kayser."

A few thin strands of hair fell down around her eyes. She pushed them out of the way in the manner of an old habit and said, "A case against whom? Do you mean to file suit against Dr. Lipsky or against my husband?"

"I'm afraid I can't file charges. It isn't within my power."

"Oh, of course it isn't." She bit her lip and looked out between the bars of her cell. "You're the only one who's ever bothered to ask about any of this, or to hear my side of it. But there's no point in telling you about it, if you can't do anything."

I couldn't stand to hear it put to me that way. "But I am here to do something about it," I whispered. "Sheriff Heath says that you should write to an attorney. They won't let you send a letter from the asylum, but you can write as many as you'd like while you're here. I'll post them myself, and if there's another message you'd like me to pass on, I will do it. Or I could . . ."

But what else could I do?

Mrs. Kayser shook her head slowly and patted my hand. She reminded me, in a way that made me ache a little, of my own late mother: fatigued and resigned, but with her own kind of warmth.

"You know I haven't any lawyer," she said, "and who would pay his bills, even if he were to read my letter and take up the matter? He'd run straight to Charlie for his fee, and that would put an end to it."

"Isn't there anyone who could help with the fees?" I sounded

67

a little desperate, but what else could I do? "A neighbor or a relation?"

Mrs. Kayser gave me a faint smile. To my astonishment, she reached up and touched my cheek, the way one comforts an anxious child. No inmate of mine had ever tried a thing like that.

"Go on," she said. "I'll think on it. If anyone comes to mind, I'll write that letter before I leave."

I hated to go home. Surely she needed me beside her until Dr. Ogden came for her. But she must've guessed at what I was thinking, because she said, "You aren't to wait here all day with me. I'm just going to close my eyes for a little while this afternoon." To prove it, she stretched out on her bunk, leaving me no choice but to get up.

I had the most horrible feeling that if I left, I might never see her again. But what else was I to do?

"Deputy Kopp," called Sheriff Heath, from the top of the stairs. He was going to evict me if I didn't leave of my own accord.

❧ 10 ❧

NORMA RATTLED THE newspaper as soon as I walked in the door.

"What is this nonsense?" she shouted from the sitting room, before I could shake off my scarf. I peered through the dust into the face of the standing clock in our foyer and saw that the afternoon papers would've just arrived.

"'Girl Sheriff Dives' was the first headline I saw," pronounced Norma as I dropped onto the divan, "and you can be sure I didn't have to wonder which girl sheriff it might've been."

She lowered the paper and peered at me over the top. Her hair was flattened from the wool cap she wore outdoors all day. "Although I've never known you to dive. If anyone in this house has ever submerged herself into any body of water larger than a bathtub, I didn't hear about it. You smell like a swamp, by the way."

Fleurette came out of her sewing room with a pincushion on her wrist and a pair of thread snips over her thumb. "I used to go in the ocean. We haven't been in ages. Why don't we—"

"The last time we went to the seashore, Constance's gangsters tried to burn down our house."

Norma had a way of stringing information together that made it seem as if entirely unrelated events had some causal link: trips to the seashore and arson attempts, for instance. She also liked to make it seem as if any sort of criminal mischief that came our way was my doing. The gangsters didn't belong to me, and it was entirely outside the bounds of ordinary grammar to refer to them in the possessive, but it was useless to explain any of that.

"I wouldn't mind a trip to the shore," I said, just to oppose Norma. "If we have another stretch of warm weather, we'll go."

Norma grunted at that and shifted around in her tattered leather armchair. "I thought you were to stay out of the papers until after the election."

"That was the general idea," I admitted.

"Then why did you have to go and jump into the river after a man? You know they can't resist a story like that. Look at this headline: 'Woman Detective Rescues Lunatic.'" She rattled the page at me but wouldn't actually let me look at it.

"It sounds like a moving picture," Fleurette said.

"The *Hackensack Republican* agrees," Norma said. "I can't tell if I'm reading a newspaper or *Moby-Dick*." She pushed her spectacles up and read it to us.

Sabbath morning dawned dark and gloomy. A north-easter of indeterminate force, varying from breeze to half-gale, carried snowflakes that covered the earth with a pure white mantle save where soggy roads turned the fleecy crystals into drops that were lost in the mud which stretched away through the town and country, monster black serpents, thick with pasty, oily slime. As the day advanced into afternoon and the storm ceased, sputtering like a weary runner, the sun shone forth, and night tossed her dark robe over a world rejoicing in a rosy sunset. The moon, passing into its first quarter and

attended by a tiny star, rode in brilliant glory,
while the constellations and the Milky Way honored
the Queen of Night. Quote we now from the Newark
News . . .

"'The Queen of Night'?" I put in. "They're embarrassing themselves."

"They're trying to embarrass you. I'll spare you the account of
the rescue itself, on the grounds that you're already acquainted
with the facts, and go right on to the quotes they've invented for
you, presented, they explained, to illustrate the fact that the 'deputy sheriffess is susceptible to the weaknesses of ordinary women.'"

"Please don't," I said, but she did.

We quote the Tribune, to the end that no element
of this serio-farcical romantic comedietta may per-
ish from the earth.

"I will never forgive myself," she said, after
a night's rest under the care of a trained nurse.
"I really wasn't scared though. I was just awfully
tired when I got my man ashore."

"It was wonderful, Miss Kopp," beamed Sheriff
Heath, who stood by.

"Not so wonderful," protested his deputy. "He
was my prisoner and I was responsible for him."

"That's all right," insisted the sheriff, "but I
consider you one of the most efficient county officials that we have."

"Thanks awfully, Sheriff. Everything is all
right now except," and Miss Kopp hesitated, "except
my suit."

"We'll go to New York and get a new one. The county owes you that."

"You have not been to New York to look at dresses without me!" Fleurette cried. She'd taken to wearing a string of wax-filled glass beads meant to resemble pearls. They had not yet made their New York debut.

Norma knew her business and liked to work Fleurette into a state. "That's what it says. Apparently Mrs. Heath took her."

"Mrs. Heath!"

"Of course she didn't," I assured Fleurette. "Do I look like I've been to New York to shop for dresses? They stole most of that from the *Tribune,* and invented the rest."

"Then how did the *Tribune* find out? I hope it was a man under a lamp-post with a notebook and an evil glint in his eye," Fleurette said.

"That's how they do it in the pictures, but in this case, Sheriff Heath had to go over to the courthouse and explain why the inmates hadn't yet been sent away. The reporters heard just enough to get going on it."

"Or maybe one of the guards is being paid to slip scandalous news to the papers," Fleurette suggested, ever hopeful for more drama and intrigue.

"Our guards wouldn't do that to Sheriff Heath," I said. "Besides, there's nothing scandalous about it. Inmates do try to escape. It's our job to put a stop to it. That's all I did."

"The real scandal is that you stayed at work all day after you went for a swim in the Hackensack River," said Norma. "I don't believe that particular odor has ever been introduced to our parlor before, and we do live on a farm."

I was a mess. It was no wonder I'd been so ill-treated by Dr.

Lipsky and Dr. Ogden. "I've come home for a bath and a fresh suit. I intend to use every one of Fleurette's soaps and potions."

"Not all of them!" Fleurette shrieked, and ran upstairs to put away her lavender talc and *savon violette*.

I was starting to stiffen on the divan, so I groaned and forced myself up. "I'll tell you the scandal that ought to be in the papers," I said to Norma. "The woman I was to have taken to Morris Plains has been committed by her husband for no reason that I can see. Her doctor insists that it's nervous hysteria, but even he admits that he hasn't so much as spoken to her."

Norma didn't bother to look up from her paper. "If she's been committed, there must be something the matter with her. She managed to hide it from you, but some of them are clever that way."

"What do you know about it?"

"I know there's nothing you can do if the judge has ruled. You oughtn't to try to save every errant girl who comes your way."

"She's hardly a girl. She's well over fifty, and do you know that this is the fourth time her husband has had her committed? I had to do something."

Norma looked up at me, suspicious. "What did you do?"

"I just told you. I went to speak to her doctor, but he had nothing more to say on the matter. It seems to me that she should have another physician examine her, but how is she to arrange any of that?"

"Don't they have doctors at Morris Plains?"

"Of course, but have you ever heard of an asylum doctor turning a patient away because she seemed too sane for commitment?"

"No," Norma admitted. "I suppose what she needs is a lawyer, not a doctor. Does she happen to have one of those in her pocket?"

"She does not."

I was already on my way upstairs. I paused on the third step and turned around. "But . . . there's no reason I shouldn't speak to a lawyer."

"I can think of all sorts of reasons," Norma muttered, but it was spoken entirely out of habit. She'd already turned back to her papers and the words came out reflexively.

I thought it over as I soaked in the bath Fleurette had drawn for me, which was laced with the only toiletries she would permit me to use: a bath salt scented of cheap lilac, and a bar of soap meant to smell like cashmere, although even Fleurette couldn't explain what odor cashmere possessed.

It didn't matter. Even her least favorite toiletries brought about a tremendous improvement in my spirits and banished the miasma of New Jersey waterways from my person.

Sheriff Heath had made it plain that his office had no jurisdiction over Anna Kayser's commitment. But what was to stop me, in the privacy of my own home, from making a personal inquiry of an attorney? If I could find someone to help Mrs. Kayser, the sheriff's office need not be involved at all.

That night, I wrote a letter to a lady lawyer I'd met once in New York. I didn't even know what branch of the law she practiced, and had only shared a congenial dinner with her and her friends when I found myself at a hotel on another case. Nevertheless, I hoped she might be sympathetic to Anna Kayser's plight, and I thought it best not to involve a Hackensack attorney whose loyalties would be unknown to me.

Dear Geraldine,

I write to ask your advice concerning a woman under my care at the Hackensack Jail. She has been committed to the lunatic asylum at Morris Plains and will no doubt have arrived there by the time this letter finds you, as I have no way of keeping her any longer. She is as sane as anyone I've ever met. Both her doctor and her husband are bent on locking her up, for reasons they cannot satisfactorily explain. Hasn't she any legal rights?

I'm acquainted with a lawyer or two in Hackensack, but everyone here seems to take it as a matter of course that women go to the asylum for no apparent reason.

Your wise counsel would be received with gratitude.

I remain,

> Yours in the inglorious pursuit of justice,
> Constance Amélie Kopp
> Deputy Sheriff, Bergen County

☙ 11 ❧

OWING TO THE events of the last few days, I'd skipped my weekly probation visits. It was near the end of the month and I owed Judge Seufert a report.

The probation program was my idea: I perceived a need to keep troubled but not troublesome women (as I liked to call them) out of jail, or to get them released if the charges against them were unfair. Young girls in particular were, naturally, more willing to confide in me than in a male deputy, which meant that I was often able to get at the root of their problems and to help them to see a way out.

In some cases, this meant persuading a girl to return home to her strict father and overbearing mother, and to put more effort into her school-work. In other cases, I was able to negotiate some freedom for girls who wouldn't have had any otherwise. I could persuade a judge that a girl who'd been reckless once might not be again, after she understood the consequences. I could negotiate a truce between a mother and daughter by persuading the mother to drop a charge of delinquency or incorrigibility in exchange for allowing the daughter a measure of freedom unheard of in the previous generation.

And for women who trafficked in the more ordinary styles of

crime—theft, arson, fraud, and assault—I could investigate their background and, in some cases, argue that the crime was brought about by circumstances that wouldn't occur again, if only the woman in question could be released and freed from her association with the unsavory characters who had led her astray.

As a result, I had acquired a growing list of women under my supervision, not at the jail, but out in Hackensack and the surrounding small towns. With my oversight they went to work, lived in respectable rooms, and comported themselves in such a way as to avoid running afoul of the law again. I don't mind saying that I took a great deal of pride in the fact that I'd kept so many out of jails, reformatories, and state homes. It might sound bad for business for a deputy sheriff to keep people out of jail, but the plain fact is that a criminal mark will do nothing but impede a woman from her return to a respectable life. If I couldn't put her on a better course, I would only see her in jail again and again, and that wouldn't serve the public interest.

For this reason it had become a regular part of my duties to carry a little dark green notebook with me and to visit these women. Once a month I wrote a report that celebrated their small triumphs and commiserated over their minor setbacks. Judge Seufert, to whom I was required to submit the reports, told me that he enjoyed them on their literary merits alone. He looked forward to my monthly missives as one would a new installment of a Sunday serial. I'd begun to suspect that he agreed more readily to release women to my care simply to see the cast of characters expanded.

I made my rounds on no particular schedule, preferring to catch my probationers by surprise. Fortunately, both of my Hawthorne girls were at home when I stopped by.

I found Fanny Langer in front of the shop where she worked, washing down the windows with a wad of newspaper.

"I have a story for your little book," she called when she saw me. She put her newspaper down and wiped her hands on a canvas apron that was so large it wrapped around her twice.

"I'm glad to hear it," I said. I had trained my girls to produce some amount of descriptive detail on command, knowing how it would please Judge Seufert. It wasn't enough to merely jot down that they were in good health and staying out of trouble: he liked a story with a moral and an uplifting conclusion.

Fanny walked over and stood on her toes to look into my notebook as I wrote. "First, you should put down that I turned seventeen last week, and some of the neighbors brought over a little cake. Don't you see, that means that I'm making friends and that I'm well-liked."

This girl was quite the self-promoter. I wondered if she'd considered going into sales. I wrote that down and asked her if there was anything else to tell.

"There is, and you'll like it so much! I'm allowed to run the cash register now. I've been doing it for two weeks, and not a penny has gone missing."

"I would never expect otherwise," I said.

Fanny was no thief, and I knew it. She got into trouble when she worked for a junk dealer who could neither read nor write. For that reason Fanny handled his check-book, indicating where he was to make his mark when a check had to be written. After only a few short weeks she made a check out to herself, knowing that he couldn't tell the difference. A watchful bank clerk told the junk man about it, and Fanny was arrested.

That was not the entire story—of course, it wasn't! Fanny couldn't have told the truth to a male officer, but she made her confession to me on the first night. The girl had no family to speak of, her mother having died a few years earlier and her father gone to Cleveland to pursue a business opportunity. Finding herself without a roof over her head, she was obliged to rent a room at the back of the junk dealer's shop.

It's easy enough to guess at what came next. The man began paying unwelcome visits to her late at night. She took the money because she couldn't see any other means of escaping and starting over in some new position.

I had a little difficulty explaining the matter to Judge Seufert in language suitable to the formalities of the court, but he caught on readily enough and agreed that I might find another position for Fanny. A shop-woman in Hawthorne (known to my brother's wife, Bessie, who worked a little persuasion in the form of flattering words and raspberry preserves) proved sympathetic to the situation and was willing to give Fanny a job as long as it didn't involve handling cash. The junk dealer agreed to drop the charges, provided the money was repaid. Fanny took a room above the shop; worked diligently at sweeping, dusting, and other such chores; and gradually discharged her debt.

It was a relief to see Fanny doing so well. "Keep this up, and I'll write you out of my green book for good," I told her. I stepped inside to have a word with the shop-woman, and then let them get back to their business. I didn't like to keep anyone too long if there weren't any problems. The reward for sticking to the rules should be that the deputy sheriff isn't hanging around all day.

My next stop was just a few blocks from my brother's house, where I looked in on Katie Carlson, a Swedish girl arrested for waywardness. Hers was an unusual case to fall under my jurisdiction, as it hadn't originated in Bergen County, but in Philadelphia. Katie had gone before a lady judge at the new girls' juvenile court established in that city on charges filed by her parents. She was out of control, they alleged, and had been staying out all night at dance halls and coming home under the influence of liquor.

In her defense, Katie had nothing at all to say and merely

snapped that the charges were true and that the judge ought to send her to a state home. After a few more gentle questions, it developed that Katie resented going to work every day and bringing every penny she earned home to her mother, while her father spent his paycheck at the saloon. She thought she ought to be entitled to do as he did.

"I hate him," she told the judge, "and you would too, if he were your father."

The judge saw no reason to argue with that. She called the father before the bench and lectured him about his family obligations, then arranged for Katie to be sent to New Jersey to live with an aunt willing to take her in. The aunt was to make sure that Katie finished her schooling and that she stayed away from liquor and dance halls. It fell to me to see that the judge's order was carried out.

The aunt lived in a comfortable and well-tended bungalow. As I walked up to the front door, I thought about how pleased Katie must've been to have landed in such comfortable circumstances. But when the door opened, it became immediately clear that Katie was not at all pleased.

She was such a pretty girl, with angelic light hair and eyes the color of the sky, but she was not at all agreeable to look at when she was angry. Her mouth turned down at the corners, her nose was red, and she refused to grace me with so much as a glance.

"Oh, that's just fine. Now the lady deputy's come to write her report." Katie marched back into the parlor, but left the door ajar so I could follow. The aunt appeared to be out of the house. I took a chair across from Katie—they were old carved oak chairs of the sort my own mother's family had brought over from Vienna in the last century—and waited to hear the worst of it.

"I can't say anything right, so you might as well put down whatever you want in that book of yours," she snapped.

"I can only put down what you tell me. What's come over you?"

"Only that I have no time to myself, and no friends to talk to anyway, or anything else to do but dust this old parlor and polish the silver."

"Don't you go to school?"

"Yes, and it's dull and I hate it. I'd rather go back to work."

"But your aunt gives you work to do, and you complain about it."

"Then I'd rather just go home. It was better than this. At least I did what I liked."

"And for that, they arrested you."

Katie sniffed and flung her legs over the side of her chair. I would've thought a sixteen-year-old too mature for such theatrics, although I had to admit that Fleurette had been just the same at that age.

That gave me an idea.

"What is it, exactly, that you miss about your old life? Is it your parents?"

"Of course not. I can't stand my father, and I can do without my mother."

It gave me a little pain to hear a girl say a thing like that, but I pressed on. "What is it, then? Your friends? Tell me, or I can't help you."

She picked at an upholstery tack with her thumbnail and said, under her breath, "I used to go to the dance halls, and learn all the dances. I bet there are a dozen new ones now, and I haven't even heard the songs. There's not any sort of music in this house, nor anywhere for me to go hear any."

There it was! Having raised a girl with aspirations for the stage, I recognized one in Katie.

"Well, what would you think about taking some dancing lessons?"

Katie looked up with interest but said, "I'm not allowed out."

"I'm not talking about a saloon. I mean that you could take lessons at a girls' academy. It's not so terribly expensive, and perhaps your aunt wouldn't mind paying for it, if you worked a little harder around the house. Isn't she a teacher?"

"Yes, which is why I never have any fun at school. She's always watching me."

I wasn't there to listen to the girl complain, so I rose to go. "I'm sure she's very busy at school and would appreciate it if you'd do a bit more at home. Help with the cooking. Couldn't you do that?"

Katie shrugged. She clearly wasn't prepared to strike any sort of bargain. Nonetheless, I wrote in my little green book, "Katie does everything asked of her at home and has stayed with her schooling. She shows some musical promise and hopes to enroll at a girls' academy of music and dance. Deputy Kopp to speak with her aunt at earliest convenience."

It wasn't much of a report, as I was forced to omit Katie's rebelliousness and her litany of complaints. There was some drama Judge Seufert didn't need to hear.

"Be good to your aunt," I told her as I left. "You were given a second chance. Not everyone is."

⇥ 12 ⇤

WHEN I ARRIVED at the jail later that day, an automobile from the Hackensack Hospital was waiting to take Tony Hajnacka and Anna Kayser away. Dr. Ogden stood alongside it, looking every part the aggrieved chauffeur. With him was a young and timid-looking nurse who stared up at the jail's glowering façade. She was trying to keep the worry from her face, as nurses are trained to do. She obviously hadn't had much experience with it yet. I could only imagine Dr. Ogden telling her that the lady deputy couldn't handle transporting lunatics, so she'd been conscripted to take my place.

Sheriff Heath was just walking out to greet him. "I'll bring Hajnacka down myself," he told Dr. Ogden, "and Deputy Kopp here will deliver Mrs. Kayser to you. I take it you'd like the men in the front and the ladies in the back."

Dr. Ogden had a way of tucking his chin down and peering over the tops of his spectacles to express disapproval. It reminded me of a very similar expression of Norma's. "The inmates can ride in the back."

"I wouldn't put two inmates together, Bill," the sheriff said. "You want an officer alongside. We'll chain them to the door so they can't escape. I'm sure Nurse Schilling will feel perfectly safe alongside her charge. Mrs. Kayser is as docile as a lamb and might well be quieter if she had a nurse for company."

"Of course," the nurse said, eager to prove her mettle. "It's no bother."

Dr. Ogden glared at the sheriff. "We'll do it your way, but if there's any trouble . . ."

Sheriff Heath laughed and slapped Dr. Ogden on the back in a show of friendship he surely didn't feel. "If there's any trouble, you're to blame, Bill! That's the burden and the blessing of public service. What happens under your watch is credited entirely to you. Now, let us deliver your inmates."

Sheriff Heath turned to go and I went along with him.

"The nurse can bring Mrs. Kayser down," Dr. Ogden called, and the nurse quite visibly quaked.

But Sheriff Heath just waved him off. "My jail, my rules, Bill. Inside my four walls, we handle our own inmates."

When we were inside, I said, "I don't know how you manage to stay civil."

"Staying civil is the one absolute requirement of elected office," Sheriff Heath said. He was almost buoyant about it. "And speaking of elections, you're to meet my successor in a few minutes. Shine your shoes."

"You can't be serious," I said. My boots were atrocious, but it was impossible to keep them otherwise.

"Just take a look at mine." Indeed, I could almost see my reflection in Sheriff Heath's everyday shoes. "Remember, Mr. Conklin used to be sheriff. He likes a clean uniform."

"All right," I grumbled. I parted ways with him and went upstairs to fetch Mrs. Kayser. She was perched on the edge of her bunk, waiting for me, her coat folded neatly across her lap with her handbag on top. She could've been waiting for a street-car.

"I'm sorry, Mrs. Kayser, but it's time."

She looked at me with such kind affection. "It's not for you to apologize, dear."

I opened the cell and when she stepped forward, I whispered, "We only have a moment. I've written to a lawyer friend on your behalf. As soon as I hear from her, I'll get word to you. I'm not sure how I'll do it, but do watch for some kind of message from me. It might be . . ."

She smiled tentatively. "Written in code?"

"I don't mean to make a game of it, only to say that I'm pursuing this on my own. No one else knows."

She squinted up at me. "Your sheriff doesn't know."

It was embarrassing to hear her put it like that. What must she think of me? "It's . . . it's a little out of bounds. If there's anything else I ought to know, tell it to me now. You don't know me very well, but I don't give up easily."

I couldn't delay any longer. I led her down the stairs. "You're a good girl," she said, and once again I felt more like her daughter than her jailer. "But in there, hope makes the time pass even more slowly. Send word to me if you can, but I won't expect it and you shouldn't feel disappointed if you can't."

We were by that time at the bottom of the stairs. "Isn't there anything more I can do for you?" I asked as we went past the interrogation rooms and out into the damp, gray afternoon.

Anna sighed at the sight of the auto and the nurse standing alongside. "Get word to my daughter if you can. Tell her I'll be fine. Tell her I'll be home before she knows it."

"I will."

There was nothing left to do but to lock her inside the machine. She held her wrists out willingly. Her hands were cold. I warmed them with my own before I let her go.

• • •

SHERIFF HEATH AND I watched the auto roll away. There was a secret standing between us now: my letter to Geraldine, my promise to get word to Mrs. Kayser if I could. It was a small secret, hardly worth keeping. Why not just tell him that I'd written to an attorney on her behalf, as a private citizen? I'd even posted the letter from home. What difference could it possibly make?

I might've said something at just that moment, but as we turned to go back inside the jail, a man's voice called out from behind us. "Just hand me the keys, Bob, and I'll take it from here!"

There was no time. I spun around to meet my new boss, realizing as I did that I hadn't bothered to shine my shoes. I made the mistake of glancing down at them, and so did he.

I could tell in an instant that William Conklin was nothing like Sheriff Heath. He was robust in the red-faced, loud-mouthed manner of a man who was once captain of the college football team, and thought of as great fun at parties. Sheriff Heath might've had a number of good ideas about the running of the jail, and he was wily enough to catch a criminal and enjoy doing it, but no one would ever believe him to be fun at a party.

"Deputy Constance Kopp," Sheriff Heath said, "may I introduce Mr. William Conklin."

I offered my hand and Mr. Conklin took it. His own hands were enormous and surprisingly warm. There was something about him that reminded me of a furnace.

"So this is our lady deputy!" He was one of those men who had a tendency to shout, even in close quarters, and he spoke with a trace of a Virginia accent. "Bob told me all about your good work with the girls upstairs. That's just fine."

He flashed a row of perfect teeth at me. Although his face was lined and leathery, with deep crinkles around the eyes and an impressive cleft in his chin, there was something about him that seemed impervious to age. He had a vigor that could fill any room. I understood at once how he won elections.

He slapped Sheriff Heath on the back, and the three of us stepped inside and down the hall to the sheriff's office. Mr. Conklin arranged his long limbs into the nearest chair and said, "Bob, go ahead and finish with your girl here. I must be early."

Sheriff Heath cleared his throat. "I asked Deputy Kopp to join us. She'll be a great help to you on this campaign."

Mr. Conklin leaned back in his chair and pulled a pouch of tobacco from his pocket. "That's awfully decent of you, Bob, but I've got a girl down at the office who does my calls and letters. I won't need any—"

"I'll be your deputy, not your stenographer," I put in, and immediately regretted it. I had hoped to sound light about it, but it didn't come out that way.

Mr. Conklin's face looked vacant for a minute, then he reassembled it into a visage of amiability and said, in the noncommittal manner that politicians have when they want to duck a difficult conversation, "Of course, ma'am. Just as you say."

Sheriff Heath said, "We didn't have female deputies when you were sheriff last time, so you ought to know something about what Deputy Kopp does. It's proving to be of great interest to the voters."

There was a flash of something in William Conklin's eyes. I couldn't be sure, but I suspected he'd already formed his own opinion about female deputies. He covered it quickly and said, "That's why I'm here, Bob. Why don't you tell me all about it?"

I didn't wait for Sheriff Heath to answer. "Just a few days ago I caught a thief running out of Mr. Giordano's shop," I offered. "He gave quite a chase, but I had no trouble in catching him."

"Catching him! Do you mean to say that you went chasing him down the street?"

I couldn't tell if Mr. Conklin was teasing me or not: he had that way about him.

"Of course she did," Sheriff Heath said.

"Was he a boy?" Mr. Conklin asked, genuinely curious.

"No, he was a Polish gentleman of about forty," I said.

"Ha! Another Pole out thieving." Mr. Conklin slapped his knee. "I'm sure old Johnnie Courter would rather lock up a German if he could get one, but he'll take a Pole. Looks good to the voters. He can say he's doing something about the immigrant problem."

Then he looked me over and added, "I'm sorry, ma'am. You're not German, are you? Name like Kopp, I suppose you might be. Ever think of changing it?"

I had no patience for that kind of talk and didn't like to hear it coming from the man running for Sheriff Heath's office. The whole country was getting whipped up into a frenzy over the war, and a man in the fever of combat will see enemies everywhere. Americans were turning against not just the Germans and the Austrians, but also against the Poles and any other flavor of European they found disagreeable—all of whom were viewed as sympathetic to the eastern front, and as refusing to take up American ways. They posed a vague threat never properly explained, but that didn't stop politicians from making a campaign issue of it.

"Unless you see the job of sheriff as that of putting people into jail before they commit a crime, I don't see how anyone's nationality comes into it," I said in the awkward silence that hung about the room.

"There's no point in debating Mr. Courter's positions," Sheriff Heath said hastily. "He's unfit to carry the keys to this jail and the voters know it."

In an effort to turn the conversation back to my duties, I said, "I also stopped an inmate from escaping a few nights ago."

"I might've read something about that in the papers, miss," he said. "I wonder why we bother to hire any fellows at all, if you ladies are going to run out and collar criminals all by yourselves."

"She does good work with delinquent girls," Sheriff Heath put in quickly, "and you know our men can't get a word out of those girls."

I realized that Sheriff Heath had meant for me to tell about my probationers, this being a better example of the kind of situation where a woman could succeed when a man could not. William Conklin didn't need a woman to chase down thieves and clearly didn't want them to.

"I never did like those delinquency cases," Mr. Conklin said. "Impossible to prove, wastes your time."

"But the girls get sent away without cause," I said, "and that's a waste of a life." I'd given up on trying not to sound stiff and rigid. Mr. Conklin seemed to bring it out in me.

He seemed as discomfited by the conversation as I was. "Well, all I'm saying is that it's not the best part of the job."

"What is the best part of the job?" came a voice from the doorway. It was Cordelia Heath, looking every the inch the politician's wife in a rose-colored serge suit with a flag-patterned ribbon pinned to her lapel.

Mr. Conklin was back on his feet in an instant. "Is that Cordelia? Cordelia Heath? You don't look a day over twenty, and you never have. I wish you'd give your beauty secrets to Mrs. Conklin. Now, don't you tell her I said that, pretty girl." He leaned over and planted a kiss on her cheek.

Cordelia's complexion turned the precise color of her dress. "Bill, you know I tell Loretta every word you say, so watch yourself."

In all the time I've known Cordelia, I have never seen her sparkle like that. She was usually so restrained, and always on the verge of expressing her displeasure. Ordinarily, a smile from

Cordelia was a token to be issued when protocol demanded it, but now she grinned and blushed and lapped up his flattery like a debutante.

I looked over at Sheriff Heath in surprise, but he didn't seem to find anything unusual in it and in fact seemed relieved for the distraction. He rose to pull a chair from the corner of the room for Cordelia, but Mr. Conklin beat him to it, and offered Cordelia a seat at his side, having pushed my chair away. I didn't take offense: I wasn't looking to be kissed on the cheek by the next sheriff of Bergen County.

I would've been happy to make my escape, but Sheriff Heath nodded for me to stay and said, "Bill, I want you to have a look at the program Cordelia's put together for this campaign. She has me speaking at every club and church supper in Bergen County over the next month, and we'd like to have you along. I'm campaigning on my record, which is to say that I'm telling the public about the good works of this office. It seems only natural that they'll want to meet the man who's going to carry on with what we've started here at the jail. I've also put some photographs together so that people can see for themselves. Deputy Kopp is sometimes on hand to answer questions about our programs for women, which seems to hold a special interest at the ladies' clubs."

Mr. Conklin leaned forward in his chair so he could take another look at me. To my astonishment, he winked at me. "I do love those ladies' clubs. They put out a spread like you will never see at a Rotary supper. There's a group of ladies down in Fort Lee who do an entire table of pies. Pies like you can't imagine. Pork pies, chicken pies, potato pies, and then every kind of fruit and cream pie. One of them does a maple sugar pie, and I told Loretta to get that recipe but she never could. You ladies like your secrets, isn't that right, Miss Kopp?"

I was entirely unprepared to answer a question about pies and secrets. "They do feed us well" was the best I could muster. "But they also very much want to hear about our programs, and I know they're eager to meet you."

"Oh, they've met me." He leaned back in his chair and stretched his arms above his head, then laced his fingers behind his neck so that Cordelia had to duck to avoid his elbows. "I don't mean to say anything against your traveling picture show, Bob, but nobody really wants to know the sheriff. They'd rather not think about the sheriff at all if they can avoid it. Now, a mayor is someone people like to meet. And a congressman." He laughed genially at that. "That's you, Bob! The congressman. That's who they're coming out to see. They don't need to see Mr. William Conklin. They all know me, and they know to put a mark next to my name on Election Day. They've been doing it for years. Tax board, Freeholder, sheriff, garbage man, dog catcher . . ."

He laughed at his own joke again. Sheriff Heath cleared his throat and said, "The voters do appreciate your service, Bill. I don't expect you to have any trouble at all in this election. Mr. Courter goes around making a fool of himself, and you're right, people like an even-tempered sheriff they can just forget about."

"That's me, Bob," Mr. Conklin said, grinning again at Cordelia. "Just forget about me."

"How could we?" Cordelia said, and handed him the schedule she'd written out. "I hope you'll join us when you can."

Sheriff Heath said, "I think you'd particularly like to make an appearance right here at the jail next week, when we put on Captain Anderson's Salvation Army program. He's going to speak to the men about turning their lives around. Deputy Kopp's sister is going to lead the group in song."

"Is that right?" Mr. Conklin said.

"She's been practicing for weeks, with a friend of hers," I said. Cordelia put a hand on Mr. Conklin's arm. "Please do come,

Bill. I've invited some ladies to attend the concert and take a tour of the female section."

This was the first I'd heard of a tour of the female section. I didn't like the idea of putting my inmates on display. I glanced at Sheriff Heath, but he wouldn't return the look.

"I've invited the wives of the ministers, and of the Freeholders and a few businessmen—all the old families. We'll put out a nice spread. You'll want to be there for the cakes and pies alone."

"Well, then, I won't say no. With all your ladies working their magic, we can't lose." He reached around for the hat hanging on the back of his chair, which seemed to signal that the meeting was over. I was entirely sure that Sheriff Heath had hoped to spend the next hour poring over every detail of the jail's budget, programs, and daily operations, but Mr. Conklin didn't seem interested.

"The public doesn't expect much, Bob," he said, as he shook the sheriff's hand. "Just keep the criminals on the inside, that's all anyone cares about."

Mrs. Heath coughed and looked sharply at her husband. No one looked at me.

"Aw, what did I say this time?" Mr. Conklin said, in the awkward silence that followed. "I know you didn't mean to let that fellow run off. Don't worry about it, Miss Kopp."

"I didn't let him run off," I said. "He ran off, and I caught him."

Mr. Conklin looked between us, confused. "Well, who did let him get away?"

"Bill, you know from your time as sheriff that things can go wrong, even for a good deputy," Sheriff Heath said. "It's better not to name names. You never did."

"Well, but I never had a lady being insulted back then! Go defend her good name, if she wasn't to blame! John Courter's out there making speeches about it."

This was the first I'd heard of any speeches about me from Mr. Courter. Sheriff Heath didn't so much as blink—I have to credit him that. "Mr. Courter doesn't have a say in whom I employ or why. If I let him force me into a debate over my deputies, there will be no end to it. Don't you see? I refuse on principle."

Mr. Conklin chuckled at that and gave a little bow to me and Cordelia. "Ladies, I'm going to leave you to Mr. Heath and his principles. I'll see you next week. Save one of those pies for me."

⊰ 13 ⊱

AFTER MY MOTHER died, my brother's wife, Bessie, took over the responsibility for hosting our family dinner once a month, to everyone's relief. Francis had married the best sort of woman: a sturdy and energetic creature who turned out the most savory of dinners and the most delectable desserts, ran an orderly household, raised well-behaved children, and imbued the entire family with her rosy good cheer. She seemed to approve of everything we Kopp sisters did, and believed our lives to be one grand adventure after another.

She also played the role of mediator between me and my brother. He saw it as his obligation to point out the dangers inherent in my profession, and its overall unsuitability as an occupation for a sister of his. It unnerved him to see my exploits written up in the papers. I suspect that he took some ribbing over it at work: while he sat behind a desk at a basket importer's office, I was out chasing down escaped fugitives, wrestling thieves to the ground, and extracting confessions from recalcitrant witnesses. Even when I was doing nothing more than watching over striking workers at a textile mill, the papers wrote up a breathless account of it, and Francis undoubtedly had to hear about it at work.

Every time I saw him, he had a new idea about a more appropriate profession for me than that of deputy sheriff. At our Sunday dinner, I was treated to his latest. He offered to set me up in a millinery shop, where I might spend my days putting feathers into hat-bands.

Norma put a stop to him before I could. "I wouldn't expect you to know a thing about women's hats, but surely you're acquainted with your own sister and her manner of dress."

"There's nothing wrong with her manner of dress," Fleurette said. "I dress her myself."

It was true. I reached six feet in height at the age of twenty, and never did find a thing to wear in the shops after that. Fleurette knew my measurements perfectly, and started turning out dresses for me as soon as she could work a sewing machine. It fell to her to invent my uniform, as the sheriff's department had no provision for a female deputy's suit. I'd never felt more authoritative in my life than I did the first time I stepped into one of Fleurette's fine uniforms.

"I only mean to say," Norma continued, "that her style of dress, and the cut of her hat in particular, is not one to be emulated by the well-to-do ladies of Hackensack, upon whom she would depend for clientele. If her hair would fit under a conductor's cap, she'd wear one of those and be perfectly happy about it."

"I do like those caps," I admitted.

"Then why not set up a shop making uniforms for lady officers?" Francis asked. "You could send circulars to the larger police departments. There must be a call for it."

"Why on earth would I sew uniforms for lady officers when I can be a lady officer?" I asked in astonishment.

Francis was seated at one end of the table, in front of a platter of sliced ham. I was seated at his right, and his children, Lorraine and Frankie, were next to me, eyeing the steaming dish of scalloped potatoes, the basket of rolls, the buttered peas, and the string beans in hot bacon. It was difficult for any of us to wait.

Francis pushed the ham aside to make room for a dish of creamed spinach. "I only thought that with the election coming up . . ."

"We're not to speak of politics at the dinner table," Lorraine pronounced. In just the last year, she'd grown from a playful little girl into a prim young lady who liked to remind others of the rules.

"Well, I approve of that. I'd rather not speak of politics at all. Where did these tomatoes come from?" I said as I took a plate of them from young Frankie. "I thought yours were done for the year."

"Don't you recognize them?" Bessie asked. She'd come in from the kitchen without her apron, which was our signal that dinner could begin. "Those are from your garden. Your sisters brought them over."

"Constance didn't so much as look at the vegetable garden this summer," Norma said.

"I paid for a boy to take care of it," I answered. "Isn't that enough?"

"Could I pay for a girl to do the washing as well?" Fleurette asked.

"Try to pay your own keep first," Norma returned. The scant wages Fleurette earned as a seamstress, and her predilection for spending them on herself and not on the household expenses, were an endless source of disagreement between them. In fact, my wages, along with a few small leases of our land, kept all three of us, and I saw nothing wrong with that arrangement.

The conversation continued along those lines while the platters went around. I'd never had such a good dinner in my life until Francis married Bessie. She only asked us over once a month, probably because Norma, Fleurette, and I ate enough to feed a small nation when we sat at her table. Even a woman of Bessie's hearty constitution must've been exhausted by the effort. We tended to deplete her supply of jams and pickles, too, as we couldn't be bothered to do our own.

A few satisfied moments of silence followed as we could do nothing but murmur appreciatively at the culinary miracles Bessie had wrought.

"I understand you fished a fellow out of the river last week," Francis said.

"Saved his life," I said, and buttered another roll to fortify myself. "Now I'm trying to help a woman who's been committed to Morris Plains under suspicious circumstances."

"Yes, only she can't tell the sheriff," Fleurette volunteered. "She's written off to a lady lawyer to enlist some help, but it's to be kept a secret because the sheriff can't afford another scandal in the papers."

"That isn't the reason," I said. "Sheriff Heath never said a word about the papers. It's simply outside of our jurisdiction to be involved in a commitment case. I've written to a lawyer as a private citizen, nothing more."

"But he was thinking of the papers," Francis said. "Nobody gets elected on a campaign of letting nuts out of the nut house."

"She isn't a nut," I said. "The voters wouldn't want to see a housewife locked away without cause."

Francis laughed at that. "The voters or the housewives? Because one will be lined up at the ballot box and the other won't."

I wasn't about to get into an argument with my brother over votes for women. I could see that Bessie didn't want to either, for she jumped up and took away Francis's empty plate. "I have a lemon cake and an apple pie. Shall we take a vote, in the spirit of the campaign?"

There could've been no more welcome diversion. Bessie made her lemon cake with a milk frosting that no one could resist, but her pies were also legendary. There is something about a lattice crust, brushed in butter and sprinkled with tiny boulders of brown sugar, that renders whatever is underneath superfluous. But of course the apples were coming into season and promised to be excellent.

I begged pitiably for both and the children joined in. Our votes won the day, and soon we were settled in contentedly with our dessert plates and coffee. Bessie, trying to keep the conversation light, said, "Mrs. Heath has taken a real interest in the campaign, which I think is all to the good. I see her at the library every week. Her mother's quite encouraged by it."

"I've only met Mrs. Westervelt in passing," I said. Cordelia's mother was possessed of a community spirit that Cordelia seemed not to have inherited. Mrs. Westervelt ran the library (where Bessie volunteered her time a few afternoons a week), directed the historical society, and wrote the history of Bergen County in multiple volumes. She belonged to every club in town, could speak extemporaneously on subjects ranging from botany to road construction, and seemed to know all of Hackensack by name. Her daughter could not have been more different.

"Well, as you can imagine, Mrs. Westervelt is quite relieved to see Cordelia doing something to help her husband rather than fight him every step of the way."

"I suppose. She does seem happier when she's busy. I didn't know it was all her mother's doing."

"Oh, yes. Mrs. Westervelt has very firm opinions on how a wife ought to conduct herself."

From the other end of the table, Norma said, "I'd like to hear that."

"According to Mrs. Westervelt, a wife ought to stay busy," Bessie said, "and have a reason to get out of the house, such as a club or a charity. If she can, she ought to find some small way to involve herself in her husband's business. 'Just enough to make for better conversation at the breakfast table,' as she likes to say. She told a woman to bring her garden club downtown to plant flowers along the street where her husband runs a shop. Do you know the lady did it the very next day?"

"What has she told you to do?" Fleurette asked.

"It wasn't a bad idea," Bessie admitted, taking a sip of her coffee. "She thought I ought to take the most popular line of wickerwork that Francis sells, and get a group together to fill decorated baskets for the needy. We'd have our picture made for the paper, and credit would go to Francis for the donation."

"I'd rather have credit for selling baskets than giving them away, as that's more our line of business," Francis said.

"Well, I think it's lovely," Bessie answered, "and the children want to have a hand in it, too."

"Cordelia's gone beyond flowers and decorated baskets," I said. "She's in the sheriff's office every day and gets quite involved in his affairs. She's the one who wants to keep me out of the papers right now."

"I don't know why she's so worried about what gets said in the race for sheriff, if her husband's running for Congress," said Fleurette.

"It's because he's running on his record," Francis said. "He's never done anything but serve as sheriff and undersheriff, so the voters will judge him by it. William Conklin is the one running against John Courter in the sheriff's race, which means that Conklin will have to take a stand for Sheriff Heath or stand against him."

"What do you think of Mr. Conklin?" Bessie asked me. "Will he make a good sheriff?"

"I don't know yet," I said, but it took a great deal of effort to keep my voice from betraying me. "I only just met him and haven't yet formed an opinion of how he'll run the jail. He was sheriff back in 1910, and he hired Sheriff Heath as a deputy, so I suppose they think alike." I'd seen no evidence of that, but I was reluctant to criticize the man who was to become my boss.

Francis raised an eyebrow at that. "I've seen Conklin at my club a time or two. I don't think he has much in common with your sheriff, but in this election that might work in his favor."

"Francis!" Bessie scolded. "Sheriff Heath is a friend of this family and always will be after what he's done for your sister. Now he'll be a congressman, which is terribly impressive. Have you ever known one personally?"

"What I mean to say is that Mr. Courter is going around criticizing Sheriff Heath for hiring a lady deputy in the first place, and coddling the inmates, and for letting them escape—"

"I very particularly stopped the man from escaping," I interjected, but he went on.

"And all anyone will remember is the accusation. It puts a picture in the minds of the voters that isn't so easily erased. There are those who never will tolerate the idea of a lady cop. Plenty of them vote. You must know that. John Courter certainly does."

My brother was overly fond of making gloomy predictions, but there was a clarity to his words that worried me. Was I to be turned into a weapon against Sheriff Heath?

⊰ 14 ⊱

A LETTER ARRIVED from Geraldine. She thought it best to pay a visit to the Kayser household straight away, and asked me to meet her train from New York the following Tuesday. Sheriff Heath wouldn't want me to interfere further—I'd done enough already, by writing to a lawyer—but I couldn't beg off now.

"If it isn't sheriff's business, I don't know why you'd get involved," Norma said, when I put the matter before her.

"But don't I owe it to Mrs. Kayser? She's sleeping in an insane asylum while I spend the night in my own comfortable bed. Besides, I promised to get a message to her daughter."

"Why don't you go in disguise?" Fleurette asked.

"I don't think there's any disguising you," Norma said. "The trick is to make sure that Mr. Kayser doesn't go to the sheriff and complain about you. Do you think you can behave, for one afternoon, in such a way that won't cause a man to lodge a complaint?"

I considered that. "He wouldn't have reason to complain, if he thought it merely routine to check on the welfare of the children."

"That might work," Norma said, "except that he probably never had a lady deputy stop in before. Hasn't he sent his wife away half a dozen times already?"

"But there never was a lady deputy before!" Fleurette said triumphantly. She loved nothing better than to craft a plausible lie. "You can tell him it's the new way of doing things, now that you're in charge."

"Make it sound routine," Norma said, "and you might get by. No one wants to speak to the sheriff if it can be avoided. He won't, if you don't give him a reason."

It was as good a plan as any. On the appointed afternoon, I turned up early at the Rutherford station and passed a quiet half-hour with a magazine and a particular type of hot cinnamon bun that one could only purchase from a little stand next to the ticket-window. I had often tried to inquire as to the source of the cinnamon buns, hoping to discover a bakery that specialized in them, but the girl who worked at the stand spoke only Turkish and seemed not to understand my hand gestures and attempts at getting the idea across in English, German, or French.

The train arrived and Geraldine stepped off in her smart city tweeds and a checkered silk blouse of the type professional women wore. I felt a little dowdy in my uniform, but Geraldine rushed right over, made a great fuss over my badge, and had me turn around in a circle so she could admire the sight of a lady deputy.

"Aren't you something!" Geraldine cried. "We have girl cops in New York, too, of course, but all they ever do is stand around in dance halls disapproving of things. You, on the other hand, look like quite the dashing heroine. I wish someone would snatch my handbag right now, just so I could watch you chase them down."

"I'm trying not to attract attention to myself today."

"Oh, you can't help that." Geraldine hooked her arm through my elbow, and we walked out of the train station and down Park Street, past the little shops and offices that made up Rutherford's downtown. "When do you think Mr. Kayser gets home?"

"Soon, I suspect," I said, "and there's a fifteen-year-old daughter, too."

"I wouldn't mind catching the daughter alone if we can. Children will say the most astonishing things about their parents."

"It's good of you to come and look into it," I said, "but I don't know how you're going to get paid for any of this. Even if Mrs. Kayser is released, I'm sure her husband handles all the money."

"Oh, I'm counting on a plummy divorce at the end. It's a bit more effort than I might usually put into winning over a divorce client, but I'm intrigued by it. Did I ever tell you that I had a great-aunt who was locked up in one of those monstrous old places upstate?"

We chatted about the great-aunt and her misfortunes all the way to the Kaysers' home. The place was just as I remembered it: neat as a pin, with nothing so much as a loose shutter to suggest any kind of difficulty within. Perfect mounds of shrubs waited under the windows for winter to come along and blanket them in snow. Autumn chrysanthemums shone from flowerpots. There was a little wooden seat on the porch, draped in a tidy canvas cover.

Geraldine snorted. "If she's insane, I'm hiring a lunatic to keep house for me."

"That's just the trouble. It's a well-kept home and Mrs. Kayser herself hasn't so much as a hair out of place. She raised a fuss when I turned up to carry her away, but anyone would."

A lamp came on behind a curtain. It was nearly five o'clock.

"Someone's at home," Geraldine said. "Let's find out who it is. Don't say anything in particular about me. Let them think I'm your assistant."

"I'm going to tell them that we're always required to look in on the children after we remove the mother. It needs to sound ordinary. This can't get back to the sheriff. I don't want to raise any suspicion."

"That's perfect, then. Say as little as possible about your reasons, and let them talk."

I rapped authoritatively on the door. My knock was answered by a slender and elegant woman of about thirty-five who became so agitated at the sight of my badge that she hardly heard the introductions. I stepped inside as if I'd been invited, and Geraldine followed.

"I'll only take a minute of your time, Miss . . ." I waited for the woman to supply her name, but she didn't.

"I can't imagine what you'd be wanting with us," she said, waving a bony hand around. There was a cigarette between her fingers, and the smoke followed in a fine blue stream.

The place was just as I'd seen it last: the magazines on the table, the glass lamps, the little hooked rug. Only a few framed photographs of Anna Kayser were missing. A new hat-rack stood by the door, and on it perched a dozen or so small fancy hats, looking for all the world like a flock of exotic birds that had just landed.

I was about to ask about the daughter, but just then she appeared. When she saw my badge she went right up to me, as if she knew me.

"Is it about my mother?" She looked up at me anxiously, a freckle-faced girl of about fifteen with fat cheeks and braids.

"Your mother's fine, dear. Tell me your name."

"Charlotte Kayser. What sort of trouble is she in?"

"No one's in any trouble. Your mother is safe and I'm sure her care is good. She was very sorry that she couldn't say goodbye to you when she left. She promises to be home before you know it."

The woman, who still hadn't given her name, put a hand awkwardly on Charlotte's shoulder. "Go on back to your school-work. Finish your French."

Here I saw my opportunity. *"Du français? Vous le parlez bien?"*

"Correctement," Charlotte answered flatly.

The woman looked alarmed at that and said, "You can see why she needs to practice."

"Are you her tutor?" Geraldine asked. "We like to see the children keep their schooling up."

The woman looked surprised but said, "I see to it that she does her lessons. Of course I do."

Geraldine had taken on the brisk, officious air of a city clerk. "We haven't learned your name," she said, pulling a notebook out of her handbag.

Charlotte, who had ignored the instruction to go back to her school-work, said, "This is Miss Virginia. Father always brings in a lady when Mother goes to the hospital."

I risked another question in French. *"Est-ce toujours la même dame?"*

"Non" came Charlotte's one-word answer.

Miss Virginia looked shocked at the turn the conversation had taken and gave a nervous laugh. Ashes from her cigarette fell onto the carpet and she looked around for an ash-tray. Geraldine handed her a little bronze dish stamped with the insignia of a printing company. "Do you look after the house, too?"

Miss Virginia seemed relieved to have the ash-tray to occupy her other hand, and smiled more calmly. "Yes, I manage the running of the household. Now, if you'll—"

A knock came from down the hall. She turned around but didn't go to answer.

"Please don't let us keep you," I said.

"It's only the grocery boy," she said. "He can leave the box."

"But you'll want to look it over."

"I never do." Miss Virginia was keeping her eyes on Charlotte. She obviously didn't want to leave the girl alone.

I nodded to Geraldine. "Why don't you go along with Miss Virginia to bring in the groceries? Charlotte can show me the other rooms, and then we'll be on our way."

But Miss Virginia wasn't having it. "I'll show the kitchen to all of you, and make some tea while we're there. Come with us, Charlotte."

She took the girl by the shoulder and steered her down the hall. Geraldine and I followed. In the kitchen, Miss Virginia opened the back door and carried in the box of groceries.

"I'm glad to see a well-stocked kitchen," Geraldine said. "I know the cost of care at Morris Plains can be a terrible burden on a family."

The cost? I wasn't expecting that from Geraldine, but it had a surprisingly purgative effect on Miss Virginia, who unleashed a torrent of complaints, without any regard for what young Charlotte might hear.

"Oh, it's crippling. You haven't any idea what Charles goes through. The poor get everything for free, of course, but if you have any sort of salary or a roof over your head, you're expected to pay and pay. And it isn't his fault, is it? He couldn't have known when he married her what a burden she'd be. It puts a man in chains, having a lunatic for a wife."

Charlotte had been backing away from Miss Virginia during her speech. She reached the door just as Miss Virginia said the word "lunatic" and shouted back at her, "She's not a lunatic! You don't know a thing about her!"

She ran off down the hall. A door slammed, and the three of us stood in wary silence.

Miss Virginia drew herself up and sniffed. "I forgot to ask if you were here under any sort of order. Have you a letter or a warrant giving you the right to inspect the premises?"

"We've only come to see about the child's welfare," I said. "It's a routine check."

But Geraldine was pulling me to the front door. "That's fine, Miss Virginia. We ask only that the girl be looked after, and we can see that she is. She'll calm down soon enough. We're sorry to have disturbed you."

When we were back on the street and out of earshot, I said, "Why did you drag me out of there? I wanted to speak to Charlotte alone."

"It doesn't matter. We've had a stroke of luck. Mr. Kayser is paying for his wife's commitment."

"Is that unusual?"

"They do try to collect from the family if it seems that someone has money," Geraldine said. "But I'm beginning to think that this was a voluntary commitment."

"Oh, I promise you that Anna Kayser didn't go voluntarily. She cried and fought and begged."

"Yes, but . . ." Geraldine thought about it as we walked, tilting her head from the right to the left as she considered it. "Her husband, acting on her behalf, might have committed her voluntarily."

"Do you mean that he volunteered her for a year at the insane asylum?"

"Yes. It would still require the approval of the judge, but only as a formality. If the husband is paying the fees, he wouldn't be refused."

"And if he stopped paying the fees?" I asked.

"They'd probably release her."

"Then I don't see what we can do about it," I said. "If a man can have his wife locked away with nothing but an order from a sympathetic physician and a bank-book fat enough to cover the fees, then I suppose Anna Kayser's done for."

"I think we should pay a visit to Mrs. Kayser. We need to know how far she'll go. A woman who claims wrongful imprisonment by her husband but then doesn't want to divorce him might be suspect. I can't proceed until I know her intentions."

"I don't believe they allow visitors."

"They've no choice but to admit an attorney. This time, you'll be my assistant."

My stomach turned over at the thought of going into the asylum against Sheriff Heath's orders. "I just don't—"

"Do they know you at Morris Plains?"

"I don't believe so," I allowed.

"Then you won't be found out. Have that sister of yours dress you like a lady lawyer's assistant."

"She'll enjoy that."

We walked along in silence, mulling it over. "What did you say to that girl in French?" Geraldine asked.

"I asked her if her father always has the same woman come and look after her when Anna goes to the hospital."

"Oh, that was a clever question. And does he?"

"Non."

⇥ 15 ⇤

"THE BOARD OF Freeholders are about to start their meeting,"
Sheriff Heath said when I turned up at work the next day. I'd had
a change of heart about going around behind his back to look into
Anna Kayser's predicament and had resolved to come clean about
what I'd done. I would have—at least, I'm fairly certain I would
have—but Sheriff Heath was going on with such enthusiasm that
I could hardly get a word in. It is also true that some small part
of me was pleased to have gotten away with my own covert investigation.

Regardless, before I could make my confession, he said, "Have
you forgotten? I'm putting in for a medal for you. I want you to
be there."

I hadn't forgotten. I'd merely assumed he was only saying it
to contradict his wife and had no intention of following through.
"I don't want a medal. I believe Mrs. Heath is right this time. We
shouldn't make more of this than it already is."

"Mrs. Heath doesn't run this jail, and you know very well that
I put in for commendation any time a deputy of mine puts his life
on the line."

"It was hardly life-and-death. The Hackensack River is nothing more than a filthy ditch this time of year. I practically just walked across it to grab him."

Sheriff Heath said, "Nonsense. It was a ditch filled with fast-moving water over six feet high and a sewage pipe. Tony Hajnacka was in handcuffs and could've drowned in a foot of water. You saved his life and gave no thought to your own when you did it."

"I didn't have to think about my life. I had only to think of my job, which required me to capture the inmate and bring him back."

"For which you will receive a medal."

There was no arguing with him. For once, I wished I'd worn a better hat.

THE HAT WOULDN'T have saved me. I knew it the minute I walked in and saw Detective Courter and Dr. Ogden seated in the front row. They appeared entirely at ease, leaning back in their chairs and nodding as their friends filed in. They didn't turn to look at us, but I had the queasy feeling that they knew we were there nonetheless.

"What's Mr. Courter up to?" I whispered.

"Nothing. He's here every week," Sheriff Heath said.

"And Dr. Ogden?"

"He attends too, sometimes."

"Then you don't suppose they're here because of us?"

"I wouldn't mind if they were. My deputies do fine work and they ought to hear about it."

He seemed so resolute, and I did admire him for his convictions, but I couldn't help but wonder if his wife was the shrewder politician. The medal meant nothing to me. Why invite trouble?

Nonetheless, we took our places in the back of a noisy and crowded room. The Freeholders were seated on a kind of dais at the front, where they had the look of an august group gathered for a portrait: to a man they were gray-whiskered and packaged in good tweed, each of them wearing an expression of immense satisfaction over the responsibilities they'd been given and the attention they commanded. At one end sat an urn of coffee and one of tea, each attended by a harried-looking page who was also called upon to pass around a tray of finger sandwiches and dainty sweets brought in for the occasion from a bakery in Rutherford. The tray was of great concern to the Freeholders: one time, when it failed to arrive, the meeting was postponed until some other provisions could be found. The sliced salami was of particular importance to our elected officials, so much so that the page was obligated to distribute it first, before the meeting began, to ensure that each man had his fair share.

The last round of sweets was being offered as we took our seats. "They make an awful fuss over that tray," I whispered.

"It's the reason they run for office. They like their Tuesday afternoons and their tea and cake."

Deputy Morris appeared just then, and took a chair next to me. He'd been out of work since his fall, and walked now with a cane and a metal brace around his leg.

"Is it very bad?" I whispered.

"For a deputy, it would be. For a man of leisure, it's nothing. I'm taking retirement a little early, that's all."

I hated to see him go. "Couldn't we find something for you at the jail?"

He shook his head. "I'm only retiring a few months early. Don't worry yourself over me. I'm here to see you get that medal."

Sheriff Heath was turned away, talking to the man next to him, so I ventured to say in a low voice, "I wish he wouldn't go to all this trouble. It doesn't mean a thing to me."

"But don't you see, miss? He's doing it to protect you. If you've been bestowed a medal for your good work, it puts your reputation on a firmer footing. It'll be of use to you when he's no longer sheriff. He wants to make your accomplishments a matter of public record."

Sheriff Heath was listening now. "I did the same for you, Morris. It's what William Conklin taught me when he was sheriff. Always put the good works of your deputies forward. I earned a medal myself when I was deputy."

"Then it's a tradition," I said, seeing the futility of arguing over it. They were paying me a compliment by allowing me to take part in the rituals of their fraternity and to be thought of as one of them. But I knew that no matter what Sheriff Heath and Deputy Morris said, I wasn't the same as them, and my actions wouldn't ever be seen in the same light as theirs.

At last the Freeholders were ready to get on with their business. We sat through a debate over the funding of road repairs, which concluded with the decision being put off until the following week, and an argument over the Freeholders' use of county cars and chauffeurs for trips into New York and up to the Berkshires over the summer. It was decided that the trips had been perfectly in order and in support of county business. Sheriff Heath looked as though he had an opinion about that, but didn't say.

His request came next. Freeholder Morrison called out, "Sheriff Heath is here to honor one of his deputies for bravery. Come on up and tell us about it, Bob."

The sheriff went to the podium and addressed the board. "As you know, it is the responsibility of my department to transport inmates to Morris Plains or any other such place as a judge may see fit to send them. Last week, I sent two of my deputies to do that very thing, only to be waylaid by a storm and the impassibility of the very roads I believe you gentlemen were just discussing."

That got a little murmur of agreement from several on the board, but a few of them looked awfully displeased. From my vantage point in the back of the room, I saw a man rise from one of the front benches and go to stand along the wall as if he were next to speak. It was John Courter.

I knew then that a trap had been laid for Sheriff Heath. I only wished I'd tried harder to dissuade him.

"My deputies had no choice but to turn back," the sheriff continued. "Upon their return to the jail, one of the inmates broke loose and ran for the river in an attempt to escape or drown himself, we know not which. My deputy chased after him and succeeded in rescuing him from drowning, and brought him to shore at great personal peril. For that reason I ask this board to bestow a medal for bravery. Let me introduce the deputy. Miss Kopp?"

It should not have come as a surprise to anyone in the room that the deputy in question was a woman, for they must've all read about it in the papers by then. Nonetheless, there was a considerable amount of murmuring and shuffling as every eye in the room turned toward me. I stood and nodded to the Freeholders, the assembled audience, and the reporters busily scribbling in their notebooks.

Sheriff Heath went right on with his speech, which allowed me, to my relief, to take my seat again. "I hired Deputy Kopp to serve as jail matron and to handle the many difficult cases involving women and children in this county. She's done an admirable job in that regard, but she's also proven herself to be as capable a deputy as any other when it comes to chasing down a criminal or putting herself in danger to protect an honest citizen. Miss Kopp is the best police officer and detective in the state of New Jersey. She does not know the meaning of fear and with her bravery she uses brains. Her rescue of this inmate shows both quick thinking and fearlessness in the face of danger. For that I ask the Freeholders for their commendation."

He'd gone too far and I knew it. The Freeholders murmured to one another. One of them looked over at Detective Courter, still standing on the side of the room, waiting his turn.

"I believe Mr. Courter from the prosecutor's office has something to say about the matter," one of the Freeholders said.

"I wasn't aware Detective Courter was present at the moment this rescue took place," Sheriff Heath said, but it was no use. He was asked to yield the podium and he did. Detective Courter marched up in that prideful manner he had, with his chin held very high above a stiff collar.

"Gentlemen, citizens, and members of the press," he began. I sighed and slumped down into my seat. "I've said before that the sheriff has no business transporting inmates and should never have been entrusted with the job. He's proven that he can't reliably keep hold of a man outside the confines of the jail. I don't have to remind you that one of his deputies allowed an inmate to escape last year from the Hackensack Hospital."

I could see only the back of Sheriff Heath's head. I would've rushed to his defense if I knew how, but I could think of no course of action other than to sit by and watch Detective Courter do his damage.

"Now we have another escape, and it comes at too high a cost of public safety, not to mention the monetary expense. Sheriff Heath insists on keeping a matron on his staff, at the same salary as any other deputy, in spite of the fact that there are eighty or ninety men in jail on any given day, and fewer than a dozen women. Why they require the paid services of a full-time attendant passes understanding, unless they are to receive a fresh coiffure every morning and change into formal gowns for dinner."

That brought a laugh from the audience and a few expectant glances in my direction. Did they think I'd laugh at his joke? I did not. Morris sat alongside me, equally stone-faced.

Detective Courter went on. "Now, I don't blame the lady deputy for allowing this inmate to escape. She never should've been given charge of him in the first place. It was sloppy work on the sheriff's part that led to this mishap. But to hand out awards at a moment like this would be a misuse of the duties of this board. Instead, I asked that the Freeholders issue a letter of censure to Sheriff Heath over his mishandling of the case, and that they permanently revoke from him the authority to transport inmates.

"The county physician, Dr. Ogden, whom you see here today, took charge of carrying two lunatics to Morris Plains after Sheriff Heath failed to do so. It is my recommendation that the county physician take responsibility for all inmate transportation henceforth. This is a matter not only of the inmates' health, but also of public safety. We cannot risk another criminal breaking free on his way to the lunatic asylum. And if an inmate escape isn't enough, consider this: the girl deputy was so heartbroken over the commitment of Mrs. Anna Kayser that she took it upon herself to march down to the office of that lady's personal physician and argue for her release. The sheriff's office seems determined to set lunatics free, for reasons that escape my understanding." He put a special emphasis on the word *escape,* which seemed to delight his friends on the board.

With that, he stood apart from the podium and gestured at Sheriff Heath, as if to give him back his place. It was a nasty trick on Detective Courter's part to fling accusations at the sheriff and force him to defend himself in so public a forum, but the sheriff didn't hesitate.

"Gentlemen, I didn't come here tonight to hear criticism of my decisions, or to open up for discussion the question of the transportation of inmates. But you're entitled to hear about it and to make your own decision. This office never asked to be responsible for inmate transport. If the Freeholders believe that the county physician is better qualified for the job, he is welcome to it. Now, as for the subject I brought before you. It shouldn't matter whether the deputy is a man or woman. Inmates will try to escape. It is in their nature to do so. You would, too, if you were facing a sentence at Morris Plains."

This brought a smattering of laughter from the Freeholders and a nod from one of them to the page, who hastened to pass the tray of cookies again.

"I will answer to any man who has questions about the expenses I incur in the running of this jail. As to the employment of Deputy Kopp—many of you didn't realize that we had been running the jail without a woman on staff to look after the female inmates!"

The Freeholders looked a little uncomfortable with that, but the audience mumbled its assent. "You didn't realize that. You don't seem to understand that had your wife been arrested, and brought to the county jail, and lodged in a steel cell, unable to get away, that a man would hold the keys to all those doors. Would you like it? Of course not. We want a matron in that county jail, and the taxpayers ought to appreciate the fact that we are doing the work with one matron, not three. And when it's necessary, Deputy Kopp stays there all night in her own jail cell, without a word of complaint. She goes out on calls when a woman is to be arrested and carries out all the other duties of a deputy. I can assure you that she puts herself in danger and steps willingly into the most desperate of circumstances to offer help to those in need, and to protect you, the members of the public. If you had any understanding of what my deputies do, you would award each one of them a medal on the spot. But if you instead want to haggle over expenses, and argue over which of your public servants is best qualified to handle one or more of the endless number of difficult duties we perform every day, please go on. I have nothing more to say on it."

With that he left the podium. The Freeholders' clerk reminded the board that they had a motion before them to award a medal to me.

I would've rather marched out of the room than stand there and watch them take a vote on an honor I hadn't asked for and didn't want. But there were too many eyes on me, and on Sheriff Heath, who had come to the back of the room to stand alongside me. So I did the only thing I could have, which was to keep my face perfectly composed and to stand calmly, with my hands at my side, as the vote went around the room and the Freeholders defeated the motion.

❧ 16 ❧

NO MEDAL FOR MISS KOPP

HACKENSACK, N.J. — The Bergen County Board of Freeholders, instead of giving Miss Constance Kopp, the
only woman Deputy Sheriff in New Jersey, a medal,
passed a resolution today taking from the sheriff's
office the privilege of conveying insane persons
or prisoners to Morris Plains or other asylums.
This followed on the heels of Miss Kopp's rescue
of an insane man who had plunged into the Hackensack River. Miss Kopp was in charge of a crazy man
and an insane woman when the man got away. County
Detective Courter in his report to the Freeholders
said that "the escape should not have been possible."

"I CAN'T SAY that I disagree with him," Norma said. "Sheriff
Heath put you in an untenable position. I don't blame you for it,
of course."

"If you're going to blame someone, you have to blame me," I
said irritably. "If I'm to be given all the responsibilities of the job,

I have to accept all the blame. What they don't understand is that every inmate wants to escape. They try it all the time."

"But he was Morris's man," Norma said.

"Morris was ill that day. Anyone could've taken a tumble in that mud. It's precisely why we go out in pairs."

"I'm only saying that Mr. Courter is right to criticize the sheriff," Norma said.

"I believe you're obligated to oppose Mr. Courter, if you live in this house," Fleurette put in.

"It is simply a fact that we never used to have inmates escaping like this," Norma said, as if the inmates were somehow hers to lose.

"I'm sure we did," I said, "but the goings-on at the jail were never of such concern to this household before. What you don't see in the papers is that Sheriff Heath is going around and telling everyone exactly what he's done in office, and what he'd like to do in Congress. William Conklin is saying the same. They've been well received every time they've gone to speak. They're doing just fine."

"Oh, I'm sure they're fine," Norma said, "but that's not the same as winning votes." She shoved a plate of sandwiches across the table as if to bring the matter to a conclusion, which was fine with me.

Lunch at our house took place around the kitchen table and was usually hastily assembled by Norma and prepared to Norma's tastes. On that particular day, the sandwiches were of brown bread, chipped roast, and pickles. Fleurette ate the bread only, with far too much butter. I ate two of the beef sandwiches and would've had a third had Norma not taken it, so I rummaged around and found some cold chicken instead.

None of us were terribly good cooks. We were raised on plain Austrian food by a mother who was distrustful of foreign influences at her kitchen table, and accordingly rejected every competing cuisine that had ever shouldered its way into Brooklyn's markets during our childhood. An occasional dish from the French countryside was not entirely out of the ordinary, as my grandmother had been French, but for the most part, we subsisted on potatoes and cabbage, sausages and roasted meats, buttered noodles and dumplings. Norma didn't like to cook any more than I did, but I was home so unpredictably that it simply fell to her. (There was no question of Fleurette cooking: she considered toast and jam a perfectly fine dinner.)

As we finished our lunch, there came the sound of an auto in the drive. Fleurette ran over to the window to look. It belonged to Norma's friend (her first and only friend, as far as anyone knew), Carolyn Borus. The two of them had become the oddest of acquaintances: Norma was no nicer or more generous to Carolyn than she was to anyone else, but Carolyn was mysteriously blind to Norma's social deficits and, equally inexplicably, fascinated by messenger pigeons and thoroughly in support of any plan to deploy them that Norma contrived.

In an effort to avoid hearing any talk of pigeons, Fleurette dashed into her sewing room and I washed up the dishes from lunch. I ventured into the dining room a little later, where I found Norma and Carolyn at the table, bent over a set of cryptic drawings. The discussion revolved around axles, hickory shafts, and hinged rear gates. They appeared to be designing a buggy of the sort used to transport goats or ponies.

"What happened to your pigeons?" I asked.

"This has everything to do with pigeons and nothing to do with you," Norma said, without looking up from the drawings.

I sat down across from them and unlaced my boots.

"I wish you'd go upstairs and take a bath and not put your feet all over everything," Norma said. I picked up a metal protractor she'd unearthed from Francis's school things, and she took it away from me. "You didn't tell us what happened with the lunatic."

"Lunatic?" asked Carolyn with interest.

"She's not a lunatic. That's just the point," I said. "Her doctor had her committed on complaint of her husband. The woman herself was never examined."

"What does our lawyer say?" Norma asked.

"When did she become our lawyer? You wanted nothing to do with this."

"I don't know why you don't answer simple questions."

"We went to pay a visit to the husband. He wasn't home. He brought a lady in to clean, but she's nervous as a cat and doesn't seem to have charge of the household at all. It's suspicious."

"Well, I don't know what else you can do about it," Norma said.

"We're going to the asylum."

"You don't mean to say you're visiting a lunatic asylum?" put in Carolyn. "You Kopp sisters aren't afraid of anything, are you?"

"I don't have anything to fear from the asylum, but if Sheriff Heath finds out that I'm sneaking around on this Kayser case, that's another matter."

Norma's pencil lead broke and she reached for a knife. "In a month or so, he'll be in Washington or wherever the voters send him. What he thinks about your inmates won't matter much longer."

"Well, I think it's wonderful what you do with the less fortunate," Carolyn told me. "You should get some sort of award for it."

"We've rather soured on awards around this house," said Norma.

But Carolyn was still looking at me pensively. "I can just picture you out giving lectures. You should go around to other cities and tell them how you've done it here in Bergen County. I'm sure that every policewoman who comes into the job must feel as though she has to invent it for herself. You ought to go around and tell them how to do it properly."

I confess that I'd thought of doing that very thing. I hadn't dared say it to Norma, because to go and give a lecture would require travel, and Norma was constitutionally opposed to venturing too far away from home or having any of her relations do so. But, in fact, a policewoman in Los Angeles had formed an international association the year before. Now they were holding conferences and electing officers. I imagined that I might have a place with a group like that someday.

I could see myself visiting other cities, and meeting other policewomen, and giving a speech about the good work that I'd done in Hackensack with Sheriff Heath. By then he'd be a congressman, which I wouldn't mind boasting about.

There was no reason, really, why I couldn't help to write the book on how a woman's version of policing ought to be done. Such were my ambitions on a grand scale.

But I hadn't said a word about that to either Norma or Fleurette, and I was surprised that Carolyn had guessed at it so easily. If it weren't for my obligations at home, I would've liked to advance to a more prominent position in a big city. New York had already hired a lady detective. Chicago and Philadelphia had women commanding their own units. I could rise in the ranks, if only I were free to go.

But what would Norma do without me? And how could I leave Fleurette?

Norma noticed my silence and looked up. "I'll send a pair of pigeons with you to the asylum. If you run into trouble, you can send word."

"You don't suppose a pair of pigeons under my coat might attract suspicion?" I pushed aside a stack of newspapers—which

Norma was using for her mysterious sketches, as she hated to waste clean paper—and dropped my elbows on the table.

Norma hoisted an eyebrow aloft and said, "You'll be the only deputy using trained pigeons in all of New Jersey, or I suppose anywhere in the country, and you'll be in the papers all over again, although I don't suppose you'd get as many marriage proposals out of it, which is just as well, because you're ill-suited for matrimony."

Norma had a way of sending a conversation into any direction, however unexpected, as long as it allowed her to make a final pronouncement and put an end to the matter. She took up her ruler and made another set of marks.

⇥ 17 ⇤

GERALDINE ARRANGED AN auto from New York City so we wouldn't have to rely on trains and trolleys to get us to Morris Plains. She'd worked herself into a state of genuine excitement over the case and didn't mind making the investment in car fare.

"What the public doesn't realize," she said, as we rode together to the asylum, "is that so many of these commitments are private affairs, with little more than a nod from a sleepy judge who simply takes the good doctor at his word. A woman can hire a lawyer and put up a fight, but most of them don't know that and, anyway, who would pay for it? The husband certainly wouldn't give her the money if he's the one having her committed."

"Then these cases must not come before you very often," I said.

"Almost never, in my corner of the law. It's nothing but wills and trusts, and the occasional business matter, and all those divorces. I might see an accusation of insanity in the course of a divorce hearing, but it's my duty to keep things civil and to see the matter carried through without anyone being locked away. I've never had a client committed, and I've certainly never seen the inside of an asylum. Have you?"

"My inmates have been committed to Morris Plains, but I never had reason to go inside."

"I'm sure it's dreadful," Geraldine said.

We arrived at Morris Plains just before the appointed hour. Behind the gates sat an imposing building of heavy gray stone, five stories high, topped by a mansard roof sheathed in copper. Stone columns stretched for three stories above the entrance, giving it a look of grandeur, but there was something grim and fortress-like about it, too, particularly in the way the narrow windows were covered in metal grates. Alongside the main building sat several smaller structures in the same style, as the facility seemed to be in a constant state of expansion. The grounds went on as far as I could see, and in the distance there were fruit orchards and a truck farm.

A guard at the gate was expecting us. He told us to drive through, and showed the driver where he could wait. A nurse came out to meet us.

"Dr. Evans will speak to you first. He has charge of Mrs. Kayser's care." She didn't ask our names and seemed not to wonder why there were two of us, but Dr. Evans did.

"I approved a visit from a lady lawyer, but I wasn't told to expect two," he said when we were brought into his office. It was the usual wood-paneled affair with a leather chair and desk for the doctor and uncomfortable oak chairs for the visitors. The doctor had only the most listless streak of hair plastered against his head, but to compensate for it he bore a mustache much wider than his narrow face. He wore a coat of some stiff silk material that gave him the air of an Eastern mystic. Although he was an altogether peculiar-looking man, there was something forceful about him that made me straighten my spine.

Dr. Evans put his cigar in a tray and regarded us suspiciously as we eased into our chairs. "A meeting like this can be very disturbing to the patient and only prolong her illness, but by law I'm obligated to allow it. I hope it's important," he said.

Geraldine gave her name and her card, and said that she was an attorney working on a private family matter, which was not entirely untrue and seemed satisfactory to the doctor.

"All right, but I'm giving you only a quarter of an hour. Don't say anything to excite her."

The nurse was waiting outside Dr. Evans's office to take us to Mrs. Kayser. She led us down a labyrinth of corridors, all narrow and dark, until we were hopelessly turned around and deeper inside an insane asylum than either of us had ever wanted to be. We passed nothing but locked rooms: no windows, no furnishings, and nothing to give an indication as to the purpose of that particular wing of the building. Through the doors I could hear chairs being scraped across the floor, and the sound of metal banging against metal, and voices too muffled to understand. Geraldine raised an eyebrow at me as we followed the nurse, but neither of us dared to say a word.

At last we turned the corner and found ourselves in a sort of bright atrium, with potted palms in stands and rugs on the floors, and cushioned armchairs where a few women sat knitting or reading books. They were all clothed in simple shirtwaists and plain dark skirts, with their hair done up in the most ordinary fashion. On one wall hung a display of embroidered tea-towels and other fancy-work.

"Isn't this nice," Geraldine said under her breath.

"This is the cooperative ward," the nurse told us as we walked through it. "If they aren't violent or delusional or sent here under a criminal charge, they can stay here."

She took us into a little sitting room furnished with four stuffed chairs and a dainty table. There was a cross on the wall and a watercolor of a mountain scene. If it weren't for the bars on the windows, we might never have known that we were inside a lunatic asylum.

The nurse stood awkwardly in the doorway, prompting Geraldine to make polite conversation. "It seems that most of the women are older" was the most she could manage.

"Yes, it tends to be the older ladies who have a calm enough disposition to earn their way into this ward. Some of them have been here twenty or thirty years. They're very comfortable."

At the thought of living at Morris Plains for twenty or thirty years, I very much wanted to run outside, through the gates, if only to test my liberty and confirm that I was still in possession of it. Geraldine sat gingerly on the edge of her chair, as if she, too, was ready to bolt.

"I'll go and fetch Mrs. Kayser," the nurse said. She slipped out and closed the door behind her. I reached over to turn the knob and was not surprised to find it locked.

"I have a touch of lunacy coming on already, and I haven't been here half an hour," Geraldine said. "Twenty years? Think of it!"

I went over to the window, which was covered in dust and the white calcification accumulated over years of snow and rainfall. There were bars on both sides, making it impossible to clean from within or without, just like the windows of a jail. Through the murky glass I could see only a stretch of lawn, and what might have been a caretaker's cottage.

After a few minutes, a key rattled in the door and the nurse made another appearance, this time with a much-diminished Anna Kayser in tow.

"Fifteen minutes," the nurse said. She pushed Mrs. Kayser in and closed the door behind her. The three of us stood staring at each other. I wasn't sure, at first, if Mrs. Kayser even recognized me.

"Please sit down," I said, and she did. Up close, the asylum's uniforms were actually quite shabby. Mrs. Kayser's skirt had been patched and hemmed repeatedly, and her shirtwaist frayed at the collar. I knew her to be a neat and well-kept woman and thought it must've bothered her to wear such miserable and anonymous garments.

Geraldine and I sat down across from her. "This is Miss Rodgers, a lawyer from New York," I said. "She wants to help you if she can. How are they treating you?"

She shrugged resignedly. "It's worse than before. The attendants have us doing their chores. They sit in the evenings and play cards while we scrub the floors. A lady complained about it last week and was judged to be paranoid and sent for treatment. The rest of us don't dare say a word. We do whatever they ask. The nurses come in the mornings and the floors are gleaming and the attendants collect their pay."

"Would you like me to speak to the nurse about it?" I asked, although I knew the futility of complaining about an inmate's treatment. I didn't like to hear such grievances from my own inmates.

"It wouldn't help," Anna said. "They'd put me in for treatment, too, and I'd wake up not knowing my name."

"What I want to do is to send you home," I said. "I've been to see your doctor, and he won't give an inch, but a few days ago, Geraldine and I went to your house."

She snorted. "To plead with Charlie? I could've saved you the trouble."

"Charlie wasn't there, but we did see your daughter. There's a housekeeper looking after her."

"Yes, there usually is," Mrs. Kayser said with a high uncertain laugh. "It always takes me a week to put my kitchen in order when I come home."

Geraldine was writing in a little notebook. "Am I to understand that this is your fourth time here?"

"Yes, I was here for a year after my youngest was born, and then I stayed for six months another time, and almost a year the third time. I suppose I'll be here through the winter, at this rate."

"And when you're released, do the doctors tell you why you're allowed to leave?"

"They don't say a word. One day a nurse will just come for me and say that my husband's arrived to take me home."

"Have you any friends who petition on your behalf?" Geraldine asked. "Sometimes people will get up a little committee."

Anna Kayser's face crumpled at that. "I've always been the kind to keep to myself. I had four children to look after. I hardly had the time for friends."

"Of course," Geraldine murmured. "I just wondered if we might have witnesses to attest to your sanity."

"On most days, I only ever saw the milkman or the grocery boy," she said, sounding downtrodden about it.

I recalled the scene at her house and said, "Then I wish we'd spoken to the grocery boy. He knocked when we were there, but Miss Virginia didn't want to open the door."

Anna looked up suddenly. "Who?"

"The housekeeper, Miss Virginia. I looked through the Rutherford directory and didn't see a woman listed by that name, but there's no reason to think that she lives in Rutherford ordinarily," I said.

"Virginia isn't her last name," Mrs. Kayser returned sharply. "It's Townley. My husband works with Joseph Townley. Virginia's his wife. Slender, red hair? A good twenty years younger than me?"

"That's her," I said quietly. I leaned forward, cautiously, the way one might approach a wild animal. "Do I take it you know Virginia well?"

"Oh, I know of her, but I've only ever met her in passing. Joe and Charlie are the best of friends. They used to try to get up a foursome for supper and bridge, but Virginia wouldn't have it. She's so much younger than Joe, and she says she doesn't like his old friends. Old! Well. Joe's first wife passed away some years ago, and Joe married this flighty young creature who doesn't know anything about running a home and doesn't care to."

I hated to ask, but I saw no choice. "If she doesn't know anything about keeping a house, why is she working for your husband?"

Anna was staring out the dim window. I leaned forward and took her hands. "Quickly, before the nurse comes back. Tell us about this Joe Townley. What sort of man is he? Has he a temper? Does he drink? Who is he?"

She turned to me, her face fallen. "He's a salesman, like Charlie. He always seemed like a reliable and solid friend. He helped Charlie build a patio one summer and put awnings across the back of our house. Charlie did the same for him. He's that sort of man."

I could hear the nurse's footsteps in the hallway. We were out of time. Geraldine said, "Anna, listen to me. If we learn that Charlie's done something wrong—if he's up to no good—would you speak in court against him? Would you divorce him?"

Anna was just staring back and forth between us, taking it in. "Has it come to that, then?"

"If you're willing, I need to you sign a letter giving me permission to file on your behalf." Geraldine pulled out an envelope. "I might not be able to get much news to you. You'd have to allow me to act in your best interests."

The key rattled in the lock. I tried to stall by jumping up and blocking the door. "Thank you, Mrs. Kayser," I said, in my most officious voice. "This has been a great help."

Mrs. Kayser signed the letter Geraldine put before her, but I worried that she hadn't properly taken it in. She moved slowly, as if in a fog.

The nurse stepped in to take Anna by the arm just as Geraldine tucked the papers away.

I hated to leave her like that. But just as she was being led away, she seemed to come around. She turned and looked directly at Geraldine. "Yes," she said. "Yes, of course."

We were left alone for a minute in the sitting room, but we didn't dare say a word to each other. It wasn't until we'd been escorted outside, and were settled into the back of the automobile, that either of us could even take a breath.

"A married woman, keeping house for her husband's best friend," Geraldine said.

"It would be terribly nice of her, if she were a nice woman," I said.

"But she isn't. What do you suppose her husband would have to say about it, if we went and spoke to him?"

I was putting it together the way a lawyer would, and I very much liked the idea. "He might not approve of his wife keeping house for another man. Surely he doesn't know what she's doing."

Geraldine slapped her notebook against her knee. "I like our chances. I was ready to go and have it out with Charles Kayser, but I think we ought to let him shift for himself for a while longer. Joe Townley might just be our man."

⚜ 18 ⚜

THERE WAS NOTHING better than a solid lead. Most of the time, it doesn't go this way: the interview turns up nothing of use, the victim isn't any help at all, and the inquiries made in desperation up and down the street, searching for witnesses, lead nowhere. But this was different. We had a name, and a hunch.

Geraldine was to track down Joseph Townley and make an appointment with him. I would've loved nothing more than to run to Sheriff Heath with our findings and to put him on the case, too. But after the disastrous meeting at the Board of Freeholders, I was quite sure the sheriff wouldn't want to take any more chances. Besides, I'd gone too far to make a confession now. I'd enlisted a lawyer, visited the Kaysers' home, and lied my way into Morris Plains—all, possibly, for nothing. Joseph Townley might refuse to talk to us, or might have an entirely ordinary explanation as to why his wife was in Charles Kayser's employ. Why risk telling the sheriff what I'd done, if I didn't yet know what was to come of it?

So I stayed silent on the matter and returned to my everyday duties at the jail while I waited for word from Geraldine. Sheriff Heath was out most days, giving speeches at any club that would have him, and Cordelia was bustling about, making preparations for the Salvation Army program and jail tour. Because her friends —wives of influential men, men who might throw some votes toward Sheriff Heath—would be in attendance, she wanted those sections of the jail that they would visit scrubbed from top to bottom. A crew of inmates was put to work with brooms and mops, and a new coat of lime-wash was rolled onto the walls. The jail smelled fresher than it had in some time, and had more the look of a hospital about it than a place of punishment. That was fine with me: I appreciated the effort, and my female inmates seemed to enjoy sprucing up their quarters.

On a fair afternoon, I went out to visit my probationers and managed to speak to the aunt of Katie Carlson, the sullen girl in want of a dance and music education. The aunt, being a teacher herself, recognized the need immediately and only regretted that she hadn't thought of it sooner.

"I'm in the business of finding ways to keep children interested in the world around them," she told me. "If there's nothing in their lives that seems worthwhile, they won't sit still for their lessons." Over the years, she'd encouraged parents to let a child with a love of animals keep a horse or a flock of chickens, or to let one with an affinity for tools knock about in his father's woodworking shop, or to put out pencils and paints for children with a love of art. "I know she used to sneak out to the dance halls," the aunt told me, "but I hadn't thought to ask if it was really the dancing, and not the boys, that drew her to it."

I assured her that Fleurette had come to no harm at Mrs. Hansen's Academy, and that Katie might benefit from an association with girls who shared an interest in the theatrical arts. It was simple enough to arrange.

My other cases that morning were equally straightforward: girls arrested on charges of disorderly conduct or drunkenness were under more watchful eyes, a woman charged with assaulting her husband had refrained from doing so again, and a grand-mother accused of neglect after allowing five grandchildren (placed in her care after their mother died) to run wild had hired a housekeeper and now had her situation well in hand.

I found it very satisfying, as I always did, to visit my proba-tioners and to write up my account of their successes in my green notebook. Of course, they didn't all fare so well. The first two girls placed under my supervision had run off, allegedly to join one of the wartime volunteer services in France, although I suspected they'd merely moved on in search of better employment. One or two had been arrested again, usually for offenses of a drunken or disreputable nature. I couldn't help all of them, but I'd kept most of them out of jail and living a more productive life than they would've had behind bars.

It was the most rewarding work I could've imagined for myself. My ambitions for what I might accomplish in this line stretched over decades: a small army of women, kept out of the criminal life and free of damaging accusations, however petty or false, that would have otherwise ruined them. They would go on to raise children of their own, or to find useful work, and perhaps one or two of them would be inspired to do what I had done, and to enter into a life of public service. If I succeeded at that, I could ask for nothing more.

FLEURETTE HAD BEEN trying lately to persuade me and Norma that she should spend her nights away from home as I did, owing to the demands of her job. She'd been working as a seamstress at one of the new moving picture studios down in Fort Lee. She sewed costumes primarily for May Ward, a vaudeville actress who gave us quite a shock the previous spring by allowing Fleurette to run away with her troupe. To our relief, Fleurette returned home safely, after only a few mishaps, and I saw no reason why she shouldn't continue her association with the actress as long as the terms of employment were fair.

The trouble was that it was nearly impossible for Fleurette to go back and forth to Fort Lee on the train every day, as the journey took more than an hour from door to door. Her idea was that she should spend the night on a little cot in some dark corner of the movie studio. This was met with instant and outright disapproval by both Norma and myself. The fact that I slept at my workplace was not an effective argument, as I was locked in a jail cell, with guards patrolling the building and the sheriff living downstairs. Fleurette on a cot in a movie studio was, as Norma put it, a bird of an entirely different feather.

Instead, Fleurette was obliged to leave very early in the morning, while it was still dark, and ride a train to Fort Lee, where she would spend the day taking measurements and pinning costumes together. She would then haul the work back on the train with her in an enormous carpetbag and work on Mrs. Ward's costumes from home for several days at a stretch.

She wasn't at all happy about this arrangement and did her best to make it uncomfortable and difficult for Norma by insisting that Norma take her down to the train station in our buggy on her Fort Lee days and return again in the evening to collect her. Fleurette tried missing her return train a few times, just to make Norma wait at the station and understand what an inconvenient arrangement it was, but Norma found a way to take the upper hand. Every time Fleurette missed her train, Norma would, at some point in the future and without warning, fail to turn up at the train station to retrieve her. This forced Fleurette, who couldn't possibly carry her carpetbag all the way home, to hire a buggy at a considerable dent in her wages.

Fleurette and Norma quarreled mightily about this every time Norma failed to meet her at the station. Fleurette would argue that she hadn't missed a train in weeks and didn't deserve the punishment. But Norma never forgot a slight and kept a perfect scorecard of grievances in her head at all times. She could recite with dead accuracy a timetable of every train Fleurette had failed to catch, and whether a penalty had yet been inflicted or not.

Just such a drama was playing out as I arrived at the Wyckoff train station after having spent several nights in a row at the jail. I stepped off the rail-car (intending to walk, as I wore sturdy shoes) and found Fleurette stranded on the platform with two heavy bags by her side, staring impatiently at the station clock. Her friend Helen Stewart sat peacefully on a bench, waiting for the situation to sort itself out.

"Did Norma leave you stranded again?" I asked, coming up behind her.

Fleurette spun around delightedly. "Oh, now we'll have to hire a buggy."

"I suppose you expect me to pay the fare," I said.

"Either that, or we can walk, and you can carry one of my bags and Helen the other." Fleurette beamed up at me. She always knew how to work me over. For my part, I didn't mind being worked over once in a while. I was resigned to appreciating any sort of attention the girl would give me.

"I could've had my father drive us from the Paterson station, if I'd known we'd be such a bother," Helen said, which naturally left me in the position of insisting that neither one of them could ever be a bother.

I went out to look for the old stableman who ran his buggy around town. Wyckoff was nothing but a village clustered around a rickety platform and a whistle stop, but there were still plenty of people in the countryside who didn't run automobiles and had to be met at the train from time to time. I was fortunate to find the man at the stables next to the station and secure a ride home for us.

When we arrived at home, the girls flew up the stairs and ran down half an hour later, attired in matching gowns of angelic white. The dresses were made of a pearly silk chiffon, and draped about them in the fashion of the moment, with low-slung waists and hemlines a little higher than I might've liked.

"We're ready for jail!" Fleurette announced.

"Is this your costume for the Salvation Army program?" I wanted very much to pull the gold ribbons out of their hair. They were too extravagantly dressed for a night at the county jail.

"There was a time when you would've been locked up yourself for wearing a dress like that," Norma said pointedly as she glanced up at the girls and returned to scribbling on those cryptic drawings of hers.

"They're perfectly respectable dresses for 1916," I said.

Fleurette hopped over in her stockinged feet and showed us the pretty piece of old lace she'd added to the necklines and hems. "It's even more modest with the lace, isn't it?"

"I suppose so," I said, although the lace seemed altogether too fine for a jail program. Since Fleurette's tour on the stage with May Ward, her everyday wardrobe had grown more cosmopolitan and there seemed to be nothing I could do about it.

She and Helen had been practicing their duet for weeks. Captain Anderson had sent word asking the girls to rehearse a song called "Sinners Seeking Pardon." Fleurette had a great deal of fun with it, and had been delivering the lyrics with so much gusto during their practice sessions that it came across as more of a barroom shanty than a hymn of repentance.

When looking back upon the past
Of wasted years of sin and shame
I wonder if the die is cast
And hell is written 'gainst my name

Those didn't sound like suitable lyrics for a girl to sing, but the captain insisted. The second verse belonged to Helen. It began:

I know I've broken all thy laws
And am the vilest of the race

It only got more preposterous from there, as sweet and pretty Helen recounted the sins of a broken man in her unspoiled soprano. Nonetheless, it was the song the captain had chosen, and no one could say they hadn't put a great deal of effort into learning it.

I only hoped the inmates would summon up some semblance of good manners and behave like gentlemen in front of the girls. Norma must've been thinking the same thing, because she said, "I don't know why the sheriff has to recruit two girls to entertain the prisoners. They aren't soldiers at the front. They've done nothing to deserve a concert."

"It isn't entertainment," Helen said, as she spun around and admired her reflection in the darkened kitchen window. "It's a program of moral enrichment."

"I wouldn't have thought your father would allow you to step foot inside of a county jail," Norma said to Helen. "I don't know why we are, either, except that we seem to be on ever more friendly terms with criminals. I half expect Constance to start bringing them home for supper." Norma didn't even bother to look up as she said that. She just let the words come out in one long breath, like a line she'd memorized.

I slid my foot over and nudged Norma's under the table to get her attention. "I'll be there to keep an eye on the girls. If any of the men misbehave, I'll haul them upstairs and lock them in their cells."

"Which is where they live, so I don't see how that punishes them."

⁌ 19 ⁊

NORMA'S DISAPPROVAL NOTWITHSTANDING, the concert went ahead the following night. I spent the day at home, putting my uniform in order and polishing my boots, and that evening the sheriff collected me, Fleurette, and Helen in his wagon following some business he had in Trenton.

We found Captain Anderson waiting for us in the Heath family's sitting room, alongside Cordelia. He was sitting very stiffly in the manner of a military man—he'd fought in the Civil War—and although he must've been seventy-five years of age, only his wiry white hair betrayed him. He sprang out of a dainty armchair with the vigor of a much younger man and pounded the sheriff on the shoulder.

"Bob Heath! I hope it was only the company of these charming ladies and not some criminal mischief that delayed you," he said, while the sheriff glanced at the clock. It was only one minute past six. We hadn't been delayed at all.

Mrs. Heath rose from a stuffed chair whose armrests had been elaborately embroidered in a pattern of lilies and sweet peas. Since the campaign had commenced, there was a directness about her, and a sense of purpose, that had been missing before. Perhaps Cordelia's mother had been right: to take an interest in her husband's profession would make for a happier marriage, and would, perhaps, ease the strain between them. Cordelia had always carried around a terrible burden of unaired complaints. What she couldn't say spoke louder than anything she ever did say.

That was certainly true when she turned to greet me. I was, at that moment, the most serious problem in her husband's campaign, and we both knew it. But it wouldn't do to speak of it in front of Captain Anderson, so she gave me only a slight nod and turned her attention to the girls, complimenting them on their gowns.

"Captain, these are your singers," Sheriff Heath said. "Miss Fleurette Kopp is the youngest of the Kopp sisters, and this is her friend Miss Helen Stewart. They've been in rehearsals for weeks."

Captain Anderson pressed each of their hands into his. "I know how much the men will appreciate your singing. It's a good influence on them to hear spiritual music. I've seen with my own eyes how it can mend a man's broken soul."

"What about a woman's broken soul?" Fleurette asked. "Aren't we to sing for the ladies?"

It was impertinent of her, but I'd asked the same question when I first heard about the program. Sheriff Heath told me that I was the salvation program for the female inmates, and the men didn't have anyone like me. I tried to point out that there was such a creature as a male deputy, too, but Sheriff Heath only waved me away and said that the other deputies weren't suited to that sort of thing.

Captain Anderson looked down at Fleurette in astonishment. "Well . . . I . . . Our program is more for the hardened and unrepentant criminal. I don't suppose your ladies' matron sees many of those."

"Oh, she has murderers and arsonists and all the rest," Fleurette boasted.

141

"That's true," I said. "We have a kidnapper upstairs, too." It seemed strange to brag about them, but I didn't want to give the impression that my charges were any less deserving of concerts and special programs than the others.

Captain Anderson stared back and forth between me and Fleurette, entirely flummoxed by the idea that the female inmates might have need of his program. "Yes, well . . . It's a fine thing to have a ladies' matron. I was just telling Mrs. Heath that in so many places I visit around the country, the sheriff would be run out of town for taking the side of the suffragists. You must tell me how you manage it."

"Deputy Kopp manages just fine," Sheriff Heath said.

If there was one thing Cordelia disliked, it was to have the conversation center around me for any length of time. "I've left my mother in the kitchen for too long," she said. "We have a group of ladies joining us tonight, and she's putting out the refreshments."

"And I understand I'm to meet the next sheriff of Bergen County," Captain Anderson said.

Sheriff Heath looked around as if he might find William Conklin hiding in a corner. "I expect we will, but let's not wait on him."

The sheriff led us through the jail's massive kitchen and into the dining hall, where Cordelia's mother was overseeing the setting out of refreshments along with her kitchen-maid.

I had only met Mrs. Westervelt once, in passing, when she and Cordelia's father paid a visit to the jail. She was a woman of considerable vitality and intelligence, just as Bessie described her. She greeted me with a spirited handshake and said, "Your brother's wife speaks so well of you that I just knew Cordelia had it all wrong. She hasn't made it easy for you, has she?"

I looked around in surprise and was relieved to see Cordelia across the dining hall, out of earshot. Mrs. Westervelt had a frank and open face, and was obviously accustomed to speaking her mind. She went on before I had a chance to reply. "Cordelia is one of those women who isn't sure of herself unless she has a grievance against someone else. She's always been like that. I try to talk her out of it, and then her grievance is with me."

"It doesn't matter," I said, and very nearly meant it, as Mrs. Westervelt had a way of appealing to my charitable side. "I know the sheriff is glad to have her help with his campaign."

Mrs. Westervelt was standing over a silver tray, dropping little slices of shortcake into frilled paper cups. "I've always said that it is incumbent upon a wife to take an interest in her husband's affairs. Cordelia did nothing but oppose Bob, and I never saw the percentage in it."

"I believe you're right," I said, although I didn't care to know about the inner workings of Sheriff Heath's marriage. Sheriffs are forced to live above the shop, so to speak, which makes for a disagreeable mingling of family and business.

Mrs. Westervelt brushed the crumbs from her fingertips and picked up the tray. "She'll be a fine wife for a congressman. It's a relief to her father and me."

"I suppose you'll miss her when she moves to Washington," I said.

By then a guard was admitting the first of the guests to the dining hall. Cordelia swept across the room gracefully to meet them. Mrs. Westervelt stood in the doorway, the tray of shortcake still in her hands.

"Quite the opposite," she said. "I'd rather have her far away and settled down contentedly, than underfoot all the time and unhappy about it. Grown children can be more of a nuisance than one might imagine. Consider yourself lucky not to have any."

She meant to be friendly, but she didn't know the truth. Although it was never spoken of in our family, Fleurette was in fact my daughter, but raised as my sister to prevent the scandal that inevitably follows when an eighteen-year-old girl carries on with a sewing machine salesman. It all happened a long time ago, and had become such a settled point in our family's history that it caused nothing in the way of hand-wringing anymore. I might confess to indulging Fleurette a bit, but youngest siblings are often the pet of the family, so I saw nothing wrong with that, and Fleurette didn't seem to find it unusual that one sister coddled her more than the other.

Regardless, as Mrs. Westervelt said those words, I was watching Fleurette and Helen work out their plans with Captain Anderson across the room. It wasn't easy for me to imagine her far away, or settled down, or both.

About thirty women had paraded into the dining hall by then, in groups of three or four, and took their places at the tables nearest the front, which had been draped in Mrs. Heath's good tablecloths for the occasion. They obviously thought it quite a novel experience to take their evening's entertainment in the jail, where the spartan furnishings and drab walls made even their most sensible dresses look outlandish. The room rang with the rustling of coats, laughter, and exclamations over the cunning flower arrangements, which consisted of individual chrysanthemums sitting under little white cages meant to represent the steel bars of a jail cell. Even the air had changed: atop the odor of the soap we used to scrub the floors now floated a layer of a dozen different French perfumes.

It embarrassed me to see an evening at the county jail treated as a lark, when it was anything but for those incarcerated there. The sound of the women's laughter could carry easily to the upper floors of the jail. I couldn't help but wonder what the inmates must've thought. If this was what a campaign required, I was glad I wasn't running for office.

As soon as the guests were furnished with their cakes and coffee, Sheriff Heath took the lectern and gave his opening remarks.

"Ladies, I've met most of you before. I see the wives of clergymen here, and of businessmen, and of more than a few elected officials. It's the scandal of the year to have you all in jail at once."

This was greeted with giddy laughter and the rattle of cups in saucers. Cordelia Heath and her mother, seated together at the front of the room, looked on approvingly. Helen and Fleurette had come around to the back to sit with me.

"You all know why we invited you here tonight," the sheriff said. "When the good men of Hackensack put me into this office, they were voting for my ideas. I said that I could run the jail with a businessman's efficiency, and I have. I took away the contract for kitchen service and put the inmates in charge, at a considerable savings to the taxpayers. Those who are able to do hard outdoor work put in honest labor at our farm in the summer, and stock the kitchen with corn and potatoes they grow themselves.

"But a jail can't run on business principles alone. It must run on Christian principles, too. I want to get to the man before he goes to jail, and to give him something in the way of education and a model life to strive for. When my deputies go out to make an arrest, we visit the very breeding ground where crime is allowed to take root. It is a place of poverty, neglect, and ignorance.

"I do what I can for my inmates while they're here, and I do it because I know they won't be here for life. Every man who is housed upstairs is awaiting his release. If I'm to return him to the streets of Hackensack—to your community, where you live and raise your children—then I want to make sure he's a better citizen upon his release than he was upon his arrest."

It was a passionate speech, spoken with considerable eloquence. He'd been delivering some version of it all over the county in the previous few weeks, always to a round of applause. Even Fleurette and Helen were impressed and clapped mightily.

The sheriff continued. "And it isn't just the men. I brought in a female deputy because the women we house on the fifth floor are mothers and daughters themselves. Their needs are every bit as great as the eighty or ninety men on the floors below them. Of course, there are practical considerations that make it a necessity to employ a jail matron. The female inmates shouldn't be under the watch of a male guard. You wouldn't want to be, if any of you were arrested."

This brought a round of laughter from the audience again, and Sheriff Heath gestured for me to stand. I had a feeling that every woman in the place had heard about John Courter's speech at the Board of Freeholders meeting, and the board's refusal to award a medal for my actions, and as a result I felt more than a little self-conscious as I stood to let the ladies have a look at me.

"A female deputy can do something in the line of preventing crime before it happens, too. She can win a confession or issue a word of warning in all manner of situations where a male deputy would be ineffective. I'll never forget the day, just last year, when she came to the aid of a factory girl whose mother had accused her falsely. I'm sure I wouldn't dare to get between a feuding mother and her daughter, but Deputy Kopp did, and it came out all right."

That earned me a polite smattering of applause, but I couldn't help but feel that he was trying too hard to defend me. He finished his remarks and told the ladies that they would be led upstairs for a tour of the female section while the rest of the inmates were brought down to the dining hall for Captain Anderson's sermon. Once the men were settled, the ladies would be allowed to return and sit at the rear of the room to observe the program.

Helen hadn't realized that she'd be taking a tour of the jail and she looked a little nervous about it. "Couldn't we wait here?" she whispered to me.

"I'm afraid not," I said. "Protocol requires us all to stay together." I didn't want to tell Helen that the women were being taken out of the room for reasons of safety. The jail had only one elevator for transporting inmates, which meant that they would be brought down in groups of ten or so. It took every guard on duty to manage the movement of the inmates, and it couldn't be done if they also had to oversee a few dozen society ladies. By shepherding the ladies upstairs all at once, I could keep them confined until the men were settled.

And that's exactly what I intended to do, until I stepped into the hall and found John Courter waiting for me in the shadows.

"There you are," he said quietly—too quietly. He had something to say that he wanted only me to hear. We were alone for just a moment. I had the odd feeling that I'd been trapped.

I looked at him evenly and said, "Of course I'm here. I work here."

He was eyeing me with such calculated calm. "You don't work at the asylum, but you were there Wednesday last."

I froze. Sheriff Heath had spotted him from across the room and was coming toward us. Mr. Courter turned around and saw him.

"He doesn't know, does he?"

I couldn't gather my thoughts. What was his purpose?

"I went against his orders," I said at last. Better to take the blame myself and spare Sheriff Heath.

He didn't have time to answer before the sheriff was upon us. "Mr. Courter! Pardon me, I didn't realize you'd be joining us tonight."

He turned to Sheriff Heath and said, "I saw all the ladies being brought in and thought you'd arrested an entire garden club. What is this?"

It occurred to me that Mr. Courter might take a dim view of the sheriff holding a campaign social at the jail. Was there anything wrong with what we were doing?

"It's a Salvation Army program for the inmates," the sheriff said. "These ladies have taken an interest. They're here to help."

"Punishing criminals with entertainment and refreshments? I suppose that's another of your modern ideas. I didn't come for your party, although I notice I wasn't invited, either."

He turned to go, giving me one last glance as he did. "Your girl deputy keeps busy."

Sheriff Heath looked a little puzzled at that, but he just called out to Mr. Courter's retreating form. "She's a hard worker."

When he was gone, the sheriff turned back to me. "Strange for him to drop by of an evening like this."

I hoped my face wasn't as flushed as it felt. "I'd better get the ladies upstairs."

⊰ 20 ⊱

A DOZEN OR so of our guests were willing to make the climb to the fifth floor, up a narrow circular staircase lit only by the lanterns we carried. Those unable to manage the stairs went by elevator with Mrs. Heath.

I could only hope that I was behaving as if nothing unusual had happened, but inside I was boiling. What was John Courter's purpose in coming to me? If he had a complaint against me, he could've taken it up with Sheriff Heath, or aired it in the papers as he had done so often before. Why keep it quiet? What effect did he hope to have on me?

There was no time to think about any of it. I had my inmates to consider now and Mrs. Heath's guests. At the top of the stairs, we crowded together into a small room meant as a guard's station, equipped with a bunk, a chair, and a desk. The women looked around them in awed silence.

"Is this where you spend the night?" Fleurette whispered.

That drew nervous laughter from the others, who must've assumed Fleurette was joking. I pulled myself together as best I could and said, "Most of the guards stationed on night duty would stay here. But I prefer to be out among my inmates. I sleep in a cell just like theirs. I want them to feel that they can talk to me, so it's better if I live as they do."

I waited while the women murmured and whispered to one another about that, then I made ready to tell them a little about the inmates they'd be meeting on our tour. Before I could, the elevator clattered into place behind us and the rest of the guests stepped out, accompanied by none other than William Conklin.

"Ladies! I hope somebody set aside a plate for me. Mrs. Higgins, is that your cinnamon loaf I smelled downstairs? Now, who's ready for a jail-house tour?"

There were cries of delight and, I must admit, relief from the audience assembled around me. William Conklin made a far more attractive tour guide to a group like this. I could hardly object to letting him take center stage—after all, he was the one running for sheriff—but it did irk me that he turned up with no preparation, having asked me not a single question about my inmates, and never having bothered to even glance around at the fifth floor before that moment.

Nonetheless, he had full command of the group. He knew most of them by name and grinned down at them as they fluttered around him. Even Fleurette and Helen were drawn to him, and lined up to be introduced.

I put an arm around each girl and said, "Mr. Conklin, I'd like to present my sister Miss Fleurette Kopp and her friend Miss Helen Stewart. Captain Anderson was good enough to invite them to sing tonight."

Mr. Conklin turned and took a step back in surprise when he saw them. He bent down slightly, his hands on his knees, the way one does when addressing a child. As Fleurette was only five feet in height, this was not entirely out of order.

"Just look at you girls!" he said, grinning at them. "In my day, we wouldn't let a pretty girl set foot inside the jail. But don't you worry—stay right here by my side and I'll make sure you're safe."

He looked like he was ready to carry one of them away under each arm. I kept my grip on their elbows and said, "That's fine, Mr. Conklin. The girls will stay with me. We have only a few minutes for our tour. Shall we begin?"

He looked at me like he thought I was spoiling all the fun. Maybe I was. The inmates could hear every word we said. I didn't like the implication that they posed some threat, but were nonetheless to be put on display.

As he didn't have a set of keys, I unlocked the gate that led to the inmates' cell blocks and ushered the guests along. To one side of us was the grid of whitewashed steel bars that encircled the jail's central rotunda. Through the bars one could hear the echo of the elevator clanging, the inmates shuffling along, and the guards calling out orders. On the other side, at intervals as we followed the rotunda around, were the entrances to each cell block.

I had told my inmates to expect special guests, and had promised them a smuggled portion of leftover refreshments as long as they kept quiet and gave only the shortest and most polite answers to any questions put to them. But I hadn't had time to discourage the guests from asking questions about the inmates' circumstances, as it would be nearly impossible for some of them to answer truthfully without speaking indelicately. There was no opportunity to say a word about that before Mr. Conklin swept into the first cell block he came to, and they all stood peering between the bars at Providencia Monafo.

It pained me to see her rise from her bunk and stand perfectly still in the middle of her cell, like a wild animal on observation at the zoo. She made quite a sight to those unprepared to greet her, with her unruly black hair falling almost to her waist, her stooped shoulders, crooked teeth, and an eye that hung half-closed and gave the impression that it could see beyond this world and into the next.

What could I do but make the best of it? I elbowed my way to the front of the crowd and said, "Mrs. Monafo, I'd like you to meet Mr. Conklin."

Providencia turned and squinted at him, sizing him up in that mystical way she had. He seemed not to take her in particularly and merely said, in his pleasing baritone, "How do you do, ma'am?"

She didn't answer but looked over the crowd of women behind him. "This is Mrs. Heath and some of her friends," I said, my voice cracking a little under the strain of a pretense at good cheer. "They've come to see how we do things on the fifth floor."

Cordelia Heath stepped forward and extended her hand, probably out of habit, for one does not generally shake hands through the bars of a jail cell. Providencia took it before she could change her mind and promptly turned it over to examine her palm. She traced a ragged old finger down the center of it and squinted up into Cordelia's face.

"You live downstairs with your children. I see you."

The ladies around her murmured, a little alarmed. "From the window," I hastened to explain. "The windows open just a bit. As you can imagine, the inmates appreciate a little fresh air and sunshine, so they tend to crowd around on fair days and watch people come and go. I'm sure Mrs. Monafo has seen you from the window at the end of her cell block from time to time."

"I never realized," Mrs. Heath said, under her breath.

Providencia let go of her hand but kept staring at her. "This is not your home." She said it with great conviction. Her words had a way of stabbing at a person.

"Mrs. Heath has made a fine home for her family," I said

brightly, and turned with the unreasonable hope that the rest of the crowd would follow me, but they seemed quite transfixed by Providencia.

It was at this moment that Mrs. Pattengill first made herself known to me. She stepped forward with a proprietary air and said, in the sort of loud, halting voice that wealthy women use to address their immigrant servants, "Please do tell us how you came to be here. What did you do—or rather, what was it in your circumstances—I mean to say . . ."

This was exactly the question I'd been fearing. The answer was that Providencia had been arrested for a murder she didn't intend to commit. She shot and killed her tenant, but she'd been aiming for her ill-tempered, drunken husband. Never had a sheriff seen a killer so eager to confess and take up residence behind bars, but then again, never had a wife such good cause to fear her husband's revenge. Providencia Monafo saw jail as a refuge and served her time contentedly.

"Oh, that's not necessary," I said hastily. "I'm sure our inmates would rather not revisit—"

Mr. Conklin interrupted. "Now, Miss Kopp, I believe Mrs. Pattengill asked a question, and she would like an answer. Go ahead and tell us, Mrs. . . . ."

He had forgotten her name. Providencia didn't bother to supply it. Her chin wobbled and her lips worked to put the words together.

"That poor man stepped in front of my gun," she said solemnly.

Mrs. Pattengill's mouth fell open. The ladies seemed to have heard quite enough and turned to shuffle away.

"Thank you, Mrs. Monafo," I said. "Perhaps Mr. Conklin is ready to move along."

A few of the women looked a little green, but they all scurried along behind Mr. Conklin, who marched over to the next cell block as if nothing irregular had happened. There they encountered Nancy Fyfe, who held her hand out graciously, but this time no one dared to take it.

"Oh, you don't have to worry about me, ladies!" she called cheerfully. "I'm only here for a night or two. The nice officer thought I didn't know how to handle my automobile, and he brought me here so that I wouldn't miss his point."

This elicited a cheerfully sympathetic response from the guests, many of whom admitted that they didn't know how to handle their automobiles, either, at least in the eyes of police officers.

"Didn't they send for your father, dear, or anyone who could come and collect you?"

It was Mrs. Pattengill speaking again. She seemed to take pride in knowing how to address the inmates and wanted everyone to hear it. I confess that I was impatient with her from the beginning. She had a nosy and interfering manner about her and took a proprietary air with my inmates.

"I should remind our guests that these are sensitive legal matters best discussed in privacy, and only with those who need to know," I said, a little too loudly. In the awkward silence that followed, Miss Fyfe took it upon herself to smooth things over.

"Oh, I don't mind saying. My father would come to my rescue, but I don't dare tell him. It's all right, though. Miss Kopp has been awfully good to me and has helped me to post letters to every friend and acquaintance I know. Someone will be here in the morning, I'm sure. But I don't mind, truly. I've been made quite comfortable."

"I've never heard an inmate call a jail cell comfortable," Mr. Conklin said, and moved down the block to Ruth Williams, who, even in her jail uniform, looked like an actress. She had a wide, flashy smile and had managed to style her hair into alluring waves, which was no small feat given how little the inmates had in the way of curlers and lotions. Her eyes were of an unnatural blue that could be mistaken for purple in the right light.

"Well, hello," she called when Mr. Conklin came into view. "Is this the sheriff? I expected to have a private audience with the man who ran the jail, but I suppose that's why you have a matron. The sheriff can't be bothered to come up and have a look at us poor girls."

This was exactly the sort of pouting and preening to which Mr. Conklin was susceptible. He took a step closer, leaned toward the bars, and said, "I'll get to know each one of you once I'm sheriff. I'm on the ballot this November. You'll tell every man in town to vote for William Conklin, won't you?"

She lifted an eyebrow and said, "I might just know every man in town."

A line like that would not have stood in ordinary society, but something about the jail-house tour was making the ladies feel a bit daring, and they laughed raucously at her remark.

Fleurette knew a trained actress when she saw one. She slid up next to me to have a better look. Ruth took stock of her in an instant and said, "Those are pretty little gloves, dear. Couldn't I try them on?"

Fleurette raised her hands to show the pearl buttons at the wrist.

"Oh, I had a pair just like them once," Ruth said, "but I've never had a dress as nice."

Fleurette turned a little to the side to show it off and said, "But this is nothing. It's so simple to make."

"You're a dear, but I know an easier way of getting a new frock."

"I wonder if they're ready for us downstairs," I put in, before this line of conversation could go any further. I was hoping to herd the group back to the elevator, but they'd already moved on to the next cell block, like visitors at a museum going from painting to painting.

We came, therefore, to the unionists, who were nothing if not organized. Three of them called out, "Good evening!" in one voice. Before anyone could return the greeting, Marie stepped forward and delivered a speech that she'd obviously been rehearsing.

"Ladies, we are the shop workers who make your dresses and waists. At the factory where we work, we must pay a fine if we make the smallest mistake, even if the fault lies with poor equipment or cheap thread. The fines are far greater than the cost of the ruined garment. And if a spool of thread is lost, we must pay the full price of it, even if the spool was empty. Sometimes the fines leave us with no wages at all at the end of the week. Does that sound fair to you?"

Again came Mrs. Pattengill's voice. "My stars and heavens! No, it does not. Shouldn't there be some provision for . . . that is . . ."

A woman standing next to her, caught up in the community spirit, stepped forward and said, "What factory is this? Is it here in Hackensack?"

"It's Daly Suit and Shirt Company," the girl said, in a proud and defiant voice.

A gasp went up among the ladies. Everyone turned to a woman standing near the back with Mrs. Westervelt. I knew with a sinking feeling that it had to be Mrs. Daly.

"I'm sure there's some misunderstanding," the woman said, tight-lipped but forcing a smile.

Mr. Conklin was at her side in a flash. "Don't give it a thought, Mrs. Daly. If you listened to everything a county jail inmate said, you'd have an awful ugly picture of the world. Leave this to the police and the courts. If I'd been told we had radical unionists up here, I never would've—"

Before he could come right out and blame me for Mrs. Daly's discomfort, a bell rang downstairs to call our group back to the dining hall. I couldn't have been more relieved.

"Mr. Conklin," I said, a bit sharply, which seemed to be the only way I knew to address him, "would you do us the honor of leading us back the way we came?"

Fortunately, Mr. Conklin took my suggestion unhesitatingly, and we wrangled the women back downstairs in more or less the same manner in which they'd been led up.

That brought a close to the most difficult part of the evening. There was nothing left for me to do but to sit in the back of the room alongside the ladies, with the inmates lined up in front of us on benches, to hear a sermon and a song. After that, the guests would be escorted outside, into a line of waiting automobiles, and I could return home with Helen and Fleurette. When we reached the dining hall and put the ladies in their seats in the back of the room, I sank down into a chair, grateful that the worst was over.

Helen and Fleurette performed beautifully, standing straight and tall behind the podium, their hands clasped in front of them, their voices ringing out like bells. The inmates had obviously been warned against pointing, whispering, or even winking at the girls. Sheriff Heath must've threatened them with the severest of punishments, because they sat like statues and did not even applaud until they were told to do so.

When they finished, Sheriff Heath took the podium. "Thank you, girls, for your singing, and to Captain Anderson for that fine sermon. I believe he hopes you'll take a pledge with him. The men, that is, not you ladies."

The women offered up a polite little laugh at that. Captain

Anderson took the sheriff's place at the podium, opened a cloth-bound book, and read from it. "Those of you who wish to join the Brighter Day League, now established in twenty prisons with a membership of over three thousand, will stand and recite with me."

The men had been ordered not to stand. All eyes went over to Sheriff Heath, who called out, "Go ahead, boys."

The inmates looked at each other hesitantly and shifted around on their benches before rising, a few at a time, to make a pledge about which they seemed none too certain.

"I pledge to read a portion of the Bible at least once a day and to kneel in prayer each morning and evening, asking God for help and guidance," Captain Anderson recited.

There was quite a bit of nonsensical mumbling but most of them got through it.

"To refrain from the use of profane language, and to be kind to my associates."

Sheriff Heath paced back and forth in front of the room to keep the men from making jokes. Captain Anderson continued his pledge. "To consider myself, from this day, an abstainer from all intoxicating liquors, except in the case of sickness, and to encourage others to do the same."

Helen and Fleurette giggled at that, as did some of the ladies around them. A general grumble of dissent went up among the men, but the sheriff repeated the pledge loudly and some of them followed along.

"To obey the rules and regulations of the institution of which I am at present an inmate, and to obediently carry out the instructions of the officials at the same."

This one drew a grin from Sheriff Heath and Captain Anderson, and a bit of good-natured laughter from the inmates, but they took the pledge.

Fleurette leaned over just then and whispered, "Who was that man I saw here earlier?"

There was a knot in my stomach as I recalled it. "John Courter."

"The one who wants to be sheriff?"

"Yes."

The captain folded his prayer book and recited the last line of the pledge from memory. "To endeavor to always live an exemplary life, and to act in such a way as to entitle me to be called a good citizen."

"He missed the sermon," Fleurette said.

The prisoners' voices rumbled through the room, repeating the words, more or less in earnest.

"It wouldn't have done him any good," I said.

⇥ 21 ⇤

"I HOPE YOU cured Cordelia Heath of holding tea parties at the jail," Norma said the next morning.

I laughed in spite of myself. I never did like the idea of the jail being treated as a backdrop for speeches and luncheons.

"As a campaign event, it was most unusual," I said. "My unionists were striking against a factory owned by one of the ladies' husbands, and my murderess answered the questions put to her a little too honestly. I wish the sheriff hadn't allowed it, but he has a hard time saying no to his wife."

"But as a concert, it was smashing," Fleurette said. "The inmates loved our singing."

"We all did," I said, but it was more out of habit than anything I could recall of the concert. "The strange thing is that Mr. Courter came to speak to me."

"What does he want with you?" Norma asked.

"He wouldn't come right out and say, but he was hinting at something. He knows I went to Morris Plains."

"I knew someone would find out," Norma said. "You're hard to miss. What did Sheriff Heath say?"

"That's just it. Mr. Courter only wanted me to know. He left without telling the sheriff."

Norma was bent over our dining room table, where pasteboard, toothpicks, glue, string, and bits of wood were scattered across the drawings that she and Carolyn Borus had been working on. She appeared to be making a miniature house and refused to answer questions about it.

She put down a little pen-knife and said, "Then he's threatening to expose you to the sheriff, but he hasn't done it yet."

"That's what it seemed like, yes," I said. "The trouble is, he made no demands of me. He didn't say what he wanted me to do."

"Well, surely he was warning you away from the asylum," Norma said.

"But why? He might not like me meddling in the Kayser case, but why not go to the papers with it? It's unlike him to be discreet."

"Maybe he doesn't want it made public that there's trouble with the case," Fleurette offered. "He might not want the papers looking into what happened to Anna Kayser."

I looked back and forth at the two of them, puzzling it out. "He's had nothing to do with her. This wasn't even a criminal case."

"Well, it's plain as day that he wants you to leave her alone, and he might want quite a bit more from you," Norma said. "He can tell Sheriff Heath anytime he wants. It puts him in charge, doesn't it? Hand me that pot of glue."

Fleurette and I were waiting for some sort of explanation about the miniature building project Norma had undertaken, but none was forthcoming. Norma never saw any reason to explain herself.

"I hope it's to be a doll-house," Fleurette said. "Mother never let me have one."

"It could be a working model of the jail," I offered.

Norma ignored us, pushed her spectacles up on her nose, and

rolled her sleeves past the elbow. When it became apparent that we weren't leaving without an explanation, she said, "You'll remember our plan for a message station in Ridgewood."

"We've been trying to forget about it, but we can't," Fleurette said. "It was only this summer. Give us time."

Norma's pigeon society, formed with such enthusiasm the year before, had, over the last several months, dwindled to only a few civic-minded women who enjoyed keeping birds and appreciated any activity that put them in the out-of-doors. One of those women owned a small lot behind the druggist in Ridgewood. Norma had the idea to build a pigeon loft there and to home a small flock, so that they could be checked out the way one checks out a book from the library. A person living in the countryside, or someone too ill to go out and post a letter, could take a pigeon home until such time as a message needed to be transmitted back to the druggist. They would simply slide a note into the tube that all such pigeons wore around their ankles, and then release the bird, which would fly directly back to its home loft in Ridgewood to deliver the message.

Believing that the druggist would be pleased to learn that a new method of relaying news between doctors and patients would be installed directly behind his back door, Norma marched in one day to tell him about it. She marched out a few minutes later, having received only scorn for her ideas and opposition to her efforts. When she persisted, the druggist even took his case to the town council, arguing that a pigeon loft in the middle of town would be noisy and unsanitary.

Norma attended the council meeting and stood her ground as only Norma could do. By the end of the evening, the members of the council had to concede that a pigeon loft would surely be no less sanitary than the horse stables that had been operating across the street for decades and would, furthermore, make no more noise than a single automobile, much less the scores of them that roared through town.

Although Norma won the begrudging approval of the town council, the druggist refused to participate in the scheme and said that no patient of his would be sent home with a pigeon under any circumstances, nor would he accept any messages relayed by pigeon post. Lacking his cooperation, Norma had put the project on indefinite hiatus.

"The druggist was only wasting our time. It's just as well that we found a more worthwhile project," she said.

"I assume that by 'we' you refer to the long-departed remaining members of your club," Fleurette said. "I don't recall more than one or two of them even being told about the druggist."

"Only one or two of them were of any use," Norma said.

"Then what's your new idea? It's hard to imagine a more worthwhile project than equipping a druggist with his own flock of pigeons," I offered, "but you might as well tell us about it."

Norma looked at me with pity. "Of course it's hard for you to imagine. You haven't been thinking about it like I have. What I've realized is that our station should be placed on wheels."

"Wheels?" I walked around the table and saw that, in fact, she'd fashioned wheels from the sawed-off ends of embroidery thread spools.

"I wondered what happened to those," Fleurette said.

"Yes, wheels," Norma repeated. "So it can be moved around."

"I understand what wheels do," I said, "but why would you want to move a loft for homing pigeons? Doesn't it have to stay in the same place so they'll be able to return to it?"

"We wouldn't home them in the cart," Norma said, exasperated. "They'd be homed in their own loft. We'll use the cart to wheel them down the road. From here to Hackensack, say."

"Wheel them? By horse?" I asked.

"A horse-drawn pigeon cart?" said Fleurette.

Norma could see that we were enjoying ourselves. She ignored us and leaned over the table, peering at an intricately designed hinge made of hammered tin.

"I'm doing my best to follow along," I said, "but I'm still having a hard time understanding what the people of Hackensack might do with several dozen homing pigeons on a cart. They can only fly back to their loft. What are the chances that someone in Hackensack would have an urgent need to send a message to the particular person who had put the pigeon on the cart that morning?"

"No one," Norma said. "We would only be doing it for demonstration purposes."

I was so vexed that I almost walked away. "Who on earth requires a demonstration that it is possible to raise pigeons in one place, wheel them to another, and then release them?"

Norma looked at me like I was a complete fool. "The Army."

Fleurette and I stared at each other and then turned incredulously back to Norma, who said, "This is just the thing they need in Europe."

Fleurette leaned over and whispered, "Is she sending her pigeons to France?"

Norma continued as if she hadn't heard. "They're going to need the cart to send messages back to our Army camps from the front. I'm building the first battle-ready pigeon transport cart. For when we go into the war."

"But I keep hearing they have telephone operators in France," Fleurette said. "Aren't they able to get messages through on the wires?"

"As long as you don't mind the Germans listening in," Norma said grimly, as if she'd already booted a couple of German spies out of the barn.

"Couldn't the Germans shoot down a pigeon? Isn't that sort of thing done for sport?"

"They couldn't shoot one of mine," Norma said. "My birds fly very fast and at a very high altitude. I've already demonstrated that." (It was true: she'd spent the entire spring sending her pigeons on long flights and timing the speed at which they flew.)

"But if the Army needed pigeons," Fleurette persisted, "why haven't they put out a call for them already? They only ever seem to ask for bandages and shoe leather."

Norma glued three little wooden sticks into place. She was building the back of the cart, where the pigeons could take some air but couldn't fly away. "The Army doesn't know what it needs. If it did, I wouldn't have to write and explain it to them."

"Does this mean you're going to Washington? Am I to be left all alone, with you off in the Army and Constance at the jail?"

Norma knew she was being teased, but she answered anyway. "I might go as far as Washington, but most of the camps are up here around the ports. I suspect I'll go to the Hoboken piers."

Fleurette considered that. "Do the other members of the pigeon society know that you're working for the military? Have they even adopted a position of preparedness on the war question?"

Norma dipped her brush in glue and applied it to a series of toothpicks that would form the bars of a detachable crate. She seemed to be counting under her breath.

"The vote was held just now," she said. "It passed."

Over the next hour or so, Norma managed to assemble most of the disparate components of the pigeon cart into a working whole. It was an ingenious little contraption that looked like it belonged in a child's toy set. I was fairly certain that if she ever grew tired of keeping pigeons, she'd have a future in the construction of miniature vehicles.

While Norma worked, Fleurette picked up one of the newspapers scattered across the table and started to read, with increasing fascination, a story on the front page. She sounded out the words the way a child would, and a couple of times she gasped and muttered to herself.

It was unlike Fleurette to notice anything in the paper that wasn't a theater review or a new dress pattern. "What's the matter with you?" I asked.

Fleurette stared up at me as if she were looking at a stranger. Then she turned back to the story. "When they say a man's face has been ruined at war . . ."

I sat down across from her and waited for the rest of it. By this time Fleurette was actually running her fingers over the words in disbelief. Finally she pushed the paper aside and turned her flushed face to me. She always looked like something blooming, and that was never truer than when she was about to cry, and the blood rushed to her cheeks, and the tears rolled onto her eyelashes. I couldn't help but notice what a very pretty picture she made.

"The Red Cross is building a hospital in Paris for the particular purpose of helping men whose faces have been entirely shot away. Entirely."

I did manage to read a daily newspaper. I knew all about the hospital in Paris but had very little to offer on the subject. Fleurette picked up the paper again and read to us.

"It says right here that a man came in from the firing line with nothing to show that he ever had a face," and here her voice floated up into a note of high alarm before she swallowed and read on. "He had only two slits under the eyebrows and a few teeth in the lower jaw. They say his face looked like the crater of a volcano."

She slapped the paper down, scattering some of Norma's toothpicks. "And do you know what he wrote when someone came in and stared at him? Wrote, because, of course, he can't speak. He wrote, 'Don't worry about me. I still have my sight.'"

"Some of them don't," Norma said.

"Then why haven't we gone to help?" Fleurette demanded. "We're a nation of a hundred million. Don't you think we ought to do something?"

"The Red Cross is helping," Norma said. "That's why they're building the hospital. And you can go down any day of the week to roll bandages or knit socks."

"That's not what I mean," Fleurette interjected, although I noticed that she didn't leap up and run into town to roll bandages. "We should go over and put a stop to it."

"If it were that simple, we would've gone already," I said. "Surely you can see that people don't want to send their sons and brothers into a war that doesn't involve us. What if Francis had to go? What would you make of that?"

"We should be prepared to go," Norma said, "which is why I'm making this cart."

"That's right!" Fleurette said. "We should be prepared. Why aren't we running drills and building ships and all of that?"

"We are doing quite a bit of that already," I said. "But no one wants to pay the war tax. Are you prepared to pay? Are you ready to give up your singing lessons, and make do with whatever old scraps of fabric you have sitting around, and to give up your sugar and your tea? Are you prepared to hand over your wages to the War Department?"

At that, Fleurette sighed and bent over the newspaper again. There we were, the three of us: a diorama of Americans' position on the war in the waning months of 1916. We were no closer to an answer than anyone else, but we all had the uneasy feeling that something was coming, and we'd be swept up in it.

I had an uneasy feeling about John Courter as well, and no better idea of what was coming, or when.

⇥ 22 ⇤

"I MIGHT HAVE tortured Mr. Townley to make him agree to see us," Geraldine said, when we met at the appointed hour a few days later. "I told him that I was a New York attorney and that I had information that might be damaging to his reputation. I believe he thought I'd uncovered some nasty personal business of his. I just didn't want him running to his wife with the entire story before we had a chance at him. This has turned into quite the house of cards, and I want the cards to fall in the right order."

There was something brassy and hard-nosed about the way Geraldine talked about him. "You're enjoying this, aren't you?" I asked her. "I think you like playing the part of the lady cop."

"I just might," she said, as we reached the little brick building that housed Mr. Townley's office. "I suspect I'd enjoy making an arrest. You do, don't you? You get a little thrill from it."

"Well, handcuffs do make a satisfying sound when they land on a pair of wrists."

A lady in a great fur coat and an elaborately trimmed hat overheard us as we went in the building and gave us a look of affront.

"I suppose it doesn't do to make a joke about arresting someone," Geraldine whispered as we went down the hall.

I hadn't told Geraldine about my run-in with John Courter. It wouldn't change what we were about to do. The possibility that Mr. Courter wanted me to stay away from Anna Kayser's case only furthered my resolve to see it through. Anyway, the damage was already done: I'd snuck around, lied my way into an asylum, and pursued a case that wasn't mine. To see it through couldn't possibly make it worse. If anything, I wanted some answers before I got caught.

Joseph Townley kept no secretary and merely called for us to enter when we knocked at his door. His was a tiny office no larger than a broom closet. A rolling desk was pushed against the wall and Mr. Townley occupied the only chair. He stood quickly and offered the chair to each of us in turn, but after some shifting about we all remained standing.

Joseph Townley was a jowly man with a prominent chin and the expressive eyes of a family dog. He had a thick head of hair that rose up from his forehead in a smooth wave and flopped over to one side. He wore heavy eyeglasses and an agreeably rumpled suit. In fact, he was, in every way, an agreeably rumpled man in the middle of life, with a pleasantly deep voice and a ready smile. Even in the face of whatever news might be coming to him, he was considerate and friendly. He seemed, in other words, too trustworthy to be involved in a scandal.

"I'm sorry we must meet under these circumstances, ladies," he said. "I wasn't expecting a woman cop and a lady lawyer. I hope you haven't come to arrest me." He gave an awkward laugh. We made him nervous.

"It concerns your wife," I said.

"Virginia? What's happened to her? I just had a letter this morning."

"Then you know where she's gone?" Geraldine asked.

He looked back and forth at us, confused. "Why—she's with

her sister, over in Newark. There's a baby on the way and her sister's been ordered to bed."

I realized all at once that we'd relied upon Anna Kayser identifying Virginia Townley from our description, but I had no way of knowing with any certainty if she was in fact Joseph Townley's wife, or another woman of the same general appearance. How many frail, nervous redheads answering to the name of Virginia were in circulation in Rutherford?

Geraldine started to say something, but I put a hand on her arm. "Pardon me, Mr. Townley. Does your wife favor smaller hats, in bright colors? Has she a yellow one, with a red silk poppy in the band? And a dark green hat with a gold military braid that comes around the side? And a floppy sort of velvet hat, with berries made of glass?" I was surprised at how easily I'd recalled that hat-rack. It was only Fleurette's influence that would ever make me notice glass berries pinned to a hat.

He looked between the two of us, astonished. "What's the matter with her? How do you know about her hats?"

"She isn't in Newark, Mr. Townley," Geraldine said, as gently as she could. "She's right here in Rutherford."

He started to sink into his chair but remembered his manners.

"Please take a seat," I said. "We don't mind. It appears your wife has taken a position as a housekeeper."

At that Mr. Townley laughed and dropped into his chair, obviously relieved. "Then I'm afraid you're after the wrong woman. My wife doesn't keep her own house, much less anyone else's. She's never done a day's work in her life. She spends the money. I'm the one who earns it. Ain't that the usual arrangement?"

He struck a match and lit a cigarette, offering one to each of us. We refused, but I handed him the glass ash-tray that was just behind me on a window-sill.

171

"It seemed irregular to us, too," I said, "which is why we looked into it a bit more. We happened to visit the house where she's employed, to investigate another matter, and found the situation suspicious. That's why we've come to you. Do you know a man named Charles Kayser?"

Geraldine and I both leaned back a little, expecting him to explode out of his chair. Instead he kept his eyes fixed on the cigarette in his hand, took a couple of uneven breaths, and finally looked slowly up at us.

"Charlie?" There was misery in his voice.

I gave a slight nod but didn't say a word.

He looked again at his cigarette. His head shook slightly back and forth, and he muttered something under his breath.

"Is he a friend of yours?" I asked after a long silence.

He nodded but kept his eyes down.

Geraldine said, "You might know that he's had some trouble with his wife. There's a daughter still at home, and he needed a woman about the place to look after her."

Not a word came from Joseph Townley. We stared at the top of his head, where his hair stood up in a cowlick at the back, and waited.

"I wonder why Virginia wouldn't just tell you the truth, if she was only going to help a friend of yours," I said at last.

He reached into his coat and pulled out a handkerchief, which he pressed briefly to his eyes. Then he pushed himself shakily to his feet and kicked the chair out of the way so that he could lean against the wall. His arms were crossed in front of him, and he was as far away from us as he could be in that little room.

"Charles Kayser keeps a woman," he said, in a quiet and resigned voice. "He always has."

I waited, but that was all he said for a minute. He took a ragged breath, swallowed hard, and started again.

"I mean to say that he has, over the years, kept a woman apart from his marriage."

He raised an eyebrow, as if to question whether we understood his meaning, and we both nodded.

"Charlie and I are in sales. I suppose you already know that. We travel together once or twice a month. Sometimes he'll have a woman in another town. He falls in love with them, or he thinks he does, and then he wants to marry them."

Geraldine looked at me from the corner of her eye. "You've seen this before," she said.

He gulped and nodded. "When his wife is ill—when she goes away—there's always a lady to come and keep house for him. It's —well, it's one of his girls."

"Are you saying," I asked, "that when his wife becomes ill, he brings a lady-friend to town to keep him company, or are you saying that he sends his wife away under the pretense of illness because he prefers the company of another woman?"

Mr. Townley turned around and banged his palm against the window. The rattle of the panes made us both jump.

"I never knew he had his eye on Virginia," he said, looking out the window at the street below. "I never knew, or I never bothered to ask. Charlie was a good friend to me when my wife died. He introduced me to . . ."

His voice trailed off as he put the pieces together. "He introduced me to Virginia."

❧ 23 ❧

WE SENT MR. TOWNLEY into a state of high alarm, but he was able to compose himself long enough to assure us of his readiness to file a divorce suit against his wife. Geraldine warned him that the next step was the most delicate: photographs of the erring couple must be taken and entered into evidence. She begged him to stay calm, and if he happened to see Charles Kayser or Virginia, to act as if nothing was amiss.

"Why, I'll be on a train to Scranton with Charlie in another week," he said, red-faced. "I'm not any kind of actor. What'll I do about that?"

"Change your plans," said Geraldine. "Come down with a case of dyspepsia or a head cold. Just stay away from him. And if your wife comes back—"

"She won't," he said dispiritedly.

"If she does, act as if nothing's wrong. Make it easy for her to go out again. The picture's the thing, Mr. Townley."

When we left his office, Geraldine pulled a scrap of paper from her purse. "This is going exactly as I'd hoped. The trouble is that I don't know a reliable photographer in New Jersey, and the rates to send someone over from New York would be awfully high. But there's an attorney in Paterson who handles divorce cases, so

I've made an appointment for us. It would be better for him to represent Mr. Townley anyway, and I'll take Anna Kayser."

"Who's the attorney in Paterson?" I asked.

She showed me the paper. "John Ward. Do you know him?"

I had to admit that I did know him. For a brief time, John Ward represented Henry Kaufman, the man who harassed my family a few years earlier. Mr. Kaufman fired him, and went into court with a poor defense, which seemed to have worked in our favor as we won the case. Sheriff Heath and John Ward were friends of many years, although the two men couldn't have been less alike. The sheriff served divorce papers on behalf of John Ward's clients, and sought Ward's advice on legal matters pertaining to the sheriff's office.

"I know him," I said. "And he's expecting us this afternoon? You must have been awfully confident about our meeting with Mr. Townley."

Geraldine waved her hand in the air dismissively. "Poor old Joe. What choice did he have?"

We arrived in Paterson with little time to spare, and walked right up to John Ward's office. I'd been there only once before but knew the way.

The door bore the name of the firm, Ward & McGinnis, in fresh stenciling, and when we walked in, I was astonished to see that the office had been completely transformed and that a new girl sat at the desk. Gone were the red carpets and the mahogany panels. Gone were the Chinese lacquer pots and the fan palms. The room had been made over entirely in white and gold, with a pale carpet of the faintest green, and a delicate chandelier dripping in gold filigree that hung over a desk of honey-colored wood.

Sitting at that desk was a Scandinavian beauty with aquamarine eyes and hair as white as corn-silk. Even Geraldine seemed taken aback.

"Have we come to a law office?"

The girl gave a little gasp. "What do you think of it? I've only just had it redone."

Geraldine turned around in a circle and said, "It is the most beautiful office I've ever seen. In fact, I don't think I've ever been in a room quite like it."

The girl looked pleased. "Mr. Ward told me to spend whatever it cost. He wanted all traces of the former . . . well, of the old ways taken away."

I thought the last receptionist was the prettiest girl I'd ever seen, until I met this one. I was beginning to suspect a pattern.

"I believe we have an appointment," I told the girl, and gave our names.

She consulted a little white calfskin appointment book. Just as she did, a crash came from the room behind her, and the sound of breaking glass. She looked up as if she hadn't heard it. "They're waiting for you."

"They?" Geraldine asked.

"Mr. McGinnis is in today as well." Something hit a wall with a dull thud, followed by muffled laughter. She lifted an eyebrow in the direction of the noise and said, "They found a game of parlor croquet in a closet, and they play it violently. It's best to knock."

She did so, rapping on the door behind her desk officiously. That brought about the sound of furniture sliding around and a low but animated argument between two men. Geraldine wore a look of delighted fascination.

"They share an office," I explained. "They always have."

At last the door opened, and we were greeted by a flushed and panting Peter McGinnis. He was a round-faced, red-haired jovial man whose green eyes and freckles made him look perpetually boyish. John Ward came up behind him, a lanky man with curly hair that flopped over his forehead and a scheming squint to his eyes. He wore a wide grin and kept a pipe clenched between his teeth.

"Ladies!" Mr. Ward called, opening the door wide. "Petey was just letting me beat him at croquet. Miss Ericson, what do you suppose these ladies might take at this hour? My aunt takes a drink called a Presbyterian, with Scotch and mint and enough ginger ale to hide the color of the Scotch. Could we interest you girls in a thing like that?"

"I don't know where I'd find the mint," Miss Ericson said anxiously.

"No one bothers with the mint," Mr. Ward said, grinning at Geraldine.

Mr. McGinnis took his croquet mallet—it was one of those toy-sized mallets, with the paint chipped off—and bent over to knock a ball against Mr. Ward's feet. "You're offering drinks to a sworn officer of the law, Jack. She's a deputy now."

"Yes, and I'm on duty myself," Geraldine said. She swept into the room and bent down to scoop up the ball and hand it back to Mr. McGinnis. "Where would you like us?"

The chairs had all been moved out of the way to make room for the croquet hoops. Mr. McGinnis hastened to put them back where they belonged, and we each took our seats. The men sat at either end of an enormous partner's desk, where a rudimentary game of table-top croquet had been set up, with golf balls and little paper tents.

"I thought a Presbyterian was gin and ginger," said Mr. McGinnis.

"It might be. A Methodist is the same drink, only with sarsaparilla. Say, now, Miss . . ." Mr. Ward turned to us, leaning across the desk on his elbows, "Geraldine, is it? I'm sorry . . ."

"Miss Rodgers," Geraldine said. "I've come to bring you a client. He might just like one of those drinks of yours."

"Divorce, isn't it?" said Mr. Ward. "It's a specialty of ours. I don't know any drinks particular to the institution, however. We should have one called the Willful Deserter. Write that down, Petey."

Mr. McGinnis did. "Yes, and what about Failure to Support?"

Mr. Ward said, "It sounds like a stingy drink, but that describes half our clients. I hope this one has some money."

I was beginning to remember why Sheriff Heath tried to avoid afternoon meetings with Mr. Ward. They started into their liquor early and rarely got anything done after three.

Geraldine said, "I'm afraid we have an ordinary adultery case for you. There are pictures to be taken, if you can manage it."

Mr. McGinnis straightened up a little in his chair. Mr. Ward said, "We manage it better than anyone else on the Atlantic seaboard. Petey's a champion photographer and a master illusionist. We've dressed him up as a theater usher, a milk-man, and a cleaning lady, all in pursuit of the truth."

"A cleaning lady!" Geraldine said. Mr. McGinnis smiled, pleased, his cheeks pink behind their orange freckles.

"I loaned him my best pink duster. He filled it out nicely," Mr. Ward said.

"The milk-man will do just fine," Geraldine said. "But the lady spooks easily, so get it right the first time."

"They all spook easily," Mr. Ward said. "Why does this one have the attention of the Gentlewoman Deputy?"

I told him about Anna Kayser's commitment to Morris Plains and he gave a low whistle. "Had his own wife committed? It's an old trick, but a dependable one. My great-uncle Pop sent his first wife away and got another one just like your fellow did. Used to call it the poor man's divorce. All it took was a doctor willing to take payment in chicken eggs or pork bellies."

"You never told me about any Uncle Pop," Mr. McGinnis said.

"His name was Whatcoat, but he wouldn't answer to it."

If we didn't leave soon, I feared we'd be there all afternoon hearing about Uncle Pop. "The picture, gentlemen," I said, rising to my feet. They jumped up and Geraldine followed suit. "This week, if at all possible. We have a perfectly sane woman in an asylum who would very much like not to sample the electrical therapy or the lithia tablets. Let's do her a good turn. And please keep this to yourselves, as I am involved in an unofficial capacity."

"Do you mean to say that Mr. Sheriff doesn't know you're here?" Mr. Ward said delightedly. "I didn't know you were capable of running a con, Miss Deputy."

"It isn't a con. Only—I'd appreciate your discretion."

I meant to leave in as dignified and expedient a manner as possible, but before I could, Miss Ericson knocked at the door and came in wearing a chinchilla set. Mr. Ward shrieked and Mr. Mc-Ginnis collapsed in laughter.

"You know that thing terrifies me," Mr. Ward said, rushing to the door and batting her away, while keeping one hand dramatically over his eyes. "I was bitten by a weasel as a small child and I can't go near them."

She giggled. "It isn't a weasel, and it can't bite you." She waved the snout at him and he fell back in horror.

"I don't know how you afford to feed that thing. We pay you too much, Miss Ericson."

"Yes, you do," she called, and waved good-night. "Lock the door when you leave."

Geraldine handed Mr. Ward her card. "Telephone the minute you have those photographs."

"I'll get them tonight, if it means I can telephone you," Mr. Ward said. "What does a lady lawyer get up to in the evenings in New York?"

179

"What does a married man get up to in Paterson?" Geraldine retorted.

"You'd never guess," Mr. Ward said, bouncing his pipe up and down between his teeth.

"Oh, I might."

⇥ 24 ⇤

I WANTED VERY much to write to Mrs. Kayser and tell her that
we were working on securing her release, but I knew the doctors
would read her mail. I had to hope that she was safe, at least, and
looked after, and that Ward & McGinnis would get their pictures
quickly.

We were now only two weeks away from the election. I hadn't
seen Mr. Courter again and had no idea whether he knew what
Geraldine and I had been up to. The business of campaigning occupied more and more of Sheriff Heath's time, so that I rarely saw
him, either. In fact, I read about him in the paper more often than
I spoke to him. The papers had nothing new or unusual to report,
only that Sheriff Heath and William Conklin were out speaking
to one group or another about their program of reform and social
change.

I'd managed to stay out of Cordelia Heath's way, too, until a
Tuesday morning when I was summoned down from the fifth floor
to register a new inmate. I went to collect her from the interviewing room where she'd been made to wait, but I found Cordelia
standing in the corridor, blocking my way. She was dressed for a
luncheon, in a stiff silk dress of shimmering pale lilac.

It was unusual to find her anywhere inside the jail proper: she tended to stay within her own apartment and the sheriff's office. She'd never once gone looking for me specifically, so I assumed she was searching for her husband.

"I'm sorry, Mrs. Heath," I said. "I haven't seen the sheriff. I'm on my way to bring in a new inmate, if you'll excuse me."

"Yes, I know," Cordelia said. "I want to tell you about her before you go in."

That was enough to stop me in my tracks. What was Mrs. Heath doing, interfering with my inmates?

Cordelia looked up and down the corridor. We were entirely alone, and the metal doors at each end were both closed. There were plenty of places at the jail where one might be overheard — the inmates even talked to one another through the steam pipes — but those stark brick walls were impervious to eavesdropping.

Nonetheless, Cordelia whispered. I had to bend over to hear her. "That's Mrs. Pattengill who's been arrested."

"Do you mean the lady from the jail tour? Isn't she a friend of yours?"

Cordelia looked around anxiously. "Yes. I don't have to tell you that she runs in all the same circles as . . . well, you know. She's acquainted with so many of my husband's friends."

I was beginning to get the idea, and I didn't like it.

"What I mean to say," she continued, as it must've been apparent that I wasn't sympathetic to her perspective, "is that those individuals most likely to endorse Mr. Heath, or to contribute to his campaign, are known to Mrs. Pattengill. It's unfortunate that she's here, but as it is unavoidable, we must show her our hospitality."

She followed that with a faint misplaced smile and a pat on my arm. I wanted very much to withdraw the arm, but fought the urge.

"Has there been some mistake, Mrs. Heath? Has Mrs. Pattengill been wrongly arrested?" I asked.

Her eyes flew open. "Oh! I haven't an idea, but I imagine so. It's something to do with funds raised for a charity. I don't pretend to understand it. Only—we can't afford a single misstep right now. You do understand that, don't you, Miss Kopp?"

"I suppose."

"Mr. Heath has been under a terrible strain lately, and we've two more weeks to go until the election. Neither one of us wish to see his office in the papers again, in such an unfavorable light."

I didn't want to stand in the corridor any longer and argue the matter, but what choice did I have? "We caught the inmate. In fact, I caught him. I don't know how that puts the jail in an unfavorable light."

She seemed as though she was trying to keep the conversation light, but it was all too plain to me that she was the one under enormous strain over the matter. "Of course you caught him. It's only that he never should've escaped in the first place—at least, that's how the papers see it—and once again, it's the lady deputy under fire. Surely you see the difficulty."

In all honesty, I did see the difficulty. Everything I did drew attention, but what was I to do about it? "I never ask to be in the papers, ma'am," I said.

Cordelia's expression hardened. "Well, the reporters seem to have no trouble finding you. They know your name all the way out in California. But just as your star rises, my husband's falls. Don't you see that? He pays a price."

I tried to interrupt, but she wouldn't let me. "And now we have an inmate under your care who requires extra . . . sensitivity. I just wanted to alert you. It's for your own good, too. A lady like her can make use of certain highly placed connections if she feels she's been badly served."

"Served? We aren't a hotel, Mrs. Heath."

She studied me for a minute and then said, "Never mind. I'll speak to my husband. I was only asking for a little kindness for a friend."

"I'm always kind to the inmates," I said, more brusquely than I should have, and went on down the hall.

By this time I was truly in no mood to receive Mrs. Pattengill. My spirits did not rise as I went through the metal door and approached the room where she was being held. Her voice could be heard all the way down the hall, and it was apparent the guards were having a miserable time of it. I always wondered what the inmates thought they'd gain by antagonizing the guards, but there was no time to ponder it, as Mrs. Pattengill and the guards were obviously in distress.

"I was told I'd have a lady attendant!" I heard her shriek.

"Yes, ma'am, we're just waiting," the beleaguered guard said.

"I should not be made to wait, after what I've been through! Bring her to me now or call my attorney!"

The guards had never been so happy to see me walk into a room. They were gone as soon as I arrived.

Mrs. Pattengill seemed to deflate when she saw me. "Oh, there you are. Now, they didn't give me a bite to eat at the courthouse, and I'm prone to dizzy spells. What I'd like you to do . . ."

That was absolutely the wrong way to open a conversation with a sheriff's deputy. "Why don't I tell you what you're going to do, ma'am," I said.

Mrs. Pattengill looked shocked at that but allowed me to take her arm and lead her to the de-lousing room.

Until that moment, I had never booked a lady into the jail as grand as Mrs. Pattengill. Most inmates arrived in the plain dress of working folk, and some wore nothing but rags. But this woman possessed a fine wardrobe, and she was not at all willing to part with it. When I told her that she was to remove every stitch of clothing in exchange for a broadcloth jail uniform, she gave another of her high-pitched shrieks.

I ignored that and further explained that she'd be removing her fine garments in my presence, to be followed by a hot shower and a scrubbing with naptha soap. I did not mention the mercurial ointment that would be rubbed into her scalp, for fear she might faint. As it was, she clutched at her chest and demanded a telephone.

"You may speak to your attorney tomorrow," I told her, and opened the door to the shower room, which smelled of ammonia and sassafras. Mrs. Pattengill stepped inside dubiously.

The door to that room was exceptionally heavy. When it closed, the place had the muffled silence of a bank vault. Mrs. Pattengill took advantage of the privacy and tried to appeal to my sympathies.

"You must understand, Miss . . ."

"Deputy Kopp. We met on the jail tour."

"Yes, Miss Deputy, you see, I don't belong in here at all. I've done nothing wrong, and the only reason the police don't understand the situation is that they know nothing of double-entry bookkeeping and the methods by which women of society solicit donations for their pet causes."

"The police know quite a bit," I said mildly, "but so do the judges. I suppose your attorney will put up an able defense?"

I wasn't particularly interested in the answer to this question, but Mrs. Pattengill had already removed her Gainsborough hat with its accompanying plumage and handed it to me, as if I were her personal attendant—and at that moment, I was willing to play the part. I had the idea that as long as I kept talking, the garments would keep coming off. That was my preferred way to do it: I never liked to wrestle a woman's clothing away from her if I could avoid it.

"Oh, my attorney will do what he can," Mrs. Pattengill said, "but you know how it is with these old family friends who only ever dabble in the law. He's very much a gentlemen's attorney, good for writing up wills and paying off inspectors, but he's not particularly quick-witted in the courtroom."

With that came her high-buttoned shoes, made of good Dongola leather. I set them carefully aside and said, "Am I to understand that you've been jailed over some charge connected to the work you do for a charity?"

"Oh, several charities, and that's the tragedy of it." She peeled off a pair of embroidered stockings, tied them in a knot, and dropped them, still warm, into my outstretched hand. "The Society for the Destitute Blind, the Home for Friendless Girls, the Imbeciles' Work-House—I am a missionary for all of them, and so many more. Why, you couldn't name a charity that hasn't had an envelope from me, and I'm always happy to do it. I consider it my duty."

Next came one of those knobby taffeta skirts that were popular a few years ago. I was enlisted to hold up the hem so that it wouldn't drag on the floor as Mrs. Pattengill stepped out of it, and I admit that I did it, as if it were an everyday occurrence at the Hackensack Jail for me to serve as a lady's maid.

Mrs. Pattengill hesitated after her outer clothing was removed. To keep her going, I said, "Most ladies are given awards and gratitude for all their good charitable deeds, and not a jail sentence. Whatever went wrong?"

"You are exactly right, Miss Deputy. They should've given me a medal. In fact, I was out raising donations for the Injured and Maimed Police Officer's Fund when one of Hackensack's own constables came up alongside me and told me to go quietly with him or else he'd put the handcuffs on me. Have you ever heard of such a thing?"

I had, of course, heard of criminals having handcuffs put on them.

At last Mrs. Pattengill went to work on an elaborate ruffled shirtwaist, obliging me to help with the dainty pearl buttons in the back. The room was close and stuffy, and the walls were still wet from the last inmate who'd been scrubbed down in there. We were both starting to sweat, so much so that she had to peel the shirtwaist away from her bosom. Her corset cover underneath was similarly plastered to her chest. She looked down in discouragement, and I feared she was about to abandon the effort.

"Am I to understand that you're widowed?" I asked.

That got her working furiously at the buttons down the front. "Oh, wouldn't that be a mercy. No, he lives and breathes, but we don't speak of him. Mr. Pattengill went off to Chicago without so much as a word of good-bye. I'd divorce him if I could find him. My attorney delivers a little stack of twenty-dollar bills now and then if I show up at his office and complain loudly enough. I suspect he knows right where Bill's gone, but he won't tell me and he says the money will stop coming if he does."

She liberated herself from the corset cover and a long ruffled petticoat or two. There was nothing left but one of those form-reducing corsets that belted all the way down to the hips. Red welts glared from under her arms where it pinched.

The time had come to reveal all.

"Do you mean to say that your husband vanished," I asked, "and refused to pay for your support, but all the while you took up charitable work and went door to door asking for donations to charity?"

The corset sprung loose and the truth was laid bare. "Yes, and with only a drop now and then for my expenses, naturally! You see, this is what the police cannot understand."

I took Mrs. Pattengill's hairpins and combs and folded everything into a tidy bundle. At last my inmate submitted to the shower and the naptha soap, and I congratulated myself for having maneuvered her into it without so much as a harsh word.

I still hadn't told her about the mercurial ointment for her scalp, which was intended to rid her of the lice she would swear she didn't have. Mrs. Pattengill was in too vulnerable a state to have more than one indignity imposed upon her at a time, and nothing was more distasteful than a struggle with an unclothed inmate. When I did invite her to sit down on a metal chair and to turn her head down so that I could comb through it with the ointment, she just sighed and gave in. We finished quickly, as her hair was fine and quite clean. She even laughed when I told her that the comb ran neatly along her oiled scalp and picked up no stragglers.

Then she dressed, and looked down mournfully at the house dress and slippers that had been issued to her.

"It's better this way," I told her. "You wouldn't want to stand out. Most of the other ladies don't have nice things."

She didn't seem to find that a cheering thought, but she went along obediently, as even the most defiant inmate would after being stripped and de-loused.

On the way upstairs, she asked, "What have they done—these other women?"

Her curiosity about the inmates, it seemed, was undiminished from her previous visit. "Why, you've met some of them already," I said. "You can ask them yourself. You'll have all the time in the world."

She stopped and gave me a meaningful look. "What I want to know is—well, is it entirely safe to put me in with criminals?"

I wondered how much money Mrs. Pattengill had stolen, and how many people she'd stolen it from. Mrs. Heath might've taken pity on her, but I didn't.

"It's a jail, Mrs. Pattengill. They're all either convicted criminals, or they're awaiting trial, just like you are."

"Oh, but I'm only here as the result of a terrible misunderstanding! I never meant to do anything but to offer my services on behalf of the less fortunate, and once it's all explained . . ." She sputtered and ran out of steam.

We were on the fifth floor now. "Nobody means to do the things they did," I said, "or at least, they didn't mean to get caught. In here, it amounts to the same thing."

⊰ 25 ⊱

FLEURETTE LIKED TO make her announcements at breakfast, when she was sure I'd be in a rush to leave for work. Norma, by that time, had already been up and outdoors for an hour or two. She came inside for coffee but couldn't be bothered to linger at the table, which was just as well, as she'd been mucking out the chicken coop and was still shedding bits of rotten straw.

"I took to heart your advice," Fleurette began, directing those gratifying words to me in her warmest tones, "about finding some way to help with the war effort."

I was very much involved with digging the last of Bessie's lemon preserves out of a jar at that moment, so Norma answered for me.

"It's about time you put your mind to something."

A remark like this would've usually set Norma and Fleurette to bickering until the dishes were cleared, but she'd obviously rehearsed her lines ahead of time and was determined to deliver them according to her design, because she said, "Yes, well, as you've both been saying, there's so much to be done, and we must all put our talents to use."

"That's a fine idea," said Norma. "I see no reason why you couldn't be turning out uniforms by the dozen."

This threw Fleurette off-track momentarily—when had anyone ever said anything about making uniforms?—but she pushed on. "Freeman Bernstein is organizing a troupe of entertainers to perform at the Plattsburg camps. He'd like me and Helen to put together a group of girls from Mrs. Hansen's Academy."

Now she had my attention. "What kind of performance? Do you mean to say that he's putting together another vaudeville act?"

"Well, he—"

"I don't think any good can come of an association with Mr. Bernstein," Norma said.

Norma's dislike of May Ward's husband and manager was well-established in our household, but not particularly well-founded. When Fleurette left unexpectedly to tour with May Ward in the spring (I preferred the term "left unexpectedly" to "ran away"), Norma was certain that Fleurette had been somehow misled or subjected to mistreatment. In fact, Fleurette had been hired on as the company seamstress, but didn't like to admit it. She preferred for us to think that she enjoyed a successful turn on the stage.

Norma and I went along with that little fiction. It was one of many such falsehoods that allowed the three of us to live together in whatever harmony we could manage.

"You needn't worry about Mr. Bernstein," Fleurette countered, still calm, still logical, quite clearly sticking to the lines she'd rehearsed. "He's doing good work for the troops. We are to put on a show of wholesome patriotic music. That's all there is to it."

"I don't think we can call them troops quite yet," I put in gently.

"Of course we can," Fleurette said. "They're training for Army duty."

It was a mistake to bring up the Army in Norma's presence, as she believed herself to be an expert in all wartime matters. I settled in for the lecture I had no means of preventing.

"The Army has no official orders to prepare for war, and that's just the problem," Norma said, as I expected she would. "They've been dragged into these volunteer camps because it looks bad if they don't at least show up and offer something in the way of a training exercise. But these are hardly troops preparing for war. The Plattsburg camp is nothing but an excuse for salaried men who are weary of their offices to escape to the countryside for a few weeks. They're having the time of their lives up there, camping and fishing and shooting off rifles."

"Mr. Bernstein says they're serving the nation, and that we are to lift up their spirits, and to remind them why they fight." Fleurette finished weakly, having failed to prepare herself for a debate on the merits of the volunteer camps.

"There's nothing wrong with their spirits," Norma said. "These are Harvard and Yale men who pay a handsome fee for the pleasure of traipsing around a lake in a khaki uniform. It'll be another matter entirely when our boys go into service."

Fleurette's ploy had succeeded in one way: I was eager to get off to work and wanted the matter settled. "I see no reason why you shouldn't go with the rest of the girls, if that's what you're asking," I said as I pushed myself away from the table.

But of course that wasn't what she was asking. She intended to go whether we wanted her to or not. She reached out to catch my sleeve as I took my dishes to the sink.

"I thought you might like to come along," she said to me, in as sincere and inviting a tone as she could muster. Her hair was pinned into two low coils, one behind each ear, according to a new style she'd seen in a magazine. She looked like a grown woman now, not a little girl who could beg for favors.

"You're nineteen. You don't need me to chaperone you," I said lightly. I did very much like the idea of keeping an eye on her, but I couldn't possibly leave work.

"Oh . . . well . . . of course I don't need a chaperone, but the other girls do. You know how it is at Mrs. Hansen's. The parents are very strict." She buttered a corner of toast and dipped it into the sugar bowl.

I didn't say a word, because I knew Norma would declare what a waste of time the whole enterprise would be. To my utter astonishment, she stood up abruptly and said, "That's a fine idea. We'll all go."

Fleurette obviously hadn't prepared for that. "You will?"

"Of course," Norma said. "I'd like to have a look at one of these camps."

"You would?" I said.

"Yes. The Army's sending someone to run the place, and it's about time I spoke to them."

"Spoke to . . . the Army?" Fleurette looked up helplessly, having been snared in her own trap.

"Yes, the Army! Our pigeon transport cart is nearly finished. Carolyn and I have been working on it all week. We should have something to show the generals any day now."

I shot a warning glance at Fleurette to keep her quiet, but I didn't have to: she and I both knew perfectly well that it was pointless to argue over something that wouldn't happen anyway. Norma hadn't managed to get her pigeon messaging station built behind the drugstore, so why should this ridiculous cart be any different? It was just another project to occupy her time.

Fleurette must've agreed with me, because she smiled to herself and dipped into the sugar bowl again without a word.

"Plattsburg is the perfect place to take it," Norma said. "We can put on a demonstration for the Army men."

"No!" Fleurette shrieked. "Don't you dare."

"You haven't even seen it yet," Norma said.

"I've been trying not to," Fleurette said.

"I don't believe it exists," I said. I'd heard her hammering away at something, but as Norma liked to pound on things as a general matter, I hadn't thought anything of it and never bothered to go see what she was up to.

But now we had no choice but to follow Norma out the kitchen door to have a look. There wasn't enough room in our barn to build the cart, as it was already occupied by our buggy and harness mare, along with a flock of chickens and the more sheltered portion of the pigeon loft. For that reason, Norma and Carolyn had been obliged to build it behind the barn and to keep it covered with an enormous canvas tarp to protect it from the elements while construction was under way (and, I suspected, because Norma believed herself to be building wartime equipment that had to be concealed from German spies).

I hadn't so much as glanced at the barn lately, much less walked around behind it to see what Norma was up to. I had noticed the accumulation of little pasteboard and wooden models of the cart, as cunning as children's toys, lined up along our mantle, but I wasn't prepared to have revealed before me a full-sized working vehicle. Norma pulled off the canvas with a theatrical flourish, and I must admit that I gasped.

"It's finished! It's fully built." I walked around it in amazement.

"Of course it's built," Norma said. "What do you think I do around here all day?"

"It's . . . well, it's so beautifully put together." I had no idea that my sister knew how to do anything in the way of finish carpentry. Of course, she did the rough work around the farm all the time: replacing fence posts, shingling the roof, shoring up a sagging porch step, and so on. But this went well beyond any of that.

Norma had built a fully functioning wheeled cart, longer than it was wide, with a coachman's seat up front and a rather luxurious pigeon loft behind. From the rear, a pair of wooden doors swung open to reveal two rows of nesting boxes, three sets of perches for the birds to roost, and a miniature ladder that led to a wire cage on top. Inside, on the floor, was a sliding wood panel that, when opened, revealed its purpose: the bottom of the cart was made of sturdy wire mesh so that the interior could be more easily cleaned and drained.

Every bit of it was perfectly done. The doors aligned just so, the hinges and locks moved silently, and there was not a bit of light between any board. I'd ridden in any number of buggies more cheaply made than Norma's pigeon cart.

"If I'd known you could do a thing like this," I said, "I would've had you repair our buggy when it was smashed a couple of years ago. Think of all the trouble it would've saved us."

"I didn't know how to do any of it until our buggy was smashed," Norma said, a bit impatiently. "Didn't you notice that I worked alongside the man from the dairy every day and helped him to do the job?"

I had to admit that I hadn't. I was guilty of not paying a great deal of attention to what Norma did, as I found so many of her activities and interests to be perplexing or even distasteful.

"Well then, you aren't very observant, for a lady detective," Norma said. "But now you can see for yourself how the cart is meant to work and how it will be of such use to the Army. We'll take it to the Plattsburg camp, along with a few pigeons, just to show them how it runs. They'll probably want to keep this one, but I won't let them. I'm drawing up the plans, and they can put a dozen of them together themselves if they like. It will give them something to do besides marching the Harvard men up and down in straight lines."

"Have you taken it out on the road yet?" Fleurette asked.

"We've only just finished it," Norma said. "Carolyn was supposed to come for lunch, and we were going to have our first trial with her horse. Dolley needs to be reshod so I don't like to make her do it."

We walked around the cart a bit more, climbed aboard, and even helped Norma to bring a few pigeons over. She showed us, a little boastfully, the cleverest bits of her design. The wire cage atop the cart detached from the rest of it and could be used to ferry pigeons back and forth from their home loft. There was even a ladder clipped to the side of the cart to make it easier to take the cage on and off.

By the time we finished loading three dozen pigeons into the cart, Carolyn turned up in her automobile.

"I thought you were to bring your horse," Norma said crossly, by way of a greeting. I never understood how Norma had managed to make a friend, but Carolyn seemed impervious to her most abrasive qualities.

"If you had a telephone I wouldn't have to come all the way out every time there's a change in plans," Carolyn returned, far more cheerfully.

"There won't ever be telephone wires in the countryside, and I'm glad of it," Norma said.

"Why don't you two exchange pigeons," Fleurette said, "and then you can send notes back and forth when you need to tell each other something?"

"We do, of course, but I sent the last one yesterday," Carolyn said, "so I'm out of stock."

Norma and Carolyn turned their attention to the cart, and I followed Fleurette inside.

"You have to convince her to leave her cart behind," Fleurette said. "We can't show up at the Plattsburg camp with that thing."

"They'd never forget you," I said.

She could still pout and toss her hair around, even at the age of nineteen. "It's not the sort of thing I wish to be remembered for."

⇥ 26 ⇤

NOTHING COULD'VE BEEN more disadvantageous to Sheriff Heath at that moment in the campaign than another jail-break, but when it happened, he took it remarkably well, and in fact seemed to enjoy himself more than he had in weeks. I suspect he was simply glad to be back at the business of running the jail, and talking to the inmates like he used to, rather than going out glad-handing with the voters.

The inmate in question was Harry Core, a jewel thief known for never cracking a window or forcing a door. At the scene of his most recent robbery—a jewelry store in Hackensack—he'd climbed in from the roof and made a hole in the ceiling so small that the police said only a boy or "a very slight dwarf" could've slid through it.

He was caught trying to sell the jewelry in Newark. With some pride he confessed that he never went inside a store to rob it, but instead rigged up a set of grappling-hooks and lowered them from his perch in the ceiling. This allowed him to smash the display cases and fish the jewelry out with a dexterity that even the police admired. Harry Core was a clever man and friendly, and had been a model inmate—until now.

I came upon Sheriff Heath talking to Harry Core in one of the interviewing rooms. A guard was watching from the doorway and nodded for me to come on down and listen in. From the conversation I surmised that a metal file fell through a hole in Harry's hip pocket at breakfast and dropped to the floor, in full view of the guards.

"Come on, Harry," Sheriff Heath was saying when I looked into the room. "What was the idea, trying to saw your way out of my jail-house?"

Harry Core kept his eyes down. He was a short man, stout, and stronger than one might, at first, give him credit for. He wore a neatly trimmed beard and had come in wearing a fine suit of the sort rarely seen at the jail, even among the better class of thieves. He sat calmly in his shirtsleeves, his cuffs rolled up, showing meaty arms and ropy blue veins. His cheeks were a robust red and I could see the blood lifting and pumping in his neck. Most men grew pale and listless in jail, but Harry possessed a remarkable physical vitality even after several weeks behind bars.

"Are you sure you won't tell me where you got that file?" the sheriff persisted. "I know you didn't have that when you came in. My guard Louis here searched you himself, didn't you, Louis?"

The guard agreed that he had, in fact, given the inmate a thorough search.

"Then someone brought it to you," said the sheriff. "Who was it? You've had no visitors."

Harry Core shrugged, offering the sheriff a bemused smile, as if they'd stumbled into an insignificant little puzzle that neither would be able to solve. In my time at the jail I'd noticed that some professional criminals—the kind who get into it for the money, not for revenge or love or passion—had no trace of menace about them and wanted only to do their jobs and to do them well. Some of them made for fairly pleasant company and weren't too put off about being locked up for a short stretch, jail being a hazard of the profession. Harry Core was that type of man.

The sheriff leaned back in his chair and gave a sigh of regret. "Well, it's a shame you had only that little file to work with. There's nothing worse than being poorly equipped for a job."

Harry seemed interested in the idea that someone else might be to blame. "How do you mean?"

Sheriff Heath looked up at the ceiling and worked his jaw back and forth as if to contemplate the question. He was a somber and dignified man, but he could put on an act when it suited him.

"Well, it just wasn't much of a file, that's all," he said. "It might've worked on soft metal, but in here you're going up against case-hardened steel. Whoever brought this to you didn't know a thing about my jail."

Harry filled his cheeks and blew out a puff of air in exasperation. "Either he didn't know, or he didn't take the time to find out."

"Now, that's just the problem, and we see it in here every day, don't we, Louis?"

The guard nodded eagerly but didn't dare say a thing.

"People just don't take the time to think a job through," the sheriff continued. "He didn't even give you any oil."

"Oil? Now, what's that for?" Harry was obviously disgusted at how ill-equipped he'd been.

"Or some lard. Even bacon grease, but we haven't had bacon in a while, have we? It makes the file smoother. Gives you a little better action."

"You see, I did not know that," said Harry in wonder.

"Well, keep it in mind if you ever get another chance. And next time, don't carry it around in your pocket."

"Oh, there won't be a next time. Mackie's gone off without me."

"Already? Whereabouts?" the sheriff asked offhandedly.

"Chicago."

"I don't recall a fellow named Mackie. What else does he go by?"

Harry blinked fast and understood his mistake. "I don't know any Mackie."

Sheriff Heath flicked his eyes over to me so quickly that no one would've noticed unless they were watching for it. As soon as he was finished with Harry, we'd be back in his office, wiring the authorities in Chicago to watch out for a man named Mackie.

The sheriff exchanged a few more pleasantries with Harry. He had a way of staying on such cordial terms with the inmates that they were often startled into making a confession when they hadn't meant to.

"If you think of anything else that might help us, just send for me," Sheriff Heath said as he left.

"Happy to, Sheriff." They shook hands like old friends. "Good of you to see me yourself like this. I only wish I'd had a drop of something strong to offer you." He patted himself down as he said it, like a man searching for his flask in a coat pocket.

"I wouldn't be surprised if you did," Sheriff Heath said, and they both laughed at that.

Sheriff Heath handed Harry off to his guard, and I walked with him to his office.

"You're in an awfully jovial mood for a man who'd just discovered his third escape attempt," I said.

"I will miss the inmates," he said.

"You'll have congressmen for company instead. Aren't they just as disreputable?"

"They're less forthcoming about it," he said.

"What are you going to do about Harry?"

"Harry's all right," he said. "We'll take away some privileges and keep an eye on him, but he was never going to saw his way out of here."

"I'm more concerned with how the file got in," I said.

Sheriff Heath said, "People do smuggle things into jail. It could've been a delivery boy, or a visitor who signed in to see someone else. I'll look into it, but a little contraband is inevitable."

"Do you mean you're not going to charge him? Isn't it a criminal offense?"

We were at his office by then, but he didn't invite me in. "If we charged him, we'd never keep it out of the papers," he said. "There was no harm done, and no one knows about it except you and Louis."

"And a few other guards, and most of the inmates. You won't be able to keep this quiet."

"Are you running my campaign now?"

How quickly I'd fallen into the trap of fretting over what the reporters would say, and what the public would think!

"Never mind," I said. "By the way, I booked in a rather elegant lady a few days ago. I suppose you know her."

"Everyone knows her."

"Apparently an unkind word from Mrs. Pattengill might influence your supporters. Mrs. Heath asked me to make her comfortable. I'm told she has important friends."

He shook his head and said, "Mrs. Pattengill's friends have already deserted her. You know as well as I do that when people go to jail, they're like ghosts who don't yet know they're dead. Their friends forget all about them and carry on with their own lives. Don't give her any special treatment. Cordelia might not know it, but the worst thing that can happen in a campaign is any accusation of favoritism. I don't want a single exception to the rules for

Mrs. Pattengill. She must do her chores and wear her uniform just like the other inmates."

I was relieved to hear that he and I were in agreement on this. "She will. It sounds like a strange case—some sort of charity fraud?"

"It's an old con. She just happened to get caught."

❦ 27 ❦

MRS. PATTENGILL DIDN'T take well to the rigors and deprivation of an inmate's life. She told anyone who would listen that she liked a hot lunch and a cold supper, but in jail it went the other way around, and she was quite taken aback that the kitchen couldn't reverse its meal schedule on her behalf.

She liked a vinegar rinse in her hair twice a week and a cream for her complexion every night, but neither was supplied. To her astonishment, she was not allowed to telephone a friend and ask that these niceties be delivered.

"I'm starting to understand why they don't issue us mirrors," I heard her call to Providencia Monafo, who lived in the cell next to her. "I'd rather not know what a sight I am these days."

"That is not why you don't have a mirror," Providencia returned.

"Then is it because there are spirits that live inside the mirrors?" Mrs. Pattengill asked, with an attempt at gaiety in her voice. She was under the mistaken impression that Providencia was a spiritualist who had been arrested for fortune-telling, having either forgotten or chosen to disregard their conversation on the subject during the jail tour.

"No, they don't give you a mirror because you might break it into pieces and slash at your neck."

That was enough to put a stop to further conversations between Mrs. Pattengill and Providencia, which had surely been Providencia's intention. I thought about chiding her for tormenting her new neighbor, but it occurred to me that she might well know best how to keep Mrs. Pattengill in line. There was no reason not to let her try.

I didn't take Cordelia's warning about Mrs. Pattengill seriously. The woman seemed to have no powerful friends or influential connections. She wrote no letters and had no visitors. She was quick to express her displeasure over the condition of her cell, the flavor of the food, the quality of the clothing, and all the ordinary inconveniences of jail life, which were, of course, considerable. It was always too hot or too cold. The men who lived on the four floors below us made noise day and night, and she groused that it interfered with her tranquility to hear them shouting at one another, arguing with the guards, coughing, spitting, groaning, snoring, and banging at the bars of their cells when they wanted attention.

"I was required by law to tolerate sleeping alongside one man who grunted and moaned and snored all night long, but I'm wholly unprepared to put up with eighty of them at a time," she told me. "It's unseemly."

I made light of her complaints, which seemed insubstantial and even understandable from a woman in her position. I reminded her that we did all we could to treat our inmates decently, but that we couldn't possibly provide all the comforts that she'd been accustomed to before her arrest. I was never strict with her, but I didn't indulge her, either.

It was a pleasure, in those ever-shorter days near the end of October, to return to the routine duties that my position required.

I went to see a few new probationers recently placed under my care. A girl had been arrested for sharing a hotel room with a man whom she claimed was her brother. I had to go to a great deal of effort to prove that they were, in fact, brother and sister. Once I did, the hotel's house detective accused her of drunkenness, on the strength of two bottles of beer ordered by the brother but never opened. The entire business was ridiculous and I had no trouble in getting the girl freed. I would've rather not put her on probation at all, but Judge Seufert insisted, it being his opinion that the more girls under my supervision, the better, for the general welfare of the town.

Also under my care was a married woman accused of blackmail. Her method was to go into New York with a man, and then, once they'd crossed the state line, she'd threaten to summon a police officer and have him brought up on a white slavery charge. Her husband (a ruinously loyal man if there ever was one) came to her defense, and the men who'd fallen for the scheme were too embarrassed to give their testimony publicly. She, too, was released to my supervision, obliging me to stop in at unexpected times and see to it that she was at home and behaving as a wife should.

My inmates had troubles of their own, but it wasn't the sort that elicited any sympathy from me. Ruth Williams, the actress accused of a little light house-breaking to pay for her supper, had managed to incriminate herself without ever saying a word, much less stepping outside her jail cell, and was now in more trouble than previously believed.

It came about like this: the room she'd once rented had been sitting empty owing to some repairs to the building, and when it was rented again, the new occupant tripped over a loose floorboard and found a cache of valuables hidden underneath. This led the tenant, naturally, to test the other floorboards and to investigate the deep recesses of the wardrobe, as well as the undersides of drawers and the backs of picture frames. All yielded valuable trinkets: ivory combs, ruby bracelets, engraved cigarette cases, and gold watch-chains.

Fearing that she would be accused of having stolen them herself, the woman turned everything over to her landlady, who went directly to the police. With so many additional counts of burglary against her, Ruth was now facing a substantially longer jail term.

"Have you ever heard of an honest landlady?" she asked despondently, as I tried, without much enthusiasm, to console her. Ruth had managed to make herself appear, even to me, like an artist devoted to her craft who happened to be down on her luck and forced through circumstances to lift a piece of silver or two. The picture now emerging was one of an inveterate porch-climber, fleet of foot and light of fingers. Her greatest acting role was in convincing the police otherwise, but now that game was up, too.

"Couldn't you put me into some kind of program of reformation?" Ruth asked, appealing to me with wide wet eyes.

"What sort of program?" I asked, mostly to pass the time. I enjoyed the ramblings of criminals, and the way they ambled around the case assembled against them, kicking at it and looking for any hole through which they might escape.

"Why, just what you've done for the other girls!" Ruth said. She could hardly be considered a girl: it had also emerged, through further interviews with the landlady, that Ruth was not twenty-six but thirty-four. ("Twenty-six is my professional age," she'd said in her defense.)

"Those other girls had been wrongly accused, or given sentences that far outweighed the crime," I told her. "In your case, the police seemed to have underestimated you."

Ruth felt she'd been paid a compliment and smiled brightly at that. "They always do."

As I waited for word from Geraldine—the waiting is always the most maddening part, and in this case it depended upon a pair of attorneys having the opportunity to secure incriminating photographs—I waited, also, for John Courter to make his next move. If he knew that I'd been to the asylum, he might also know that I'd been to see a lawyer. I thought he might send me some message, or drop a hint during one of his campaign speeches about what he expected from me in exchange for his silence. But he continued as if nothing had happened, making the same fiery speeches as before, and campaigning largely on what he believed to be Sheriff Heath's incompetence, even though Sheriff Heath was not his opponent in the race.

Sheriff Heath continued to go out and give a speech almost every night. Mr. Ramsey was hardly bothering to campaign against him, or if he was, it didn't make the papers. He ran his brickworks downriver from the jail, put in an appearance at a few club luncheons, and ran perfunctory notices in the paper stating his qualifications: "Success in Business—A Builder Looking to a Bright Future—Prosperity and Opportunity for All Americans." It was perfectly innocuous and free of controversy.

But that was the congressional race. As for Mr. Courter in the sheriff's race, Sheriff Heath had assured me that no one wanted a man running the jail who had no ideas about it other than to insult his predecessor—something no sheriff had ever done in Bergen County, owing to the deeply seated spirit of fraternity that had, until now, existed among lawmen.

William Conklin, for his part, ran against John Courter for the office of sheriff in the gregarious, back-slapping way that was his nature. He rode up to one of Mr. Courter's speeches in an ice cream wagon, cranking a hand organ that piped out a little tune, and luring Mr. Courter's audience away with scoops of vanilla and chocolate. He judged a Beautiful Baby contest for the newspaper and posed for pictures with each infant. I heard from Francis that he also popped in at any club that put on a good supper, where he ate his fill, shook hands, and passed out mocked-up ballots with his name printed on every line.

"It's the only name you need to remember on November 7," he said, all over town.

The campaign was, therefore, in every way, a fight between two men who weren't even running against each other. It was Sheriff Heath vs. John Courter, and the men actually opposing them for their respective offices seemed content to sit back and let someone else do the squabbling.

If it seemed strange to me that Mr. Courter would attack the sheriff rather than run on his own merits, it didn't seem at all strange to Cordelia Heath. One afternoon I was summoned downstairs to see the sheriff and nearly walked in on a noisy argument between the two of them. I didn't want to listen, but I couldn't help it: the door to his office was open and both their voices were raised. Even the guard at the end of the hall could hear them. He looked at me sheepishly when I rounded the corner.

I stopped short just before the doorway, then backed down the hall so they wouldn't see me.

"Forget about Courter," Sheriff Heath was saying. "He's not running against me. Let Bill Conklin take him on, if that's what he wants to do."

"Bill can't be bothered, and you know it," Cordelia said. "Mr. Courter isn't out smearing his reputation. He's going after you."

"What of it? I don't know why you want to involve yourself in the sheriff's race at all. I'm out of this office in November either way. Isn't that what you wanted?"

Cordelia made an unhappy little snort and said, "I don't think you see what's happening here, Bob. Mr. Courter attacks you because it's working for him, and that means John Ramsey doesn't have to. The voters hear it either way, and they'll remember it on Election Day. You'd say something about it if it was coming from Mr. Ramsey, wouldn't you?"

"But it isn't," Sheriff Heath said, "and I think it's awfully decent of Ramsey to—"

Cordelia smacked something down on a table—I was still lurking in the hall and didn't see what it was, but it gave me a start —and very nearly shouted her husband down. "He's not being decent. He's letting Mr. Courter run you down and he comes out smelling like a rose. They'll both win. It's a trick, and you're a fool to fall for it."

There are certain arguments that married couples have with each other over and over, to no useful end. I could tell from Cordelia's tone that this was one such well-trod line of dispute. I saw no reason to let it continue, so I took a few silent steps back, coughed once or twice, and stomped rather noisily into the sheriff's office. Never had he looked so relieved to see me.

"A telephone call came for you while I was away," he said to me, in a tone meant to indicate to his wife that he was getting back to business. "It was John Ward. You haven't found yourself in need of an attorney, have you?"

Cordelia sensed right away that something was amiss. She was watching me quite sharply.

"I can't imagine what he'd want," I said, as casually as I could. "Are you sure the call wasn't meant for you?"

Cordelia gave a high and nervous laugh. "I don't know what use either one of you would have for a divorce attorney."

Sheriff Heath kept himself composed, as he always did. He came around from his desk and took his wife's elbow, in a manner that anyone would describe as courtly, and escorted her out.

"I don't want to bore you with the running of my jail, dear," he said, in a voice that was truly gentle, "but you do recall that every attorney in town has need of the sheriff's office from time to time. We handle all manner of criminal and civil affairs here."

Mrs. Heath wasn't happy about it, but she allowed herself to be sent away. When she was gone, the sheriff turned to me as if nothing had happened.

"I suppose he might have a job on offer for you," he said.

I tried to make light of that. "I have no need of a divorce attorney, nor do I have need of another job. I'll be in Paterson tomorrow, so I'll call on him then."

If Sheriff Heath suspected anything, he didn't let on.

❧ 28 ❧

IT WAS CARELESS of Mr. Ward to call for me at the jail, after I'd warned him to keep our conversation a secret. I didn't entirely trust a man who took any sort of drink, and I suspected that a lunchtime whiskey might've been to blame for the call. Regardless, the news was good: when I stopped into his office the next day, he put the photographs before me with all the pride of a painter exhibiting his art. There was the evidence we needed, unmistakably plain: Charles Kayser and Virginia Townley, arm in arm at the theater. Another showed them kissing in an open automobile, and in another they were reading companionably in bed, as seen through the bedroom window.

"Did Mr. McGinnis crouch in the shrubs and take a photograph through the curtains?" I asked in horror.

"He did," Mr. Ward said. "I dressed him up like a cat burglar and put a few pieces of silver in his pocket."

"So that he could pretend to be a burglar if he was caught? That's a terrible story to tell the police," I said.

"I wasn't worried about the police catching him," Mr. Ward said. "The disguise was for Mr. Kayser. But no one saw, and now we have the pictures. I'll file my divorce suit on behalf of Joseph

Townley, and as soon as the salacious news of these pictures hits the papers, that girl attorney of yours will put her own lawsuit forward on behalf of Anna Kayser."

"Then—she's to be released?" I asked.

"Well, there's a bit more rigmarole to come, but I expect so. Luckily for you, it won't happen until after the election."

"I don't know why that would matter," I said, although of course I did. Setting free a lunatic wouldn't look good for Sheriff Heath's side.

"Everything matters in an election," Mr. Ward said.

HE WAS RIGHT. Everything mattered—even, as it turned out, Mrs. Pattengill's discontent. When I returned to the jail, Cordelia Heath stepped outside the minute I walked up the drive, giving the impression that she'd been waiting for me.

"I've been thinking about how kind you are to the inmates," she called, by way of greeting. I was suspicious already.

There were just a few stairs from the sheriff's living quarters down to the driveway. She skipped down them in dainty kid slippers of the sort Fleurette favored, and said, "It's such an important part of Mr. Heath's program. I hear him talk about it in every speech. Treat the inmates with good Christian compassion, and show them a better way. If they receive nothing but cruelty and hatred in jail, that's what they'll take with them when they're released back into society."

It came out in one long, breathless stream, as if she'd memorized the lines.

"Yes, ma'am," I said, because she seemed to be waiting for my reply.

She'd been wearing an expression of earnest hope, but she dropped it when she saw that I wasn't warming to the subject. She pushed on nonetheless. "Yes, well, in that spirit I wanted to speak to you concerning Mrs. Pattengill. She's to be charged formally tomorrow and she's in such low spirits. I've put a nice supper together for her and left it on a tray in the jail kitchen. If you wouldn't mind taking it upstairs . . ."

"I do mind," I said, pushing my way past. "We have women upstairs on charges far more serious than that of swindling a charity. I don't recall you putting a picnic together for any of them. Sheriff Heath says I'm to treat her the same as any other inmate. You may speak to him about it if you don't like it."

I left her in the drive and marched inside and up the stairs to the fifth floor. If there was one advantage to working in a jail, it was the fact that the boss's wife would venture only so far and no farther. The fifth floor was my sanctuary.

But when I arrived, I was greeted by a volley of complaints from the inmates, with Mrs. Pattengill leading the charge. Apparently she'd suffered a steam burn in the laundry and wanted to be excused from further duties. I asked to have a look at the burn, and when she couldn't find it on either arm, I reminded her (as gently as possible, under the circumstances) that she was in jail and was expected to do a little hard labor.

"But that old laundry's appalling," she complained. "I'm terrified of the mangle, and you would be, too, if you had to work it."

With some force of will I reminded myself that Mrs. Pattengill couldn't possibly know how her name had just been invoked downstairs, and I tried not to take it out on her.

"I have worked the mangle," I said mildly. "Just mind your fingers and go slowly."

"Couldn't I speak to Mrs. Heath about it?"

"You could not."

There it was. She made a direct appeal to the sheriff's wife, and I, just as directly, refused it.

Something tightened in Mrs. Pattengill's doughy features just then. I could see her turn against me, once and for all. I wasn't intimidated by it—there's nothing unusual in an inmate deciding to hate the guards in a jail—but I had some awareness, however dim and unexamined, that she had a bit of power, still, and was prepared to use it. I just didn't know how.

"No matter," she said lightly. "I suppose all this business about extending kindness and comfort to inmates is just to give the candidates a good slogan."

I wasn't about to be drawn into an argument over it, with all the other inmates on the fifth floor listening in, not to mention the men below us, who managed to overhear us more often than I liked.

"You've never been in another jail so you wouldn't know it," I said, "but we do extend you quite a bit of comfort and kindness. There's another principle we honor here, and that is one of fairness. We expect you to do your share of the work, and to accept the fact that while you're here, you'll be treated like any other inmate. We don't bend the rules for anyone."

She looked at me for a long time, the way a woman in her station might regard a servant she suspected of wrongdoing. She carried herself with quite a bit of authority, and I admit that I fell sway to it. Although I towered over her, and held the keys to the jail in which she was held captive, I nonetheless felt a little cowed by her expression, and exposed, as if I'd told some unintentional lie.

But how could I possibly be at fault? I was entirely certain of my position. Mrs. Pattengill was owed no special favors.

"You're perfectly right, of course," she said at last. "You have your rules, and you must follow them. The sheriff's under such scrutiny right now. Any hint of impropriety would ruin him."

There it was. It was the threat I couldn't see, the dim outline of what was to come. It was only a shadow, though, and I brushed it aside.

"I'm glad we understand each other, Mrs. Pattengill," I said.

"At first we didn't," she said, "but now we do."

⇥ 29 ⇤

THE NEXT DAY, I left the jail to look in on a few probationers, and returned to find calm and quiet on the fifth floor. I soon discovered the reason: Mrs. Pattengill had been released. I hadn't expected to see her cleared of her charges so quickly, but it wasn't so unusual that I thought much of it. A sheriff has little control over who comes in and out of his jail. Sometimes inmates are turned loose without notice or explanation.

My unionists were gone as well, having served their entire sentence without even considering paying the fine. They'd been proud of their principled stand and seemed to relish their time behind bars, thinking it would serve as proof of their fidelity to the cause. I often questioned the value of my inmates' principled stands, but they were popular among the young and seemed to propel them onward.

Providencia Monafo wanted to speak to me. As it was unusual for her to confide in me, I hurried through my rounds of the other inmates. I was just settling into her cell when I heard a commotion on the street below.

"Let me just see to this," I told Providencia, and rushed over to the window.

There was an unruly mob on the courthouse lawn below.

Someone was shouting—I couldn't hear what he was saying—and the crowd was bellowing out its approval. From above, I saw only a sea of black hats and the tops of canes lifted into the air.

This quite obviously demanded an investigation. I turned to tell Mrs. Monafo that I'd come back to her, but she was staring at me with such a look of urgency that I stopped.

"We hear everything on the fifth floor," she said

I was impatient to rush downstairs, but I said, "I know you do. What did you hear this time?"

"It's what Mrs. Pattengill heard."

"Hasn't she been released?"

"She said she found a way out just like the man downstairs did."

I had a sick feeling about what that meant. The noise from the crowd outside grew louder. I told Mrs. Monafo I'd come back to her, and ran down the stairs. On the way outside I met the sheriff. He tipped his hat at me, cordial as always.

"It's John Courter, isn't it?" I asked.

"I suspect so."

"Mrs. Monafo just told me—" But there were too many people around us now. I didn't dare say it aloud.

"Your Italian lady?"

"Never mind."

We rounded the corner together. There, on the courthouse steps, stood John Courter at a podium with a court bailiff on either side of him. A crowd of onlookers had pushed their way up the stone steps and spilled out over the lawn. None of this should've surprised me: in the waning days of the campaign season, speeches were erupting like volcanoes on Pacific atolls. One never knew when the next one might come, or how much fire it might eject.

Still, this was no ordinary speech. There had to be three or four hundred men gathered around. It was a chilly enough day that everyone had pulled out their wool and tweed. A faint odor of moth balls and cedar drifted toward us as we approached.

Mr. Courter had adopted the sing-song cadence of a preacher, but it didn't suit him, as he was far too sour and mean-spirited to lift the souls of his audience.

He had a megaphone but mostly didn't use it. Instead he kept it by his side and raised it to his mouth only when he wanted to repeat whatever line won the most applause from his audience.

And he was winning quite a bit of applause.

"I could stand up here all day and tell you what I think of our weak sheriff, but you don't need to hear that. I could say that he coddles the inmates, but I won't, because that's only my opinion. I could remind you that when a thief breaks into your home and steals your silver, Sheriff Heath rewards him with a haircut and a shave, and a new gold tooth if he'd like one."

The crowd roared and I took a step back. At any moment someone would turn around and see Sheriff Heath standing there, calmly, his hands in his pockets. They could turn on him, a mob this size.

"No, I'm not going to say a word about any of that," John Courter shouted. "Why should I? You have the facts in front of you. The inmates are walking right out of jail. You—the taxpayers, the citizens, the voters—you built him this fine stone prison, with bars on every window, and locks on every door, and still they escape! Criminals and madmen walk out whenever they please."

Sheriff Heath stayed perfectly still and kept his chin at a very dignified angle. He had a way of looking generally at the air in front of him, without meeting anyone's eye in particular, and this habit was serving him well as everyone turned around to gawk at him.

"Now, you might be thinking that the blame for these escapes rests not with the sheriff, but with his lady deputy, whose name has been in the papers in connection with last year's escape and the one that took place here just recently. No sheriff in his right mind would put a woman in charge of guarding dangerous criminals. Let them serve tea to the female inmates, and pass out handkerchiefs for the poor unfortunate girls to cry into, but anything more than that puts us all in danger. Common sense tells you that much. Can you imagine your wife guarding a dangerous criminal?"

Sheriff Heath had a calm resolve about him and seemed naturally to know how to be the better man in a situation such as this. John Courter had spotted him—of course he had. But still the sheriff maintained his posture of unruffled detachment.

I, on the other hand, was the very opposite of unruffled. John Courter was, in every way, a small-minded, petty, vindictive man unworthy of public office. I didn't care to stand at the edge of a crowd and listen to him hurl insults and lies at us.

What made it worse, though, was that the crowd seemed to love it. It was an uncertain time in Bergen County: there was labor unrest in the factories, a mistrust of immigrants who might be German sympathizers, and the very real fear that a munitions depot might go up like so many crates of firecrackers at the hands of secret agents of the Kaiser. And most of all, there was the absolute terror of war—a war we surely couldn't avoid much longer.

These people were looking for an enemy, and John Courter had one on offer.

It was infuriating. I wanted to march right up the courthouse steps and snatch the bullhorn out of his hands.

But then he continued, and it was just what I'd feared.

"Do you remember Harry Core, the jewel thief who was arrested after the fine work by our police, in cooperation with the police in Newark? Of course you do. A menace to every merchant on Main Street. He deserved to go away for a good long while, but did you know that he was locked up for only a month before he managed to smuggle a file into Sheriff Heath's jail?"

Here a gasp rose from the audience, and such murmuring and shouting and shifting about that he was obliged to wait for it to simmer down before continuing.

"No, you didn't! You haven't read about that one in the papers, because your sheriff kept it from you! My office uncovered the facts, and here they are: So light is the security at Mr. Heath's jail, and so carefree is life for the inmates, that it's no trouble at all to slip in a weapon or a file. Baron von Matthesius walked right out last year. Tony Hajnacka jumped into the river. Now Harry Core tried to saw his way out with a metal file. That's the record of the man running for Congress."

Now we had reporters rushing toward us. A few of them sidled up next to me, but I refused to look at them. I leaned over to Sheriff Heath and whispered, "This is what Providencia Monafo wanted to tell me. I believe that Mrs. Pattengill . . ."

"Shhhh" was all he said.

Detective Courter still had the podium, and went on as if nothing out of the ordinary had occurred.

"And that's not the only way they get out of jail. Just look at the morality cases you see coming through this courthouse. You read the paper. You know what I'm talking about. Girls lead lives of degradation and sin, and what's done about it? A troublesome lady policeman comes along and defends the little minx. She talks the judge into setting free a girl who is morally compromised and diseased—letting her right back out onto the streets that were her downfall. Constance Kopp—and how's that for a good German name?—would open the doors to our state reformatories and let degenerates and mental defectives walk right out. What do you say to that?"

I was starting to back away. I could sense what was coming, like a stampede of horses that can be felt before it is seen.

Over the roar of the crowd, he called, "She's done just that, gentlemen! Sheriff Heath's lady deputy has been sneaking into the Morris Plains Insane Asylum to conspire with the very lunatics your judges saw fit to send there. She has a plan to have them released, and she's found an unscrupulous New York lawyer to help her to do it. How do you like your tax dollars going to set lunatics free?"

We couldn't get the reporters away from us. They stood shoulder to shoulder alongside us, their notepads open, waiting to record our every utterance. They were so close that I could count the crumbs in their beards. One of them tapped me with his notepad and I swatted him.

I couldn't bear to look at Sheriff Heath, but he waved the reporters away in the most ordinary manner, as if nothing had happened, and walked off briskly.

I followed him back to the jail. A few reporters trailed along behind us, but most gave up when it became clear we weren't talking.

That's when we saw the leaflets. One was freshly glued to the deputies' entrance to the jail. When I turned around, I realized that they were plastered to every lamp-post, running in a perfect line all the way from the courthouse, down Main Street, past the library, and on to the train station.

"DEMON DEPUTY" read the title, in bold type across the top.

Under that odious headline was a murky portrait of none other than myself, so poorly printed that one could only make out the general shape of a woman's suit and hat, and below that a screed against me and Sheriff Heath that read:

Keep Robert N. Heath's Dangerous Ideas Out of
Congress

Temperamentally Unfit

Want of Experience

Failed in Office—Inmates Escaped

Blindly Loyal to Troublesome Lady Policeman Who
Frees Lunatics from Asylum

Trained by William Conklin, Now Running to
Succeed Him, Equally Unfit

It ended with this:

Vote John Ramsey for Congress and
John Courter for Sheriff

Sheriff Heath tried to rip the leaflet off, but it clung to the
door. "Never mind," he mumbled, and ushered me through before
the reporters caught up to us again.

As soon as we were inside, I stopped him. I couldn't bear to
walk to his office before I explained myself. When I took him by
the shoulder, I noticed how thin he'd become, and how dark the
shadows were under his eyes. This campaign had taken its toll.
Now I'd made it worse.

"I'm not trying to free a lunatic," I said, "but I did go to Morris Plains."

There was such weariness in his expression. "You saw a good
case, and you pursued it," he said.

"After you told me to stay away. It was reckless of me. I knew
I could be caught, but I thought only of . . ."

"You thought only of Mrs. Kayser. That was the right way to
think about it." There was no gladness or pride in his voice, only
fatigue. I wasn't sure he believed what he was saying.

"If it matters, I now have reason to hope that she will be freed. Her husband put her there deliberately so that he could take up with another woman. Mr. Ward has the pictures."

A flicker of recognition passed across his face. "The telephone call."

That had been another lie. "Yes. I'm sorry."

He put a finger under his collar to loosen it and said, "You shouldn't be sorry. I wish you'd told me, but I can see why you wouldn't. This damned election has everything turned around the wrong way."

I hadn't entirely unburdened myself. "I knew Mr. Courter was planning something against you, or against me. I just didn't know what. He threatened me with it the night of the Salvation Army program. If I'd only gone to you then—"

"John Courter threatened you? In my jail?"

"He made it plain that he knew I was pursuing Mrs. Kayser, but he didn't tell you about it. I couldn't understand why. He was obviously saving it for the last few days of the campaign, when we'd have so little time to defend ourselves. It still doesn't explain why he wanted me to know."

Sheriff Heath shook his head. "Don't spend your time trying to understand John Courter. And don't pay any mind to these leaflets. It only reflects badly on their side. The voters know it's nonsense."

"The voters know what they read on lamp-posts. You're going to have to put something out in response."

"If you mean that you want me to defend you . . ." Sheriff Heath said, looking a little amused by the idea.

"I can defend myself, but you're going to have to do better by your own record."

"I could do without a lecture about my campaign. I get one at home every night."

"I'm not lecturing you," I protested, so sternly that we both laughed. Something was a little easier between us. Of course I was lecturing him. Norma Kopp herself couldn't have done it better.

We turned at last to walk to his office. "I know how he found out about Harry Core."

"It doesn't matter."

"It was Mrs. Pattengill. She must've overheard something. One of the guards talking, maybe."

"I won't blame this on a guard."

"No, but it had to be her," I protested. "Is that how she got released so easily? Did she make a deal with the prosecutor's office? Was John Courter handling her case?"

He sighed. "I believe he was."

"How can you be so calm about it?"

"Miss Kopp. Don't you see that it's better for us this way? He's putting all his worst qualities right out on display for the public to see. You notice that he hasn't said a word about what a sheriff's actual duties might be, or why he's best qualified to carry them out. A man who does nothing but cast out hate and blame couldn't possibly be elected to office."

"But the crowd loved it."

"It doesn't matter about the crowd. Anyone can draw out a few hundred people. What matters is what the voters decide on Election Day. You saw all those reporters. They're all racing back to their desks right now to see who can write up the most colorful version of that speech. It'll sell papers, but the voters won't like it. What they like is a lawman with a steady hand."

"But—"

"Don't let him wind you up. He doesn't even want the job. It hasn't occurred to him that the sheriff spends most of his time in the company of criminals. He has to live with them. He can't hate them, or he'd be miserable in the job. There's simply no way to run a jail if you can't bring yourself to see things from their perspective, just a little. I don't think Mr. Courter ever will. He's been on the prosecutor's side for too long. It's his job to put them into jail, to prove their wrongdoing, and to make them out to be evil-doers that deserve to be locked away. I suppose that's well enough for a prosecutor, but with ideas like that he'd hate being sheriff. He'll be entirely relieved when Mr. Conklin wins and he can stay over there in the courthouse."

"But if he's so ill-suited to be sheriff, why didn't he run for some other office?"

"He could have, but for whatever reason, the party wanted to back him as sheriff. That's the way it works—at the beginning of the year, the party operatives sit down and have a look at who's willing to stand for election, and they parcel it out. I suspect they didn't want Mr. Courter running for an office they actually hoped to win."

"Then you don't think he has a chance," I said.

"He never did." He shrugged off his coat and dropped into his chair, gesturing to me to do the same. "Miss Kopp, please trust me when I say that the voters are with us. I've done this before."

"But—"

He held up a hand to stop me. "I've given this a great deal of thought. Please remember that I have far more at stake than you do. William Conklin will do just fine in this election, and you will still have a job and go on just as before. But if I lose, I have nothing. I'd have to get hired on in some sort of business. I'd be a clerk with a ledger-book."

He couldn't possibly be serious. "Why on earth would you work as a clerk? Some town around here must be in want of a police chief. If nothing else, you could be a constable. There's no reason to think you'd have to give up working in law enforcement."

But Sheriff Heath looked at me sorrowfully and said, "Cordelia won't have it. That is to say, she won't have me. She won't be a policeman's wife any longer. I'm not to carry a gun or put myself in harm's way. If I don't go to Congress, I'll have to set us up in a new home and find some way, outside of the law, to pay for everything that a wife and three children might want."

"Three children?" The Heaths had a little boy and a baby coming on two years of age.

He looked shocked: he hadn't meant to say it. But of course I knew exactly what he meant and wondered why I hadn't guessed at it already.

"When the time is right, please give my congratulations to Mrs. Heath," I mumbled.

I understood at that moment why he'd been out every night in the last few weeks, making his speeches and shaking hands. At first he'd tried to avoid his campaign duties, seeing it as a pleasant diversion for Cordelia but little more, but as the weeks wore on, he'd been running himself ragged.

And what took him away from his duties, what caused him to scramble his priorities like eggs in a mixing bowl, was a baby. Not just any baby, but a third baby. One baby is a call to joy, a second baby is a call to responsibility, but a third baby is a summons to put aside all extraneous concerns and to lay one's shoulder to the wheel for a good decade or two.

Sheriff Heath had the look of a man who'd just put his shoulder to the wheel and would not be looking up until he was a grandfather.

I couldn't blame him. That was the way of family obligations. I was a breadwinner myself, of course, and understood that the weight I had to bear was light in comparison to that of a man with three young children. It tore at me just a bit to see that he'd been put in the position of having to make a choice between the vocation that mattered so much to him—which was also what mattered to me—and his family.

Of course he chose his family. Anyone would.

If I had allowed myself to think of Sheriff Heath's defeat at all, I imagined that he would return to law enforcement. He might find work in another town, and he could run again for sheriff in Hackensack in only three years. I suppose I let myself believe that he'd find a place for me, too, and that we might work together again someday.

It was such a faint and fleeting notion that I only just at that moment realized that I'd been entertaining it at all. But now even that idea had been struck down—all over the prospect of a baby in a bassinet.

I am ashamed to admit how much I resented that baby.

⊰ 30 ⊱

"A THIRD ONE doesn't make any difference," Norma said as we settled onto the train to Plattsburg. "It hardly costs anything extra to feed it, and it won't take up any room at first. We used to put Fleurette in a drawer."

"You did not!" Fleurette gasped. "I'd still be having nightmares about it! That's like sleeping in a coffin!"

"We didn't close the drawer," Norma said, "except when you had the colic. It was the only way any of us could sleep."

"Never mind about the baby," I said irritably. Norma had the most maddening way of throwing any conversation off the rails. "I only meant to say that I didn't understand why he ever wanted a seat in Congress, and I've been especially mystified lately as to why he's been working so hard for it. Now I know."

"I don't picture him working in a shop," Fleurette said.

"He didn't say a shop. He said he'd be a clerk somewhere. He could work in an office like Francis does."

"Selling baskets?" said Fleurette.

"Selling something, I suppose," I said. "It's what businesses do. But it won't come to that. John Ramsey's hardly bothering to campaign, and Sheriff Heath's out every night. He's entirely certain that the voters are with him."

Norma looked up at me and raised that heavy right eyebrow of hers. "John Ramsey is certain of something, too."

The timing of Fleurette's concert at the Plattsburg camp couldn't have been worse, coming as it did right before the election, but Sheriff Heath encouraged me to go, in fact ordered me to. Although he wouldn't say it aloud, he probably thought the last few days of campaigning would be easier if I put myself on a train.

"But he didn't dismiss you, did he?" Norma asked.

"Quite the opposite," I said. "He wasn't nearly as bothered by it as he might have been. He said I was accountable to Anna Kayser above all, and that I did right by her."

"He sounds far too calm for a man whose livelihood is at stake."

"He doesn't believe it is," I said.

"We'll see about that."

Fleurette sat with us long enough to coax a few coins from me for the dining car, then left us to join the other girls from Mrs. Hansen's Academy, who were seated together several rows away. As chaperones we had no real responsibilities at the moment, other than to make sure the girls stayed on board the train, so Norma and I sat together looking, I admit, spinsterly with our books and our carpetbags alongside us.

"It's a shame we couldn't bring the pigeons along," Norma said.

I ignored that. Fleurette and I considered it our great fortune that Norma's plans to drive us to Plattsburg by pigeon cart had been thwarted when our mare picked up a nail on the road and required rest. She couldn't find another horse on short notice, which meant, to everyone's relief, that we traveled by train like civilized people. Instead of the cart, Norma had to content herself with a trunk filled with her wooden models.

"Keep those toy carts packed away" had been Fleurette's admonition to me.

"I'm not sure it's within my power," I told her.

"Aren't you a deputy sheriff? Arrest her!"

I didn't agree to do that, but I did agree to keep an eye on Norma and to make sure that we didn't embarrass ourselves.

A train trip of eight to ten hours—perhaps twelve, depending on what sort of mess the tracks were in at Albany—to the wilds of upstate New York was not at all appealing to Norma, as there was nothing to do but to sit and wait for it to be over, and Norma could not bear to lose a day to idleness. She would've labored in the engine room, had they allowed it, or run the train herself, which had never seemed to her a terribly difficult task. After all, she liked to say, the tracks only went in one direction, making it impossible to get lost. There seemed to be nothing to do but to operate a brake handle and a whistle, both of which she insisted she could manage.

But to stay in her seat and look out the window was intolerable. "Trains are a waste of time," she announced, to no one in particular, just as I became engrossed in my novel.

Having failed to win my attention, she tried again. "It seems an awful shame to spend an entire day trekking up to Plattsburg for a concert that won't last more than an hour. You'd think that someone around Lake Champlain would know how to sing, but instead they import a rail-car full of girls from New Jersey. I wouldn't have anything to do with it if I hadn't the need to speak to an Army man on urgent business."

The train was rolling merrily through Poughkeepsie just then. The tracks ran right along the Hudson and made for a pretty sight: the beeches were ablaze in orange and gold, and the dogwoods and maples had just gone scarlet. They cast their long reflections over the water like so many streaks of paint. Across the river were the fine old mansions that served as summer camps for New York's well-to-do. They represented altogether a different way of life from the one I lived at the Hackensack Jail, and I found the idea diverting. I might've liked a week at a summer house on the Hudson, if one were ever offered to me.

But Norma couldn't be bothered to look at any of it, much less to imagine a different sort of life for herself, even if it only lasted for a week in a borrowed house. She made a great show of consulting her watch and declaring that it wasn't quite time for lunch, but that we ought to eat before the train rolled into Albany and a whole new crowd stepped aboard. Norma liked her meals planned, and she liked to map out those plans well in advance and make announcements about them.

"Of course, there will be a paper in Albany," Norma added, more to reassure herself than anyone else. She had already read all the papers we picked up in the train station before we left.

I possessed only a single weapon against Norma's restlessness, so naturally I hoped not to deploy it so soon. But Norma was leaving me little choice. I reached into my bag.

"By the way, I found your magazine," I said casually, and passed it across to her without ever once looking up from my book.

Norma snatched it from me. "I thought it hadn't come," she grumbled.

The arrival of *Popular Science* was a major event in the Kopp household every month. Norma pored over the articles, which increasingly concerned themselves with the machinery of war ("Torpedoing a Submarine from an Aeroplane" was a recent feature that interested her greatly, although she'd never been near a submarine or an aeroplane), and she undertook many of the more practical experiments and projects described. "Making Artificial Eyes for Blinded Soldiers" was something she thought she might like to attempt, but she couldn't justify the cost of a glass-blowing tube. She did experiment with a coiled-wire alarm meant to stop a thief from taking a milk bottle, although our milk had never been stolen. The boy from the dairy couldn't remember to set the bottle firmly on the coil, which was how the alarm would be triggered, so it was rarely tested.

Nevertheless, *Popular Science* kept Norma entertained and for that I was grateful. Knowing that a long rail journey was imminent, I had slipped the magazine out of the day's post a few days earlier and hidden it away for this very occasion. Norma spent the rest of the trip engrossed in a lengthy pictorial of precariously balanced boulders found in nature, a history of petroleum, and a set of plans for a portable chicken-house, which excited her tremendously until she realized that it moved on skids, not wheels.

"It's only to push it around the pasture," she said in disgust. "You can't actually drive it down the road."

"To the great relief of the chickens, I'm sure," I said.

Our arrival into Plattsburg was predictably late, but the hotel sat on a bluff directly above the train station, so the porters could anticipate its arrival and roll up with their carts just as the train did. I herded the girls, all ten of them sleepy and shivering in the night air, into an open coach brought down from the hotel for that purpose. Norma and I walked up the bluff with the hotel manager, who was charged with greeting all of the camp visitors and seeing to their needs.

We were to be housed in the summer cottages behind the town's grand hotel—cottages that would normally be shuttered in the fall, but stayed open this year on account of the camp and its many visitors. In addition to singing and dancing troupes, I was told, the cottages were offered to generals stopping for the night to give a speech to the men, doctors brought in to tend to the campers' scratches and sprains, and politicians who felt the need to turn up with a reporter for an afternoon and have their picture made shoveling a trench alongside the men.

"What else do they learn, besides trench-digging?" muttered Norma as we trudged along.

I was so accustomed to ignoring Norma's utterances that I was surprised to hear the manager bother to give an answer. "Oh, it's every kind of military drill you could imagine, miss. Marching in formation, rifle-work, and combat exercises. They consider it quite an adventure to march twenty miles up to Canada and back the next day. We invade Canada once a week or so, but we follow the catch-and-release policy here, so they get to have it back when we're through with it." The manager was a portly, red-cheeked man with the air of a showman about him. Asked about any of the goings-on in Plattsburg, he was likely to wave his arms about theatrically and make the most of it.

"Is that all? Isn't there any signaling?" Norma asked.

"Signaling?" the manager inquired merrily, not having any idea what he was in for.

"They must do semaphores, at least."

"I don't know—"

"It's when they wave their flags around," I offered. We had almost reached the hotel, and I didn't want to continue the conversation in the lobby, where I feared Norma would corner the man and lecture him on military communications for the rest of the night.

"There's probably some of that," he said, in the manner of a man who had perfected the art of never directly denying a guest anything they might want.

"And I suppose there would be telegraph and Morse code . . ."

"Oh, that sounds awfully high-tailed for a four-week camp! You know, they call it a businessman's camp because it gets the office boys out of the city. I think they'd rather splash around in the streams than sit in a classroom and read through a code-book."

"There's no code-book for messenger pigeons," Norma said, entirely to herself, as we reached the hotel's wide entrance and a doorman rushed over to usher us inside.

There was such confusion in the lobby, with all ten girls wide awake and chattering away, and the poor desk clerk trying to make sense of the registry. I watched the idea of a pigeon code-book settle around Norma like a shawl coming to rest on her shoulders.

"A pigeon manual . . ." she said again, a bit dreamily. Her voice would've been lost entirely to anyone except the manager, trained in the art of attentiveness, who answered back:

"Pigeons?"

THE SHEER SCALE of the Plattsburg camp exceeded anything I'd imagined. On a spit of land between the river and Lake Champlain stretched row upon row of khaki-colored tents, presided over at one end by brick barracks. The camp ran as a small city would, with clapboard buildings knocked together for dining, washing, evening meetings, and games. Those communal buildings were arrayed along a wide avenue, like a miniature Main Street. There was an infirmary, a garage for the automobiles, and a supply hut on the fringe of the camp.

Just beyond that, right outside the gate, sat a row of wagons set up by the more inventive townspeople, to sell whatever the camp might not provide: sour pickles, sausage rolls, leather boots, pocket knives, and notions. I was told that in the evenings, when the breeze picked up and blew across the camp, a boy stood over a kettle drum and roasted nuts, allowing the smoke to travel naturally on the wind and advertise his goods.

Thousands passed through the camps, and most of them were salary-men with money in their pockets. It cost twenty-two dollars to enroll, and the men were obliged to pay for their own uniforms and equipment, so only the well-heeled could attend. They had money to spend on whatever the townspeople could offer.

The girls who made up Fleurette's singing troupe were at their liberty during the day, while the men were off in the hills, conducting their combat exercises. They seemed determined to sample every pleasure the hotel had on offer: a life-sized chessboard on the lawn, where they put on a lively performance of rooks and pawns jousting for position; a row of deck chairs for sun-bathing over the lake; and a beauty parlor where the more enterprising of the group had their hair styled and set.

We arrived at camp in the evening, where we were met at the gate by the camp matron, Miss Miner. She must've recognized a kindred soul in me, because she went directly to me and said, "I see you have these girls well in hand and there won't be a thing for me to do."

I was rather taken aback by the idea that a military training camp for men would require a matron, and told her so.

Miss Miner took me by the arm and walked me through the gate. "I'll tell you a little secret." She had to crane her neck to make herself heard. I leaned over in an effort to accommodate her, and in that way we walked together as old friends.

"I was brought in to make sure the girls from town weren't bothered. It is a rather large influx of unattached men all at once. Some of these people remember their parents and grandparents talking about Civil War training camps and the kinds of trouble those soldiers could make on their first time away from home. Naturally there were concerns."

"Naturally," I said. Miss Miner had a crafty look about her and a rather light-hearted way of explaining herself that appealed to me right away. She didn't seem to take her work too seriously, which I thought a refreshing change.

"Well," Miss Miner continued, "would you believe that it wasn't the men I had to worry about? They absolutely love coming up here and being told what to do, and they take their orders very seriously. When they were told to stay away from the girls in town, and to strictly avoid late nights in the saloons and the sort of loutish behavior that small towns have come to expect from Army camps, do you know what they did? They followed orders precisely. Honestly, I think they like nothing better than to get away from the girls for a few weeks and come up here to live out-of-doors and traipse around in the woods all day."

"That doesn't leave much for you to do," I said.

Miss Miner gave what may only be described as a hoot and said, "Oh, no! You're forgetting the other half of the equation."

Now I saw the trouble perfectly. "The girls."

I turned around to make sure I was still being followed by ten exuberant young women, plus Norma. I was. Norma lugged her case of pigeon cart models and refused to let anyone help her with it, nor would she entertain any questions about it.

"Yes!" Miss Miner exclaimed. "The girls! Every one of them came down with a case of khaki fever the minute these men rolled into town. They can't resist a uniform, even if the men are only pretending at being soldiers. You saw those wagons around the edge of camp. These girls have never been so eager to help their families earn a few dollars. They're out here every day, selling their goods and hoping to make a new friend. It's one thing to ask the men to stay away from town, but it's another entirely to expect them to resist the charms of a pretty girl selling lemonade on a hot afternoon."

"I suppose. Does that mean you're out on patrol every night?"

"I am, but there's more to it than that. I try to find something else for the girls to do. Sometimes that means sitting down with the parents to talk about more suitable ways to occupy their daughters' time. They should be in school or working, not day-dreaming about soldiers. And of course, I'm forced to play nurse as well, whether I like it or not. Most of these girls haven't had anything explained to them at all, and they won't go to see their family doctor if there's anything in the way of a . . . a worry of a private nature. I've sent more than a few girls down to an under-standing doctor in Albany."

"It isn't just happening at the Plattsburg camps," I said. "I work in the jail down in Hackensack—"

"I thought you might do something like that!" Miss Miner put in gleefully.

"Well, yes, and I see all kinds of trouble between girls and their parents. Sometimes I think I wouldn't mind our country going into the war, if only to send the men off and give girls the oppor-tunity to think about something else for a few years."

Miss Miner laughed at that and said, "Oh, that's a losing bat-tle."

By then we'd reached the meeting hall. I helped her roll open a great sliding door. Inside was nothing but a dirt floor, rows of wooden benches, and a small and crudely built plank platform at the front for a stage.

"What do you say, girls?" Miss Miner called as we strolled in. "Will this do?"

The girls seemed to think it would. They ran up on the stage and started to work out their numbers. There was nothing so so-phisticated as a curtain or a back-stage room to allow for a change of costume or scenery, but these patriotic pageants required little in the way of traditional theater craft. The girls wore white dresses with red and blue sashes, and gold stars pinned up in their hair. There was nothing to it but the singing of a dozen or so songs and the waving of little pocket-sized flags.

Miss Miner stood off to the side with me and Norma while

the girls made ready and the men assembled outside. Norma had been silent so far, but now she saw her opportunity.

"Are the classes held in here?" she asked Miss Miner.

"There isn't much in the way of classes. The men prefer to be out-of-doors and, to be honest, we haven't enough time to teach them anything of substance nor any idea what might be of the most use. These camps aren't really intended to prepare a man for military service, but only to toughen him up a bit and to put to-gether a working list of possible recruits when the time comes."

"It seems to me the time has come and gone," Norma said. "How are we to raise an army on short notice if we haven't thor-oughly trained our soldiers?"

Miss Miner seemed to be accustomed to hearing such ar-guments: it must've been all that anyone talked about at camp. "Speak to a general about it," she said lightly. "It goes beyond my authority to raise an army."

It was never a good idea to encourage Norma to speak to a general. To my relief, there were no generals in town that night, but there was a small group of commanders on hand for the eve-ning's performance, and Miss Miner saw no reason not to intro-duce us. I merely exchanged a few words and thanked them for their hospitality, but Norma had built up a full head of steam over the idea that the camps weren't doing nearly enough to prepare for war, and thought nothing of making her opinion known.

"You've taught them to be good campers," she said to a lieuten-ant, "but I don't know how that helps us when we go to France. We're going to need drivers, and pilots, and signalmen, and artil-lery men, and tacticians. It isn't enough to teach them to sleep in a tent and eat beans."

The lieutenant found it highly amusing to be lectured by Norma and encouraged her to go on. He even took a seat next to her and propped his elbow on his knee. "If you put a plan together, madam, then I should like to hear it. I'll take it straight to the generals."

"In fact, I will," Norma said, "but of even greater importance is what I've brought in my trunk. It's just outside, and you're all going to want to see it."

"I think we're going to want to see the girls put on a show," a young captain put in hopefully, as the lamps were dimmed and a few notes came from a pianist who had been borrowed from the hotel for the occasion.

"You'll never defeat the Germans by watching girls put on a show," Norma said, so scornfully that they had no choice but to follow her outside just as the audience was coming in. I couldn't imagine what they'd make of Norma's little wooden models, but I wasn't about to interfere. She couldn't embarrass Fleurette if she wasn't even in the room.

The girls stepped out on stage. I moved closer to the front to keep a better eye on the proceedings, having been warned by Miss Miner that it was not unheard of for addresses to be exchanged between the stage and the front row, or vice versa. Miss Miner stayed in the back to watch for the telltale shape of a bottle slipped into a latecomer's pocket. "Between the two of us, we'll keep them on the straight and narrow," Miss Miner said before we separated. "I wish I had you up here with me all the time."

With the two of us on duty, there was no trouble with the audience. The men cheered and sang along to almost every tune, and laughed at the little jokes that the girls made in between numbers. Fleurette's time on the road with May Ward the previous spring had served her well. She handled herself like an experienced vaudevillian, singing with full-throated clarity and winking at just enough of the men in the audience to make them think that she was in love with each one of them. I saw no harm in it:

these patriotic pageants always had about them a theatrical air of romance intended to inspire the men to defend freedom and the comforts of home.

By the end of the performance, the sky had gone entirely dark outside. The meeting hall was lit only by a few electrical lights around the stage and one at the entrance. The girls were luminous in their white dresses. The gold stars in their hair caught the light and twinkled the way that real stars did. I looked out over the men perched on the long rows of benches and saw one hopeful and eager face after another, all of them ready to shed the cares of the office and their ordinary lives for an adventure in France. I hoped that it would be an adventure for them and nothing more, but that idea seemed as fleeting and fantastical as the pageant that had just concluded.

The girls took their bows to thunderous applause and a flurry of rose petals. Miss Miner and I had, by previous arrangement, agreed to step up on stage at the end of the performance and oversee the signing of autographs and receipt of whatever small gifts the men might offer the girls. They were a convivial crowd, polite and welcoming, and if one or two of them overstepped his bounds by taking a girl by the hand and asking her to dance, Miss Miner and I were quick to interfere. The girls were so flushed and triumphant, and overwhelmed by all the attention, that they hardly noticed if one man was pushed out of the way to make room for another.

The Army commanders had returned to the tent as the last song concluded. From their expressions I took it that they'd been highly amused by Norma's toy carts and whatever lecture she delivered to them on the subject of pigeon communication in wartime. I did feel a little stab of pity for Norma, who had pursued her idea doggedly for months, only to have it dismissed by a group of low-ranking officers who would rather watch pretty young Fleurette dance than hear a lecture on wartime strategy.

Norma waited outside with her trunk. "What did they think of it?" I asked, when the evening wound down and we wandered out.

"They don't know what to think, because they're military men and they only think what the generals tell them to," she said, as if I should've known that already. "They're going to run it up the chain of command. I now have the name of a general to whom I may address future correspondence. I'll write before we leave. The Plattsburg postmark will make an impression."

"Undoubtedly," I said.

Although I wished, at times, that my sister could find a less peculiar hobby, and one that did not involve writing quite so many letters to generals, I was relieved to see her keeping herself occupied and saw no reason to interfere. The men she'd spoken to tonight would surely have a good laugh later at her expense. Perhaps I should've felt some small measure of outrage on her behalf over the way they were almost certainly speaking about her, but this was Norma's matter, not mine.

Two of the camp vehicles were pressed into service to return us to the hotel. As we walked to the garage, Miss Miner said, "I meant what I said earlier. I could use you, and a dozen more like you. There's going to be plenty of work at these Army camps when they get going in earnest. Wouldn't you like to come along and work with me? You could have your choice of posts."

"Oh!" I said. "I'm quite comfortable at the jail."

Miss Miner laughed. "I don't think I've ever heard that before, even from a policewoman."

"Hers is an unusual position," Norma put in. "The sheriff lets her do whatever she likes, and she has quite an easy time of it."

"I don't have an easy time of it," I protested, "but I'm happy where I am."

"Ask her again after the election," Norma told Miss Miner.

It irked me that Norma had to ruin a perfectly friendly conversation with such unpleasantness. "It doesn't matter about the election. I'll be serving under a new sheriff, that's all. It's very kind of you to offer, Miss Miner, but I belong in Hackensack at that jail."

"Please call me Maude. And do think about it. We're all going to be summoned to do our part for the war."

⇥ 31 ⇤

ELECTION DAY ARRIVED at last, fiercely bright and bracingly cold. Red and blue bunting sailed above all the shops. An air of spirited good cheer prevailed among the people of Hackensack, who took the exercise of their civic duty as an occasion for flying miniature flags from hat-bands, displaying little cameos of long-dead presidents, and parading around in a rag-tag assortment of mothballed military uniforms.

The lines of voters spilled out of every polling place in town, serving as a study of men's haberdashery: brown tweeds and heavy gray wools, faint pinstripes, neatly blocked bowlers and battered workmen's caps, leather shoes and the stained wooden clogs the silk workers wore. They drew on their pipes and chatted amiably as they waited, pleased to have been asked to consult on matters of the state and ready to offer up their opinions at the ballot box.

The candidates were expected to be out in their Sunday best, tipping their hats and saluting the old soldiers in uniform. This was the part of campaigning that William Conklin loved and took to naturally: I found him on the sidewalk outside the courthouse, surrounded by well-wishers. He was the kind of man who laughed louder than anyone else and tended to draw a crowd because of it.

Sheriff Heath stood a little apart from Mr. Conklin, closer to the jail, in the good blue suit he sometimes wore to court. Cordelia was on his arm, looking already like a Washington socialite who just happened to be passing through Hackensack for the afternoon. Now that I knew she was expecting a child, I could see it: she'd been letting her dresses out, little by little, and there were faint lines where the seams had been creased.

The Heaths were speaking to a much smaller group of voters, who happened to drift away just as I walked past, so I stopped to talk.

"Mrs. Heath, you look the very picture of victory," I said.

Cordelia was indeed more bright-eyed and full of cheer than I'd ever seen her. "Oh, it's just such a glorious day. Of course, I shouldn't be out here, with so much packing left undone, but I couldn't stay away."

The Heaths had been carting out boxes for days now. It was one of the hardships of having one's living quarters dictated by an elected office: once the results were announced, they simply had to vacate the premises.

"I can hardly believe you'll be gone so soon," I said. "What sort of place have you found for yourselves?"

Sheriff Heath opened his mouth to answer but Cordelia jumped in. "It's only a half-flat in Capitol Hill, but we're lucky to have it, with the Navy Yard bursting at the seams. There's a park for the children, and Bob can walk to work."

"Then . . . it's straight to Washington, is that it?"

"We leave Saturday, if the voters send us," Sheriff Heath said in that stoic and dignified fashion of his. There would be no early celebrating on his part.

"Of course they'll send you," I said. "It's awfully fast, that's all. Will you be keeping a home here in Hackensack as well?"

"Why would we?" Cordelia's voice rose an octave. She was obviously eager to get out of town.

"Cordelia's parents have shifted around in that big old house of theirs and made a suite of rooms for us if we require it," said Sheriff Heath. "I'll be back and forth like any congressman, and of course I'll keep an office here. Are you quite certain you wouldn't like to be a congressman's stenographer?"

I turned and looked up at the jail's glowering silhouette against a sky scattered with high-flying clouds. "I'd rather be here."

Sheriff Heath followed my glance but didn't answer. Any love he had for that jail could not be admitted in front of his wife.

"It's a fine place for you," Cordelia told me. There was an air of dismissal in her voice, and I realized that I was probably meant to move on and make way for more voters.

"Are you back at the jail today?" Sheriff Heath asked as I made my good-byes.

"I'm off to Morris Plains, remember? We're giving Anna Kayser the good news about her divorce." The evidence had been gathered, the papers had been drawn, and all that was required for the suit to proceed was Anna Kayser's signature. Geraldine had hired a car. She was expected at the jail within the hour.

"The divorce was in the papers while you were away," Sheriff Heath said. "I didn't realize the woman Mr. Kayser was mixed up with was Virginia Townley."

"Do you know her?" I asked.

"No, but John Courter does. He ran around with her himself, years ago. I used to see them going in and out of a disreputable house over in Tenafly."

"Are you suggesting that he didn't want me looking into Anna Kayser's case because he thought I might stumble into the history of the other woman?"

"Apparently he has high regard for your skills as a detective," Sheriff Heath said.

Cordelia Heath turned to him, astonished. "Do you mean to

say that you knew a thing like that about John Courter and you kept it to yourself?"

"What would you have me do, dear? Shout it from the court-house steps?"

"That's what he did."

He took her by the elbow in a curiously intimate fashion and said, "If nothing else, you can say that you're married to a man who wouldn't stoop that low."

I didn't wait for her response. I had one last trip to the asylum ahead of me. There was nothing left for Sheriff Heath to do but to stand on the corner and ask for votes.

⊰ 32 ⊱

WHEN AN INMATE is to be released from an insane asylum, it has to be done quickly. Otherwise, the rest of the patients go into hysterics wondering why they haven't been released as well.

This explained why Anna Kayser had, on her previous commitments, always been released without warning or explanation when her husband came for her. It had to happen with absolutely no fanfare or preparation, or it would rouse the others into a hysteria that would be impossible for the staff to manage.

For this reason, our visit caused quite a bit of trouble for the doctors at Morris Plains. With the photographic evidence of adultery now in hand, Anna Kayser's divorce—and subsequent release from the asylum—was almost guaranteed. But there was no way to bring it about without telling her ahead of time. The divorce suit would, naturally, require her presence in court. Somehow she would have to be told that her freedom was almost a certainty, without exciting the other patients.

The staff was in a state of anxiety over this conundrum when we arrived. Just as before, we were ushered inside the great hall at Morris Plains and met by Dr. Evans, who said, as soon as he had us settled behind closed doors, "Ladies, I must warn you that it is highly irregular for a patient of ours to be involved in any sort of legal action, as an inmate in an insane asylum naturally forfeits the usual rights during their commitment. Mrs. Kayser's husband would be expected to represent her in any legal matter that arose during this time. But of course, that isn't possible in this case."

"I'm surprised more women don't try to divorce the man who put them away," Geraldine said drily. I could see that she did not like being lectured on the law by a doctor.

But the doctor seemed not to notice her tone. "Well, if we let one do it, they'd all try, and then where would we be?"

He went around behind his desk and shuffled some papers. "I must ask you to make it plain to Mrs. Kayser that even if she succeeds in this divorce suit, she won't be released from care until I certify that she is entirely well. That's the way it is with all of our patients and we'll have no exceptions for her. Her husband did not put her here on his own. There was a physician and a judge involved, and there will be again. If I see any evidence that she's incited the other inmates or caused any kind of a stir on the women's ward, I'll take that as a sign that her recovery isn't proceeding the way it should."

I wanted very much to remind him that Mrs. Kayser hadn't any illness from which to recover, and that she would win her release, as well as her divorce suit, on the grounds that her husband had her fraudulently committed, but a sharp look from Geraldine kept me quiet.

"We'll tell her everything you said," Geraldine promised. He seemed satisfied with that, and soon we were once again placed in the possession of a nurse, who led us down the same maze of corridors and into a private room near the women's wing.

This time, Anna Kayser was already waiting for us. She looked more tired than before, with purplish circles under her eyes and a face that sagged generally under the weight of what it had to bear. She'd had a head cold, too. Her nose was red and her voice hoarse.

"I didn't think I'd see you again," she said, as soon as we were alone.

"Oh, we've been hard at work, and it's all due to Deputy Kopp's perseverance," Geraldine said. "But there's some distressing news, and Dr. Evans has warned us not to . . . upset you, or to excite you unduly."

Mrs. Kayser looked at us both, puzzled, so I put it more plainly. "We've almost certainly won your release, but the doctors and nurses here don't like it. They're afraid you'll stir up the other inmates. You must keep the news quiet, or they might argue that you are unwell. It's a threat, plain and simple. Do you understand?"

She nodded. "I don't have any friends here. I won't say a word."

I said, "Well, Mrs. Kayser, we arranged for an attorney in Paterson to take Mr. Townley's divorce case and to send a photographer. The pictures tell the story quite clearly. We have the evidence for his divorce suit, and for yours."

Anna nodded but didn't say anything. Geraldine cleared her throat and went on. "I suppose you might be wondering whether your husband took up with Virginia Townley after you were sent here, or whether . . ."

She trailed off but Mrs. Kayser finished. "Or whether he sent me to the asylum so he could be alone with her. It must be the latter. I don't know why I never thought of it. Charlie's just so ordinary. I didn't think any woman would bother with him, honestly. Why would she?"

I could tell that Geraldine had endured this conversation before, with other betrayed wives. "I don't pretend to know why people do the things they do. I don't suppose you'll ever know. But he's been monstrously unfair to you, when you've given him everything a man could want."

She laughed a little. "I don't know about that."

"But you've given him more than he deserves," I put in. "Mr. Townley confessed that he'd known about your husband's dalliances for years. I'm afraid this wasn't the first time. Mr. Townley believes it entirely possible that in the past, when you've come here—when you've been sent here—"

"That Charlie sent me away every time he had a girl," Mrs. Kayser said. There was no bitterness in her voice, only resignation, as the fact that he'd been able to pull off such a thing, not once, but four times, became impossible to deny.

We sat in silence for a minute, with only the faint ticking of Geraldine's watch and the shuffling of feet in the corridor outside.

Finally she coughed into her handkerchief and spoke. "I suppose you've filed the suit against my husband, and named Virginia Townley as the co-respondent."

"Yes, and the attorney in Paterson has done the same for Mr. Townley's case. We're sharing the evidence. I have a few documents here for your signature."

She looked them over and took Geraldine's pen. "And then I'm to be released?"

"We would appeal your commitment on the grounds that your husband sought to have you sent away so that he could live with Virginia Townley in a state of illegal cohabitation. The fact that he did all of this while your daughter was under his roof is particularly damning and will work in our favor. If I can find any of the other girls your husband used to—used to know—I will, as it can only help your cause. As for the doctor who signed your commitment papers, I believe I can convince him to reconsider the case. Otherwise I'll see to it that he goes to court, and I know a reporter who will make sure his name gets in the papers when he does."

Geraldine lived down the hall from Carrie Hart, a reporter who'd helped me once or twice before. These were proving to be the most useful friends a deputy could have. I understood now why Sheriff Heath made an effort to stay on amicable terms with reporters, and why he was so quick to summon a room full of them when he needed the public on his side.

"Where am I to go?" Mrs. Kayser asked. "And what of Charlotte?"

"You and your daughter will stay in the house, and your husband will pay to keep you," I said. "I'm certain of that. There's not a judge alive who would see you put out of your home, after what's been done to you."

Mrs. Kayser pushed herself to her feet. "What has been done to me," she repeated, her voice barely above a whisper.

Just then the nurse knocked and said that our visiting time was over.

"It's a shock," Geraldine said, once we were outside and clear of the nurse. "It always is. It'll be worse before it gets better. But she'll be looked after here, and soon she'll be home. It's a fine way to spend Election Day, setting someone free."

⚜ 33 ⚜

THAT SETTLED THINGS for Anna Kayser, more or less. Her case wasn't mine to pursue any longer. It was a legal matter, to be worked over first in divorce court and then in a subsequent challenge to her commitment, all of which Geraldine would handle.

I should've been gladder about it than I was. A woman wrongfully sent away to an asylum was to regain her liberty, and the man responsible was to be punished. There was every reason to call it a triumph.

But what of the next Anna Kayser? William Conklin had shown only a passing interest in anything I did. At best I could hope that he'd consider the fifth floor to be my realm, and leave me to run it as I saw fit. At worst—and honestly, this was what I suspected would happen—he'd never come to my defense, or take a risk for me, or champion one of my causes.

Norma told me that it was about time I championed my own causes. But a jail is like a miniature army (to put it in terms that Norma would understand), with a commander, and troops following orders, and a line of accountability that goes not to the president, but to an even more capricious and unpredictable elected party: the Board of Freeholders. I could champion my own causes all day long, but I could also champion myself right out of a job.

It was a dispiriting few days, then, as I, along with everyone else at the jail, awaited the vote tally and the name of the man who was to take the office of sheriff. I saw very little of Sheriff Heath during that time. He seemed to be consumed with putting his papers in order for his successor. When he wasn't working at that, he went out on as many calls with his deputies as he could, for old time's sake. I wasn't invited along, but I watched them come and go from the windows on the fifth floor.

This, too, seemed a foretelling of the days to come. I could imagine William Conklin rushing out with his favorite deputy— who wouldn't be me, I just knew it—and only realizing once he was at the scene that there were women and children to be looked after, and that he should've brought a matron to help. The idea would be a fleeting one, easily vanquished.

The results were due to be announced on the Monday after the election. Norma's newspapers arrived in batches twice daily. Because we lived so far out of town, it was not unusual for the morning editions to come in the afternoon, and the afternoon or evening editions to turn up the next day. That was fine on an ordinary day, but in the wake of an election such as this one, it wouldn't do.

On that Monday I was still in my dressing-gown, drinking coffee at the kitchen table, when Norma stumped in from the barn and ordered me to get dressed. "We'll go as far as Ridgewood and see what they have to tell us, but we might have to ride all the way into Hackensack. You'll want to meet your new boss, anyway."

"William Conklin and I are already acquainted," I said.

She frowned at that. "Fix yourself up. I want you hatted and booted by nine."

At her insistence I put on my best uniform. Fleurette was working down in Fort Lee that day, so the two of us went to town on our own.

The news-stand at the Ridgewood train station had a bit in the way of early returns, but nothing that mattered to us. New Jersey had gone for Hughes for president, and opinions were divided over whether Wilson would carry the country. Senator Frelinghuysen advanced from the state senate to the national seat, and state senator Edge won the governor's seat.

"They certainly went for the Republicans," Norma said as she squinted at the results.

"Well, everyone likes Joe Frelinghuysen, and even the Democrats wanted Mr. Edge for governor," I said.

"That's the most you've ever had to say about politics," Norma said.

"I had a stake in it. Let's go on to Hackensack."

Norma picked up a paper at the station and read it on the train. There was plenty of chatter among the passengers about the election, but it mostly concerned the race for president, and speculation on how New York might've voted. No one seemed to have a thing to say about the office of sheriff.

It wasn't until the train arrived in Hackensack that I began to feel truly uneasy. The news-stands there had no better information than what we'd heard in Ridgewood, but there was a burble of conversation all around us that seemed to suggest that the Republicans had made a clean sweep of it.

Oddly, my first worry was for Sheriff Heath. He would be out of a job, and I would not. The idea of working for John Courter had never been allowed to take root in my mind, and it was only barely creeping in at that moment.

Norma pushed her way through the crowded train station and I followed. Out on the street, it was business as usual: the bunting had come down, the campaign signs were gone, and the air of merriment and expectation had given way to the ordinary bustle of a Monday morning. The lack of any sign of the election—the noticeable absence of it—put a very firm line in my mind. There was everything that came before November 7, and there was now.

I had not prepared myself for the question of how different those two periods of time might be. I'd been so busy trying to do my job, and to stay out trouble, that I hadn't even sensed that a line was being drawn right down the middle of my life—but here it was.

There was more of a crowd at the courthouse, where the votes were being tallied and announced. I was overtaken by a sudden urge to steer clear, to duck inside the side door at the jail, and to run upstairs to the female section, where I might spend the day on the most ordinary of activities for my inmates, consumed by routine, until someone came upstairs to tell me the news.

But Norma marched right into the scrum of reporters and spectators gathered around the courthouse steps and demanded to know the latest results. I kept away from her. My face was suddenly very hot and I thought I might have a fever. There were so many people talking all at once that I couldn't take any of it in. I started to feel unaccountably dizzy until I realized that I was holding my breath.

Then Norma turned around and stared at me. There were so many people in between the two of us that our view of each other came intermittently as people passed back and forth. Norma was a grim-countenanced woman on the best of days, but I knew how to read her expressions and didn't have to be told.

I turned and tried to go back up Essex Street, to the train station, as if to turn back the morning like the hands of a clock. But Norma was too fast and caught me by the elbow.

I wouldn't look at her. The words just drifted around, attached to no one.

"It's a loss for Heath and for Conklin. John Courter's already moving into the sheriff's office. You'd better go on over there."

But I kept on. Never had a train station seemed like such a refuge.

Norma shuffled along beside me. "It's no good to run off. You knew it could happen."

I dodged three young men laughing and elbowing each other on the curb. What did they have to celebrate? I had a sudden urge to knock someone over and hoped, for the sake of general peace and orderliness, that no one stepped in my way and gave me the chance.

Norma's legs were shorter but she had no trouble in keeping up. Nothing ever stopped Norma.

"You're John Courter's deputy now," Norma called.

I wasn't and I never would be.

"Of course you're free to run home, but those inmates of yours are locked inside."

That stopped me. What of my inmates? I was their link to the world outside, to the courts, to whatever sort of future they might wish for. Their lives could change on the whim of the voters, even if they never met the man who lived in the sheriff's apartment.

John Courter would live in the Heath family's apartment. I had never even allowed myself to imagine that. It was a cramped and dull little space, but Mrs. Heath had exerted considerable effort to make it her own, with her doilies and her embroidered pillows, and the little shelf of books on the wall, and the sheriff's overcoat on a peg in the corner.

All of that was gone, wasn't it? It had all been carted off.

I stood a few blocks away from the courthouse and the adjoining jail-house and thought about what those places had come to mean to me. I had fought vigorously within the walls of the courthouse, at first to protect my own family, and then to defend my inmates.

It was there that I met Sheriff Heath for the first time. He'd stopped me on the courthouse steps when I went to lodge a complaint against the man who was then harassing my family, and as we spoke, a deputy ran over and called for him to attend to some other, more important matter. I felt so irrelevant as he ran off to answer to his duties and left me to wander on back home. He had a sense of purpose about him and I did not.

All of that changed when he hired me on.

It was unbearable to imagine going back to that old life of mine, the life I had before I met him.

Norma was right. I had no idea how John Courter would govern as sheriff, but it wouldn't do to miss a day's work just because I wasn't ready to find out. I had been called upon, in my job, to handle far worse situations than this one. Any deputy might have to face the wrong end of a gun in the course of everyday duties. Was a newly elected sheriff really enough of a threat to make me turn and run away?

Norma had her back to me, leaving me to my deliberations. But then a train whistle sounded in the distance and Norma was suddenly eager to be off, or she pretended to be. "That's my train," she said, with barely a backward glance. "Go on back to work."

With that, Norma trudged off. I watched her go, and envied the fact that she was returning to her own domestic sphere, where she was in complete command, and never had to worry about having her life upended over an election. I could picture Norma at home, walking back into the foyer and putting her hat on the rack. I felt a wave of longing for our familiar old house, even though I'd only left it an hour or two before. It was a longing for the life I had before I walked out the door that morning and the election made itself manifest.

But this was not a time for self-indulgence. I couldn't know what my job would be like under the new sheriff, but there was nothing to do but to go and find out.

I kept my mind a very deliberate blank as I walked around the courthouse and into the side door where the deputies and guards came and went. This path took me right past the sheriff's office, which I regretted at once. Somehow I thought I'd sneak into the jail and go directly upstairs. (Was I planning to do that every day for the next three years? I couldn't say.)

But it was too late: as I turned down the corridor, I saw my new boss speaking to a few men I didn't recognize. They stopped talking when I approached, and stepped back so that I might pass.

Mr. Courter was leaning in the doorway to the sheriff's office. (I could call him "the new sheriff" or I could call him "Mr. Courter," but I could not yet say "Sheriff Courter.") It would be an exaggeration to say that there was anything merry in his expression—he was not a man given to merriment—but there was a flushed triumph about his countenance, and the hard edge of victory in his eyes.

I gave what I hoped was a respectful nod and said, "I understand you're to be congratulated. I know that I speak for the rest of—"

"That'll do," he said. "You must have some things upstairs. I'll send one of my boys up to collect them."

I looked around at the other men, all of them young and burly. Had he hired them as deputies?

I wasn't sure how to answer. "I'm—yes, I do keep some things upstairs in my cell, but it's because I'm so often on duty overnight."

Already I felt the ground slipping out from underneath me. There was some small noise among the men—shuffles, coughs, a suppressed laugh—and then came Mr. Courter's voice, more officious this time.

"This office has no duties that require a lady deputy. You can go on home."

⇥ 34 ⇤

I DON'T REMEMBER walking out of the jail. I managed to get a block or two away without noticing a thing about my surroundings. By the time Sheriff Heath caught up with me, he was calling my name impatiently, as if he'd already said it three or four times.

I felt his hand on my elbow. The sensation was too familiar to bear.

He never did get over the impulse to help me onto train platforms, over mud puddles, or even, once, to steer me around the collapsed body of a rail-yard worker knocked out cold and left for dead. It wasn't an affectionate touch, necessarily, but it was confident and trusting and something to be relied upon. To feel it at that moment stabbed at me so sharply that I startled and nearly stumbled.

"Pardon me, Deputy," the sheriff said, thinking he'd scared me. (But he wasn't a sheriff anymore, and I no longer a deputy. What were we to call each other?)

"I only just found out." I hardly trusted myself to speak and rushed the words out before my voice broke.

Sheriff Heath—Mr. Heath, I would have to grow accustomed to it—stood exactly six feet tall, just as I did, which meant that when I turned around, we looked each other squarely in the eye.

There were very few men who weren't forced to look ever so slightly up at me, and I always saw the merest whisper of resentment of that in their eyes.

But Mr. Heath met me levelly. He was as unknowable to me as any other man might be—he had his own family, his own private life and worries, and moved in a world of civic affairs that was entirely closed to me—but when we stood like that, looking directly at each other, I always felt that he was in some way my mirror image.

No longer. The platform that had elevated both of us—a platform of public service, elected office, useful and prestigious work—had been pulled out from under us, and there we stood, two flat-footed mortals.

Mr. Heath seemed at a loss, so I said, "Is it absolutely certain? Aren't there any more boxes of ballots to be counted?"

"Only a few. They worked all night."

"Cordelia must be—"

But he didn't want to talk about Cordelia. "I know what John Courter's trying to do. He won't get away with it."

I had no interest in reassurances from Mr. Heath, the civilian, with all his powers stripped away. "He's already done it. He has every right to. I was hired, and I can be fired."

I couldn't stand around on the sidewalk any longer arguing over it. Everything I'd come to believe about myself was dropping away, and I couldn't take the shock of it. All at once I was nothing but an unmarried woman without an income, with still more unmarried female relations at home—but how would they live? What were they to do without my salary? One fresh worry after another came charging into my mind, each with more disastrous implications than the last.

On to the train station I marched, with Mr. Heath matching

my stride. The two of us were known around Hackensack, which meant that any number of well-intentioned citizens tried to stop and speak to us, but then thought better of it at the sight of my face going pink and white and red, and Mr. Heath's downturned brim shielding his visage.

Rushing to the station was pointless, as there was no train yet and nothing to do but wait. People were far more inclined to come and speak to us if we were simply standing about on the platform, so by unspoken agreement we hid ourselves behind the station agent's office.

Now Mr. Heath spoke quickly, as he could see that he wouldn't hold my attention for long. "What I'm trying to tell you is that you have civil service protections. It's an odd bit of turnabout, because the Republicans were the ones who pushed for it to protect their appointees when Democrats came into office. Now that they're in office, they're finding themselves stuck with Democratic appointees under the rules they wanted."

"Then someone needs to go and tell Mr. Courter that, because he doesn't seem to know it."

"Oh, he knows it. A whole gaggle of them were just down at the courthouse asking for a list of every civil servant subject to the rules, as well as every political appointee who'd be exempt."

I had no patience for this discussion. "Well, was I on the list, or wasn't I?"

"That's the trouble. There is no list. The law was only passed this summer. The county clerk is having to rush around and pull it together. I've been there all morning to make sure the records from my department were looked over in the presence of witnesses and properly accounted for."

"I'm surprised Mr. Courter didn't burn them as soon as he took possession of your office."

"He couldn't. I took them home a week ago."

"A week ago! But you were so sure you'd win, and Mr. Conklin, too!"

It hadn't occurred to me to wonder what William Conklin would do now that he'd lost his run for sheriff. I couldn't be bothered about him. He seemed like the kind of man who always landed on his feet.

"I was never as certain as Cordelia was, but there was no point in saying it. Things turned against us in the last couple of weeks. When I saw those leaflets on the lamp-posts—"

"'Demon Deputy'! My God, this is all because of me!" I had an urge once again to turn and run, but I was squeezed into a corner behind the station agent's office with Mr. Heath blocking the way.

"It wasn't you," he insisted. "There was just . . . a mean-spiritedness running through the entire campaign that I'd never seen before. I think it's the war. Everyone's ready to rush off and fight, and all of a sudden there's an enemy around every corner."

"Yes, the war. And here we are, with a German-speaking lady deputy out making trouble, and two political offices lost over it." I had never felt so bitter.

There was a train coming at last. I moved to brush past Mr. Heath.

"What I came to tell you," he said, quickly, seeing that he was about to lose his opportunity, "is that you need to hire an attorney and fight for your job. You have the law behind you."

I barked out an angry laugh, but it was drowned out by the scream of the engine's brakes. "The law? What could the law do about a sheriff who doesn't want me in his jail? How am I to work with that man? How am I to conduct my duties when he'll be looking every day for cause to dismiss me? Oughtn't I to seek work where I'm wanted? It's a shame you won't have that stenographer job open, because I could use it now."

That stung. The blank look of shock on Mr. Heath's face told me that he hadn't yet fully taken in the fact that he, too, was without employment prospects.

"Forgive me," I said. "I'll go on home and listen to Norma read aloud from the employment notices from the paper."

"Deputy—Miss Kopp." Mr. Heath had trouble saying it, too: we were both attached to our titles. "You don't seem to understand. All my men are losing their positions. He's fired everyone."

That stopped me. "Everyone? All the deputies? And the guards?"

"All of them."

"But they're the ones who know how to run the jail. And some of them have worked for five different sheriffs. It doesn't matter about the political party. Mr. Courter hardly knows most of them. How can he decide that they're all unfit for service?"

"It's what he's done. That's why he brought those men in this morning. He's dismissed everyone from the jail and he intends to make them scramble around and grovel to be let back in. I'm told he sees it as a loyalty test."

I could just picture them: the young, ambitious guards who hoped to work their way up to deputy or policeman, the older men who had served long enough to know every kind of trick an inmate might try to pull, and the deputies who put their own lives at risk every time they went out on a call. A few of them carried bullet wounds and scars from knives.

Had they all lost their jobs because of me?

In the opening left by my silence, Mr. Heath said, "I want you to go and speak to John Ward about your case. He owes me enough favors. If you can win this, Courter will be forced to reinstate everyone. It doesn't matter what you do after that. Quit, if you can't stand it. But go ahead and—"

"Why do I have to be the one to hire a lawyer and fight and beg for a job with that awful man? Why can't one of the other deputies do it? It doesn't matter which one of us it is."

The train rolled on out of the station without me. I had a feeling that I was going off to speak to a lawyer, whether I wanted to or not.

"It has to be you," Mr. Heath said. "A sheriff who wants to push out his predecessor's deputies and guards is hardly newsworthy. Every sheriff wants to. This fight is going to be carried out all over the state, in every county where the office of the sheriff changed political parties. There is nothing to distinguish Bergen County, or to draw attention to it, except—"

"Except for the lady deputy, fired because the sheriff has no use for a woman at the jail." I sounded so churlish that Mr. Heath laughed in spite of himself.

"I'm afraid so. You'll draw in the reporters. You'll make it a public fight, and Mr. Courter won't be able to hide what he's trying to do."

It had been Sheriff Heath (back when he was sheriff) who had first suggested to me that I use the newspapers to my advantage to shame John Courter and his colleagues at the prosecutor's office into doing something about the man who had been harassing my family. What was the headline that ran all over the country? "Girl Waits with Gun."

It sounded so foolish, two years later. I was no girl, and waiting around with a gun wasn't what made the difference. What mattered was not that I'd been prepared to fire a weapon at my attacker, but that I—with the sheriff—had managed to rally the public to my cause. Together, we gathered evidence and built a case. We won in court, not on a street corner with a revolver.

This, of course, was Mr. Heath's point. It was time to rally the public, and to make sure the county clerk and the elections office understood that the bright light of public scrutiny was shining on Bergen County, and even more brightly on the office of the sheriff.

When I thought about it like that, I knew that I had no choice.

⊰ 35 ⊱

MISS KOPP, OUSTED BY NEW SHERIFF, JUST WON'T QUIT

Young Woman Deputy Defies Bergen County Official and
Consults Lawyer to Begin Test Suit in Courts—Has Had
Spectacular Public Career While in Office

HACKENSACK—Bergen County, N.J., which suffered a sudden change of politics at the last election, lost its most comely Under-Sheriff today when Miss Constance Kopp was notified that her name had been dropped from the list of office employees by John W. Courter, the new Sheriff.

"There is nothing I can find for her to do," declared Sheriff Courter, regarding a long list of deserving Republicans who were willing to sacrifice their time for the county. He is understood to have notified Miss Kopp that he had abolished the office of matron and that he had never recognized her as Under-Sheriff. He ignored the thrilling incident when Miss Kopp came to New York and manacled a fugitive, to say nothing of other exploits in which she earned the name of "the demon deputy."

"My lawyer has advised me to linger about here until I am put out of the office," she told fellow employees. "I intend to do so."

Walter Scott has been appointed to fill the place "vacated" by Miss Kopp. When he appeared to be sworn in, Judge W. M. Seufert, of the County Court, refused to administer the oath and Scott was compelled to go to Newark and he was sworn in by Justice Parker in the Supreme Court.

Justice Parker specified in administering the oath of office that his action must not be construed as an opinion on the civil service controversy.

"I most certainly am here," said Miss Under-Sheriff Kopp, when questioned at the sheriff's office late this afternoon.

"Haven't you got out yet?" was asked.

"No, I haven't," replied the woman deputy with asperity. When asked what her intentions were regarding holding to her official position, she asserted that she cannot be removed because of the protections of the Civil Service law.

Miss Kopp, the despised woman Under-Sheriff, has captured several criminals in her term of office and recently leaped into a river to rescue an escaped lunatic.

"YOU OUGHTN'T TO invite this sort of attention," Norma said at breakfast, when news of my court case landed on our doorstep.

I chipped at a soft-boiled egg. "It's just one last round in the papers, then I'm quite sure I'll never be heard from again."

"That's only if you lose. If you win, you can stay in your job."

"You know I won't work for that man."

"You'll have to do something." Norma was already needling me about how I proposed to keep her in pigeon scratch if I found myself out of work, but at that moment I lacked the fortitude to be aggravated over it.

"No one wants to work for him," Fleurette put in. "Everyone hates him."

"A solid majority of the voters liked him well enough," Norma said.

Fleurette yawned. Talk of the campaign bored her before the election, and now that it was over, she had no interest in it. She wouldn't even have been at the table, as she was in the habit of sleeping late, but Norma had put a stop to that since the election. If there was any chance that we were to be deprived of my wages, Fleurette needed to be up and out the door in pursuit of an income.

"Fleurette's right. No one wants to work for him," I said. "But if I'm to fight this case, I've no choice but to proceed as if I do. Once the case has been won and the others guaranteed their jobs, I'll hand in my notice."

"As long as you find something else, because I can't possibly bring in more than I already do," Fleurette said.

"You don't bring in a thing," Norma said. "You spend it all before you walk in the door."

"But I pay to keep myself!" Fleurette objected. "Think of the savings!"

Norma would not think of the savings. "You don't pay your keep. There's food and firewood, and heating gas, and all the costs of running this place. You don't put in a dime for any of that, and now you'll have to."

"But you can't depend upon me." Fleurette managed to make

that sound entirely reasonable. "Constance will have to find something."

"I will," I said, "but Mr. Ward doesn't want me out looking for another position until my case is settled. It's better to wait until after Christmas anyway."

Never had Christmas been such a cheerless prospect. Francis would have us over, as always, and a day of Bessie's fine cooking would undoubtedly shore us up. But Francis would have his opinions about the turn of events at the sheriff's office, and the advisability of my taking this opportunity to find a quieter line of work, or perhaps (as he liked to suggest) selling the farm and settling up our affairs in such a way that Norma and I could be looked after once Fleurette was satisfactorily married.

Francis had a cozy picture in mind of me and Norma rooming together in some small cottage in town: two twin beds in an attic with a wash-stand and a toilet adjacent, and a little parlor where we'd sit in the evening and complain about the price of running the gas lights. I couldn't bear to hear about it again.

Over the next few weeks, the stories about my case ran in every paper in New Jersey and New York, and clippings were starting to trickle in from as far away as Texas and Nevada. They came in pale blue envelopes accompanied by notes from schoolgirls wishing me well. They came on official city letterhead, from police chiefs offering me a position as matron if I were to be ejected from New Jersey. (It didn't seem so far-fetched that I might be ejected from the entire state, given the controversy.) One even arrived from an inmate in Vicksburg, Mississippi, who had picked up the paper just before her arrest and persuaded a sympathetic guard to let her dash off a note to me, which she enclosed along with the article.

"Those ladies are lucky to have you at the jail" was all it said.

"Girl Deputy Fired" read the headline from Mississippi, but I wasn't fired, not yet. I followed John Ward's advice and turned up at the jail every day. Mr. Courter (I could still not grant him the dignity of his title) had no choice but to allow me inside: Judge Seufert's office was in the adjacent courthouse, and any attempt to lock me out before the civil service commission's ruling would be met with a swift court order.

I was fortunate, at least, that Judge Seufert had been the one to refuse to swear in my replacement. I wondered if Mr. Heath had a hand in it. The judge had always taken my side and very much approved of the idea of a lady deputy who could step in and take a firm hand with wayward girls. The decision concerning my fate was not his, ultimately—it fell to the civil service commission to rule on the matter—but in his refusal to swear in the new deputy, he'd sent a strong message that I was not to be trifled with until the decision came down.

Meanwhile, I went to work every day and behaved as if nothing had happened. The jail ran more or less as it always had, the only change being that a belligerent and deeply unpopular man occupied the office of sheriff. Mr. Courter must've thought he could dismiss us and have us gone that afternoon. He obviously hadn't considered the possibility that we'd be stuck working together for another month after he'd made it plain that our presence wasn't desired.

He had his supporters, of course, among the guards and deputies. They'd been loyal to Sheriff Heath in the way that any man in law enforcement was broadly loyal to his chief, but some of them were unconcerned with ideology or any particular philosophy of criminal justice. They wore the uniform, they guarded the jail, they caught a criminal now and then, and for that they were paid a good wage. It wouldn't bother them to work for Mr. Courter. He was simply the new sheriff. The inmates hadn't changed, and the criminals wouldn't change, so they were satisfied, and did what they could to ingratiate themselves to the man now occupying the sheriff's office.

Mr. Courter tended to huddle with that small band of loyalists behind closed doors, and to call on them when there were arrests to be made, inmates to be transported, or eviction papers to be served. All the routine civil and criminal work of the sheriff's office continued, except that it was conducted by a much diminished force.

I never once saw Mr. Courter walk through the jail, or speak a word to the inmates. He hadn't, as far as I knew, asked a question about how the jail was run or given us any direction whatsoever. He seemed strangely uninterested in the day-to-day workings of the facility of which he'd endeavored so mightily to seize control. He'd campaigned vigorously against Sheriff Heath over the security at the jail, and the escape attempts, but had done nothing yet to change how the place was run, nor given any indication of how his plans were to be carried out.

We deputies kept our heads down and steadfastly avoided any talk of the civil service case. We saw to it that the shifts were covered, that the kitchen ran as it should, that the laundry crew did its work, and that the ordinary intakes and discharges were handled properly. A few cast about for other jobs, but there wasn't much on offer beyond a factory shift. With the threat of war drawing ever nearer, most of the men hoped for a victory at the civil service commission and the opportunity to cling to their jobs in the face of uncertainty.

If I'd been fighting this alone, I would've been the least popular person at the Hackensack Jail. Everyone would've turned against me in an effort to curry favor with the boss. But instead, the other deputies were depending upon me. They had all gone in secret to meet with John Ward, and to have the situation explained to them.

"Miss Kopp's bearing the brunt of this," he told them, "but she's doing it for all of you, and you'd damned well better show her some courtesy. If she wins, you all keep your jobs, whether you want them or not."

Mr. Ward managed to persuade them, to my everlasting relief. The men remained quietly cordial, and helped me in whatever small ways they could, without ever attracting Mr. Courter's suspicion.

I saw Mr. Heath only once over the weeks it took for the commission to decide my case. He was walking out of a bank as I happened to pass by. The setting, naturally, brought to mind the financial difficulties the election had rained down on both of us, but on him in particular.

"Are you a bank president now?" I asked, trying to sound light about it.

"A bank clerk, if I'm lucky," he said. "They wanted to put me on guard duty, but Cordelia won't hear of it. I'm not permitted to take a job that requires me to carry anything more lethal than a pencil."

I hated to see him stripped of his badge. He looked diminished without it. I was wearing mine, of course, and he noticed. "You're still fighting. I knew you would."

"I'm only doing it to help the others. Mr. Ward assures me it's a straightforward case. He says the civil service laws are unambiguous, just as the Republicans intended when they wrote them."

"Then you won't have any trouble keeping your job."

"A job I don't want anymore." My voice broke just then, and I hated myself for it. I sounded like a petulant child. "I won't work for him. He hasn't spoken a word to me in all this time."

"That doesn't sound too bad," Mr. Heath said. "I'd work for him, if he promised never to speak to me."

"Don't make a joke of it. It's unbearable, watching him going in and out of your office, and driving off in your wagon."

He looked at me in surprise. "Miss Kopp. It was never my office. It belongs to the citizens. They put me there for three years, and then they decided to give it to him. You'd best get used to that, if you want to work in public service."

I glanced up and down the street, feeling as forlorn and desperate as I ever had. Men were going in and out of the bank in their everyday suits, women were rushing past in their new winter coats, and on the street was a steady parade of black automobiles. The world had gone on, but I had not.

"I don't know that I do want to work in public service anymore, Sheriff—Mr. Heath. The position seems to have lost whatever attraction it once held for me."

He crossed his arms in front of him and looked down at his shoes. "You might as well call me Bob. Everyone else does."

I couldn't bear it. "I don't believe I will."

❧ 36 ❧

EVEN MY OWN inmates followed the news, as the papers circulated among the guards and made their way into the jail laundry and kitchen. Everyone knew that I'd turned the fight for my job into a national scandal.

"I ought to be asking for your autograph," said Ruth Williams, the actress turned robber.

"I don't want any sort of celebrity over it," I said, "but I didn't have a choice. I'm only trying to stay in my position to look after you."

"What is going to happen to us?" called Ida Smith from the other end of the cell block. She and Louise Wilson had seen no progress in their case. They were stalwart in their refusal to testify against the young men, and claimed to have no knowledge of any other crimes they might've committed beyond robbing the chauffeur.

I never could persuade them to tell the truth. It was all too common at the jail for girls to get romantic ideas in their heads, and to refuse to testify against a man sitting in a cell downstairs. There was no percentage in remaining loyal to a man who would allow them to get mixed up in a crime, but they didn't see it that way.

Providencia Monafo was sitting silently in her cell when I went by, working at a bit of knitting with the blunt wooden needles the inmates were allowed. She never knitted or performed any kind of domestic art when she first came to jail, but after almost a year behind bars, she'd taken up a few pastimes: the sort of utilitarian knitting she'd been taught as a girl (mittens and slippers, mostly), a few solitary card games, and a simple cross-stitch meant only to enliven the hems of the house dresses she wore every day.

She looked better, too. She put her hair up in the same neat bun every day. Her skin, which had been ravaged by the effects of lice and unhygienic living, had responded to the jail's modest regimen of daily soap, water, and petroleum jelly. It wasn't much, but she was now a cleaner, better-rested, and infinitely healthier woman than she'd been a year ago.

"You can't stay," she said when I walked over and leaned against the bars of her cell.

"Well, that isn't for you to decide," I said, in an effort to be light-hearted about it.

Providencia shook her head and stared darkly at me: she was immune to anything like humor. "If he don't want you here, you should go."

She was right, of course. Even if I won my case, it was impossible to think of working for John Courter. He refused to say a word to me as I came and went at the jail. We stayed out of each other's way, and I have no doubt that he, too, was counting the days until the commission ruled.

"He doesn't want me here—he's made that plain," I said. "But I must defend my position, and the role of a jail matron. I'm doing it for all of you."

Providencia squinted at me, unsatisfied. "Who knows about me?"

"Only Sheriff Heath and I," I said. "Mr. Courter was never

told." Providencia had been quick to take responsibility for shooting her tenant, but didn't want it known that she'd been aiming for her husband, who would undoubtedly seek revenge. If I was gone, there would be no one to protect Providencia if she were to be released early, or if her husband were to try to come and visit her.

"I could speak to some of the guards," I offered.

But Providencia shook her head. "Don't say a word. When it's my time to go, I'll go."

I DID SPEAK to John Courter once, and it only showed me how ill-prepared he was to run our jail. (I thought of the jail as belonging to me, and the other deputies and guards and even the inmates, but not to him.) I was walking out of the kitchen with my own supper, late one night in the middle of December, when Mr. Courter came marching down the corridor with one of the men he'd hired on after the election.

Between them was a young woman, skinny and scantily dressed, her hair in disarray and a thin coat slipping off her bare shoulders. Even with the deputy holding her by one elbow (Mr. Courter quite conspicuously wasn't touching her), she wobbled and wove with the unmistakable gait of a drunkard.

She couldn't have been more than seventeen.

I went to them and reached out to take her, in an almost matter-of-fact way, but John Courter stepped in front of her. "Scott's got this," he said, referring to the man behind him. I knew I was at last meeting Walter Scott, the man Judge Seufert refused to swear in as my replacement.

I summoned my manners and said, "How do you do? I only meant to take the young lady for registration and . . . to get her settled."

I hated to announce in front of the girl that she'd be de-loused.

276

She would know, even under the effects of liquor, what an unpleasant proposition that might be, and would kick up a fuss.

Mr. Courter spoke to his deputy. "They think everything around here requires a woman's touch. Do you suppose you can handle writing her name in a book and tossing her in the de-lousing room?"

"Tossing me *where?*" the girl shrieked, just as I knew she would. She flailed around and slipped momentarily away from the deputy, who only had hold of her coat sleeve and not her elbow. For reasons I couldn't imagine, she wasn't handcuffed.

It gave me a wicked little taste of gratification to see an inmate escape, however fleetingly. The deputy chased after her and threw one of his massive arms rather roughly around her neck and kept her pinned to him, her head pressed against his chest. It was an unprofessional maneuver. He hadn't had any training in holds at all. In a position like that, a girl had her legs free, and might just jab a knee into whatever soft parts were suddenly in close proximity.

I can't say that I was displeased when she did just that. Deputy Scott—a substantially built man, mind you, thick of neck and broad of shoulder—shrieked and let go of her again. It was with immense satisfaction that I collared her and snapped the handcuffs on those skinny wrists.

She was a little thing, but she was fiery. I liked her already.

Deputy Scott leaned against the wall, panting and red-faced. John Courter looked disgusted with both of us.

"It has been the policy of this jail," I said, "to have a matron present in the shower room, for the most obvious of reasons."

"My policy is to station a male guard outside," John Courter said, although from the way he was glaring at his deputy, I wondered who he would appoint to the job. "I'm sure the girls can handle their own washing-up."

I hated to say anything more in front of an inmate, but I already felt as if this girl (I didn't even know her name yet) was a kindred spirit and wouldn't mind a little rough talk.

"I'm afraid you cannot," I said. "You've obviously never combed an inmate for lice. They can't do it themselves, and women in particular have such long hair. Nor would they do it, if you left them alone with a comb and a bottle of ointment. They'd pour the ointment down the drain and bring the infestation right into the jail, and then you'll have an outbreak on your hands. Furthermore, women in particular are quite expert at secreting away small items on their person, such as a file, a knife, or a hatpin sharp enough to take out an eye. That's why they strip down to their altogether with one of us watching. Which one of you would like to volunteer to see Miss . . ."

"Frederick," the girl offered.

"Miss Frederick, in the shower room, wearing nothing but her charming smile?"

Miss Frederick managed, in spite of her compromised state, to put on a charming smile.

I wish I could say that we left Mr. Courter speechless, but an incompetent man is never without another terrible idea. To Deputy Scott he said, "Those are the duties of a nurse. We can have one here from the hospital in thirty minutes. There's no need to keep a matron on day and night."

"That isn't all I do," I said. "I'd tell you all about it if you'd let me."

In fact, I wanted nothing more to do with Mr. Courter, but with Miss Frederick weaving back and forth under my grip, I had to consider the welfare of my inmates. Perhaps Deputy Scott would listen to what I had to say and persuade his boss. He'd recovered somewhat from his injuries, but couldn't bring himself to look at Miss Frederick.

Mr. Courter was having none of it. "The voters did not put me into office so that I would run this jail according to your instructions. Take the girl with you, and Deputy Scott will see about hiring on a nurse next time."

I never thought I'd miss that de-lousing room, but as Miss Frederick and I went off to do our business, I was quite mournful at the prospect of never seeing it again.

⇥ 37 ⇤

THE DECISION CAME on December the twenty-first. At Fleurette's insistence, I'd worn my very best suit, somber gray wool
trimmed in a collar of pale blue silk that Fleurette said made me
look more like a woman of the world. I wasn't sure how that would
induce the commission to rule in my favor, but I didn't bother to
ask. I felt like I was dressing for a funeral, and numbly accepted
whatever Fleurette handed me.

The deliberations of the civil service commission were private,
but outside their doors, the usual crowd of courthouse reporters
and other interested parties milled about. John Courter was called
in to answer the commission's questions, but neither I nor my attorney was permitted inside, so we waited in the hall.

"I wouldn't flatter this proceeding by calling it judicial,"
Mr. Ward said, as we sat side-by-side on a bench. "They're not
in there judging the merits of your case so much as they're trying to find out how far they can bend the law without breaking
it."

"Then why was Mr. Courter given a chance to speak?"

"Oh—well, he's the sheriff."

He was making a joke, but it didn't come off well. "They probably want to know who he plans to keep on if the ruling goes

his way," he added, "now that he's had a month to work with all of you."

"Well, he doesn't plan to keep me," I said.

It was an interminable wait outside the commission's meeting room. A few of the reporters tried to interview me, but I brushed them away. As I sat in the hall and watched the minutes tick by, I could think only of the losses, the defeats, and the failures: The fugitive who had escaped under my watch the previous year. The girls who couldn't be helped. The inmates who were too hardened by their own misfortunes to ever trust me. Tony Hajnacka, breaking loose and running for the river. It was an impossible line of work, as I thought back on it.

Sheriff Heath had always found something heartening, something spine-straightening, in the notion that our work was never done. "We're just here to hold the line against lawlessness," he would tell me, enlivened by the prospect. "I can promise you right now that you'll never rid this world of crime or trouble or turbulence. All you can do is to take a stand against it."

There was a time when I allowed myself to be cheered by that idea, too, but no more. I sat with my own miserable thoughts, until at last a door opened and interested parties were invited to step in and to hear the decision. John Ward had gone over to listen at the door and was one of the first inside. The reporters all crowded in after him, along with a few other public servants whose jobs were on the line. A couple of the other deputies had come over to hear the decision, and they, too, rushed inside.

But I stayed on my bench. There was no good outcome for me. If they ruled in my favor, I couldn't work for John Courter anyway. If they ruled against me, I'd be dismissed immediately. What difference did it make?

It will come as no surprise that I succumbed to a ferocious head cold just as the civil service commission announced its decision. The early indicators had been rolling in all morning, like clouds swarming before a storm. First came a pounding at my temples, then a raw scratching at the back of my throat, a dull ache in my hips and shoulders and every other joint, and, finally, just as the door opened, a noisy and violent sneeze.

That wasn't all. The work of a sheriff's deputy is physically difficult: even on a fairly tranquil day, one might have to hoist a recalcitrant suspect into an automobile, wrestle with an inmate who refuses to enter or exit her cell, or shoulder a basket of laundry or a tub of dishes. In a jail, there is no one else to do the heavy work. The deputies and the guards take it up equally, and, from time to time, we pay a price.

At that moment I was nursing a sore shoulder brought on by Miss Frederick slipping in the shower just as I was taking the last of her undergarments from her. Although she was dainty, she was quite wobbly as well, and tugged fiercely on my arm as she went down, wrenching it backward just enough to do some damage. Something was not quite right in my hip as well, owing to a tug-of-war with the heavy old mangle that finally had to be taken out for repair.

Both of those injuries reached their boiling point as I waited in the hall. When the decision was announced, I had every intention of rising to take the news with dignity. In fact, I could hardly heft myself off the bench, and when I planted my right arm to give myself some purchase, the shoulder gave way.

The reaction was muffled behind the wooden door, but I knew it soon enough. The door burst open and Mr. Courter—Sheriff Courter, there was no way around it—was the first one out. He went right up to me, and spoke the words he'd been waiting to say for months.

"I'll take your gun and your badge, Miss Kopp. You're dismissed."

⚗ 38 ⚗

I DID MANAGE to stagger to my feet, although I was, by then, considerably enfeebled. As such, the wrenching feeling I might've had while I unpinned my badge and slid my gun from my belt was muffled by the resurgence of my injuries and the insistent pounding of my head cold. When John Courter took those heavy bits of metal from me, still warm from having been worn close to the body, I felt that I'd lost the only anchor holding me on solid ground. I could've floated away, there was so little left of the person who had once been Deputy Constance Kopp.

I didn't march out of the courthouse so much as I limped. The reporters hounding me for a quote backed away quickly when I scowled at them from behind a wet handkerchief. By the time I arrived home, over an hour later, a fever had taken hold. I surrendered to the exquisite agony of it, even reveled in it, as there was no room in my mind for anything but my corporeal suffering. I was free from worry, from panic, from blame, and from wondering why. It was a relief to be so thoroughly flattened.

Norma took up the role of nursemaid during those first few days. Her services were much needed. My raw and swollen throat prevented me from saying more than a few words at a time. Anything I did try to get out would trigger a coughing fit that strained my ribs and further aggravated my already inflamed vocal cords. If I put my head on the pillow, I couldn't breathe, which forced me to sleep sitting up, and that meant that I hardly slept at all. No position was comfortable, owing to my strained shoulder and tortured right hip. I had no appetite and refused anything but tea and an occasional small bowl of Norma's noodles drowned in butter and salt.

Norma was up and down the stairs constantly with trays, mustard plasters for my chest, hot-water bottles for my feet, and ice packs for the shoulder and hip. A hot bath seemed to offer the most relief, so she drew one every day, sometimes twice, and carried up kettles of boiling water to add to the tub as it cooled. I hung my head over the water, my hair down around me like a curtain, and gasped and choked over the rising steam.

All of these ailments went on longer than they should have. On the fifth day, Bessie sensed that reinforcements were needed and appeared with jars of soup, delicate sandwiches on spongy bread, and every sweet that had ever tempted me: coconut cake, cherry tarts, meringues, hot cinnamon buns. Bessie was a woman of a great many talents, but chief among them was the ability to revive a flagging appetite. I rallied under the influence of her good cooking. I took a cup of coffee for the first time, and put away a cinnamon bun fresh from the oven.

Bessie sat on the edge of my bed and watched me eat. "I wake up every day and it's the same," I croaked, between bites. "I still have a horrible head cold, it hurts to move, and John Courter is still sheriff. If only one of those would change, I might do better."

She murmured sympathetically and poured a little more milk into my coffee. Fleurette had taken a chair by the window, where she worked at whatever hand-stitching needed doing, while Norma leaned in the doorway.

"The head cold is breaking up, I think," Norma said, with the air of someone describing the ice on a river. "The shoulder needs a little more time. John Courter will take three years."

"Yes, and where will I be by then?" But that was too much talking for me, and brought on another coughing fit. I could only nod in answer to questions and dab at my eyes. Bessie speculated as to whether a hot cherry compote might go down easier, and I indicated, with what hand signals I could manage, that it just might.

"I've been waiting until you're better to ask you about this," Norma said. She held up my little green notebook. "You tossed your coat down when you came in, and it slipped out."

I reached for it and Norma handed it over. There were the names and addresses of all my probationers, with notes as to their progress. What would become of them? Would Mr. Courter assign another deputy to make my rounds? And what would happen if one of them had an unfavorable report? I hated to think of any of them going back to jail because I wasn't there to intervene.

I tried to say something about it but could hardly get a word out. Norma snatched the book away. "I'm going to the jail to collect your things. One of the deputies was kind enough to gather them up for you."

"Who—" I didn't know what had become of any of the other deputies. Had they all lost their jobs?

Norma knew what I was about to ask and answered it. "In the end, Mr. Courter only disputed your appointment. The other deputies were also deemed exempt from the civil service rules, but he kept them on. The guards were obviously civil servants and never should've been caught up in that mess, so they're fine, too."

"Then there was no point to it," I croaked.

"Oh, I think there was. You delayed the whole mess by a month, and Mr. Courter had time to settle down and realize he needed those men. Morris has gone into retirement. The rest have jobs if they want them."

"Then isn't that fine for them," I muttered. It was ungracious of me to be bitter over it: after all, the feud had always been between me and Mr. Courter. He would've gotten rid of me somehow. But I wasn't ready to be gracious about any of it.

Norma was still holding the notebook. "Well? Should I hand this over to the sheriff?"

There it was, between the green leather covers: all of my good intentions. Everything I believed I could do right, and do well. The evidence of my diligent work, and of the girls' willingness to turn their lives in a better direction. If I had only succeeded—if I could only have served under another sheriff for a few more years—I would've made something substantial out of my program. I would've gone off to one of those conferences for policewomen, and held my green notebook high, and told of the good work we'd been doing in Bergen County.

What was it now, but a list of the names of formerly delinquent girls along with information that Sheriff Courter might see fit to use against them?

I shook my head and coughed again into a handkerchief. "Don't give it to him. It belongs to me. But there's something I want you to do."

⇥ 39 ⇤

NORMA PROVED HERSELF to be a dogged and efficient probation officer. She took up her new responsibilities with the same
stolid determination she applied to any other task. Whether she
was thumping on a fence post to set it upright, or warning a girl
accused of waywardness to keep her wits about her, Norma was
equally blunt and pragmatic.

"I've come to warn you that Deputy Kopp won't be looking in
on you any longer," she would announce when the door opened,
without bothering to make sure that she was, in fact, speaking to
the woman whose name appeared on my list. "In case you believe
that to be good news, it isn't. She was the only one keeping you
out of jail. Now you'll have to look after yourself, which is to say
that you'll have to behave even though there isn't anyone here telling you to do it."

Without waiting for a response, she would push on down the
road to the next address, leaving the girls to call out their questions to her sturdy tweed-covered backside. There were fifty addresses in all, some of them outdated, but Norma was nothing if
not thorough and thought it best to scatter her warnings far and
wide, in much the same manner that she broadcast seed on the
meadow in the spring.

She decided to carry out her duties by horse and buggy, as it would've taken half the day to work out train and trolley schedules. Besides, Norma liked her solitude and told us that she found the prospect of a day-long buggy journey, with only the hollow clap of Dolley's hooves for conversation, to be immensely diverting. She packed a hamper full of potato and pickle sandwiches and set out every morning for a different quadrant of the county, her route having been carefully mapped out the night before. She carried with her every town directory, atlas, and map in the Kopp family's possession to aid her if she got lost.

Naturally, she took a basket of pigeons along. Why wouldn't she? It was the perfect opportunity to travel a good distance, carry out a mission, and report back to headquarters on the outcome. For once, she had no reason to cut out a newspaper headline or to write a coded message that no one at home would bother to puzzle out. She could instead tell the truth about her whereabouts and what she was accomplishing, using the military-style language she'd adopted since our return from Plattsburg.

"No difficulty with the Swedes" read the message about Katie Carlson, lodging with her aunt in Hawthorne.

"All secure on Seventeenth Street" came the report about Mary White, arrested for soliciting men while dressed in a crepe mourning gown, with a Bible under her arm.

"Message delivered in Teaneck" was the best she could do when confronted by an aggrieved mother of five who had been arrested for drunkenness at a train station, but persuaded to return home to a life of sobriety and a resumption of her maternal duties.

It took her ten days to reach every address. The business clearly gave her a fine feeling of accomplishment, although she grumbled every night about all the chores that were being neglected in her absence, and the half-hearted efforts at meals Fleurette was turning out on her own.

"But I heated up Bessie's good soup!" Fleurette said in her defense, and I agreed, pointing out that Bessie had also left an entire coffee can filled with gingersnaps to see us through after the coconut cake was gone. We were more than adequately provided for.

My head cold did recede, eventually, and my other aches and pains loosened their grip a little at a time, but nothing could be done about the multiple sorrows that dogged my every waking minute. It reminded me of the weeks after my mother died: every morning I'd wake up, and for just an instant I wouldn't remember what had gone so terribly wrong, what had been lost. Then it would all rush back.

I slept late, went to bed early, and spent long hours during the day in my bedroom, reading novels. I did look at a newspaper now and then, but I couldn't bear to see a word in print about the sheriff's office, or to read about the cases that should've been mine.

A woman might, under such circumstances, throw herself into domestic work, but I declined to do so. I left Norma in charge of the kitchen and most other household affairs, and Fleurette handled the laundry. I was occasionally seen washing out a cup in the sink, but beyond that, I confess that I made little in the way of contributions to our household.

Weeks passed in this manner. Christmas went by unnoticed. Bessie persuaded us to come for dinner once during those bleak months, but it was a colorless affair save for the always excellent roast duck. Everyone had been warned not to say a word to me about my work, past or future, and as such they found little to say to me at all. I sat in the corner, let the conversation drift around me, and buttered one roll after another as they came out of the oven. There is nothing like a hot buttered roll to soothe a troubled spirit. Bessie put out a second batch just for me.

Fleurette was miserable, too, in light of our looming penury. It fell to her to bring home some of her own wages and to contribute to the running of the household. She was shocked at how much everything cost, and complained constantly about her own deprivation. She missed all the holiday parties down in Fort Lee because she couldn't afford a new dress, and she moaned endlessly over the extra work she'd taken on, and the difficulties of traveling back and forth to keep up with May Ward's wardrobe.

There was some talk of her opening a seamstress shop in Ridgewood, or taking a position in one of the better dress shops in Paterson. Norma and I raised no objections to those plans, if they'd bring in a reasonable salary. But we were deep into the winter by then, and Fleurette found it too cold and gloomy to make any sort of change in her own circumstances. It was all she could do to cling to her old routine, and to stick to the work that was, for her, familiar and reliable. Perhaps in the spring, she said, she would look for something new, after the ice thawed. But not now.

This was the excuse Norma and Fleurette applied to me, as well, although I never said anything of the sort aloud.

"There's a foot-long column of positions for women," Norma would declare in the evenings as she read over the women's employment advertisements in the paper. "You'll have no trouble finding something."

"In the spring," Fleurette would add.

To her credit, Norma never argued with that. It seemed that they had agreed, between the two of them, to allow me a mourning period that was set to expire when the snow thawed. I had no opinion about that one way or another. I couldn't imagine going around and telling employers why I'd been so very publicly humiliated, dismissed, and defeated. How would I explain myself to a sheriff or a police chief in some other city? Where would I begin? And how would I excuse the trail of press clippings that would surely follow me even if I went far away: the inmate I'd allowed to escape, the medal denied me by the Board of Freeholders, the stinging criticism during the election, and my final, failed effort to keep my job at a jail where I wasn't wanted?

I couldn't imagine it, so I didn't try.

On one of my better days, when I was up a little earlier than usual and managed to get my own toast and coffee together, Fleurette did venture another suggestion. "Why don't you and Sheriff Heath go together to one of the police departments and put in your applications? They might hire the two of you."

I jerked around at the sound of his name. "He's not Sheriff Heath anymore."

Fleurette rolled her eyes. "Mr. Heath, then. What is Mr. Heath doing, anyway? He must've found an occupation for himself by now. He'd have to. He has a family to support."

She said it rather pointedly, hoping I would notice that I, too, had a family to support. But I wasn't taking any hints, and I wasn't allowing myself to think at all about what occupation Mr. Heath might have found for himself. I knew, with some shame, that he wasn't lounging in bed all day reading novels. Beyond that, I preferred not to guess.

There was one bit of cheering news, delivered in the form of a letter from Geraldine: Anna Kayser's divorce case had proceeded along speedily, more or less as Geraldine said it would. Both divorce suits—Anna Kayser's against her husband, and Mr. Townley's against Virginia—were won with a minimum of fuss. Neither Charles Kayser nor Virginia Townley put up any kind of fight owing to the incriminating photographs. Geraldine impressed upon Anna Kayser's physician, Dr. Lipsky, the certainty of her cause and the unpleasantness of a scandal in the papers. She even brought our reporter friend Carrie along for good measure, so the doctor could see whom he was up against.

He agreed not to fight the appeal of Anna Kayser's commitment. Instead he went before the judge and swore that he'd been misled by Charles Kayser, as had everyone else. It was good enough for the judge. Anna Kayser was released without fuss and sent home to live in the little house in Rutherford with her daughter, and was awarded a comfortable alimony.

"Another victory for Deputy Kopp," sang Fleurette as she read the letter over my shoulder. She might've been hoping to inspire in me some of my old verve, and to rally me to go out and find another such title for myself, but it had the opposite effect. I only sighed and put the letter down, and shrugged on my coat to go outside and watch Norma pounding nails into boards.

She was still making refinements to her pigeon cart. She mounted sturdier hinges to the wire cage on top from which the pigeons were to be released, and turned the rear doors on their side, so they could serve as a sort of swinging lift-gate, making it easier to step in and out. There were more windows around the side for ventilation, and a set of brackets had been added to hold the ladder, which would be needed to make repairs on the roof, or to reach pigeons who, for reasons of their own, refused to go inside. In a surprising act of deference to the coming automobile age, a separate hitch had been mounted on the front to allow the cart to be towed either by horse or machine.

"It looks battle-ready to me," I said.

Norma looked up in surprise and nearly swallowed the three nails clenched between her teeth. "Are you sure it's such a good idea to go out-of-doors?" she said, spitting the nails into her palm. "You might get your wind back, and then what would you do?"

"I'm only saying that the cart's coming along. When is it going to France?"

"This is only the model," Norma said. "Once it's perfected, I'll make up a set of plans. The Army will build them over there."

I walked around and looked it over. "Do you know how to make up a set of plans? Of the type the military might need, I mean."

Never in her life had it occurred to Norma that she couldn't find out how to do a thing if she put her mind to it. "Other people make them. It can't be very difficult."

"I suppose not." I turned to leave. I'd grown pasty over the winter, without the daily rigor of a deputy's work. I thought briefly that I ought to take a walk, just to put a little color in my cheeks, but when I looked up the road, I saw automobiles passing by and didn't want to face them.

Instead I wandered back into the house and up to bed. I'd read the same novel three times in a row, because I knew that if I asked Norma or Fleurette to go to the library, they'd tell me to go myself, and I wasn't about to do that. It didn't matter: I wasn't really reading the novel so much as I was passing my eyes over the pages in an effort to advance the day by another hour.

As I kicked off my boots and put myself back into bed—how gorgeous were those white sheets, how comforting the smell of a recently slept-in bed, beckoning me back—I couldn't help but marvel at the way Norma simply battled on, having never received any encouragement from anyone, nor a dollar of pay, nor any hint —not even the slightest hint—that any of her plans would come to fruition.

What kept her going? What woman, in her right mind, would spend a year putting together a pigeon cart for an Army that had no need of it? Didn't Norma know that it wouldn't matter—that it would never matter? Ten years hence, the cart would still be there, moldering behind the barn, having failed at its mission and been put to no other use.

I felt a certain sympathy for the cart when I thought of it that way.

But Norma had never been deterred from an idea. Once she settled on a course for herself, she simply marched along in that direction, head down, shoulder to the wheel. She was utterly convinced that she was right, and once she had taken up a position, it never occurred to her to entertain any sort of doubt. She was a plodder. She moved on.

There was something admirable in it, but then again, she'd had no success of any kind, and rarely ventured out past our barn herself. Maybe Norma's ruthless determination was not such a fine example, after all. Perhaps it made more sense, in light of a defeat, to stop and take stock. Maybe it was better, I told myself, to know when to quit.

With that in mind, I let my book drop to my chest and surrendered to the encroaching fog of a late morning nap.

The next day, on January 23, I turned forty and no one dared mention it.

⇥ 40 ⇤

WINTER WAS ALWAYS the costliest time of the year for us: trees crashed down in storms and crushed fences, shingles blew off roofs (both house and barn), and the gravel road running past our property heaved and calved during the cycle of freezes and thaws, with each neighbor having to contribute toward its repair. We were burning firewood, heating oil, and coal at an alarming clip.

Fleurette, it must be credited, took seriously the responsibility to bring in wages to carry us through. Had it been spring or summer, she might've been tempted to fritter away her earnings on little luxuries and amusements, but as we were trapped within the frozen confines of winter, there seemed to be no choice but to soldier through the short, gray days. She tacked up signs around Paterson and Hackensack advertising her willingness to make alterations and tailor to suit, and carried on a reasonable trade that way. The movie studios down in Fort Lee kept working through the winter, and she took on as much of their costuming as she could.

It meant a great deal of going back and forth by train in snow and slush. She and Norma finally ended their dispute over meeting the train at Ridgewood: Norma took her to the station faithfully, never complaining about it, and Fleurette returned home on schedule, to be met by a once-again uncomplaining Norma. When Fleurette did miss the train—it was inevitable, people do miss trains—Norma waited stoically for the next one. There was nothing else to be done, so they pushed ahead with gloomy fortitude.

By February I'd found a bit of work for myself in helping Fleurette, who was by then running quite a little business with all her tailoring and costume work. I set up a ledger-book, with a system of accounts and orders, and a weekly tally of income and expenses, to ensure that she spent just as much as she needed on materials and still had enough for the household coffers.

One day, Fleurette came home with a copy of a New York paper she'd picked up in Fort Lee. There was a long story about a policewoman in Los Angeles who traveled the country lecturing on the subject of women in the law.

"Look at this." Fleurette pointed with a dramatic flourish to a caption below a photograph of the woman. "It says here that she doesn't carry a gun or a club, and hasn't the power to arrest anyone. She says she wouldn't want to do a policeman's job, and why should she, when there are men enough to do it?"

I squinted down at it and grimaced, having nothing polite to say, but not wanting to cause offense, as Fleurette obviously had an argument to make and was eager to do so.

"All I'm saying," Fleurette persisted, unwisely, "is that maybe it was too soon. Maybe Hackensack wasn't ready for a lady deputy yet. You might've been twenty years too early to do a man's job."

Twenty years! In twenty years, I'd be sixty. That was a cold consolation. I put myself to bed a little earlier that night.

Norma, all the while, had been busy with her war-work. The new pigeon cart was complete. With help from Carolyn Borus, she'd created a flawless set of diagrams meant to show any Army man how to build the cart. The drawings were dead accurate and cunningly put together to demonstrate each step with no captions required at all, only sets of arrows and numbers to indicate how the various components fit together. Norma and Carolyn had studied every military manual and engineering journal they could get their hands on to understand what was expected by way of a diagram, and followed them faithfully.

Then they copied out the plans, over and over, and mailed them off with lengthy letters putting forth their scheme, to every Army man whose name appeared in the papers in connection to the war effort. It was Norma's idea that they could wheel their cart to a Plattsburg camp in the spring, and on the basis of that success the plans would be distributed to all the camps, and then taken overseas as soon as President Wilson gave the order. Everyone thought we'd be in the war by summer. The United States couldn't wait much longer.

No replies ever came to those letters. I knew better than to think that any would, but it pained me, nonetheless. Norma was experiencing her own defeat in another sort of election, one carried out one man at a time, but with results just as definitive. What would Norma do, when she ran out of letters to write, and it became clear that the Army had no interest in sending pigeons to war? The war would proceed without her and her birds, of course. But what would she do next? What would any of us do?

An announcement came from Norma, who heard it in Hackensack one day, that Mr. Heath had accepted a place as an accounts-clerk in some manufacturing enterprise—exactly the sort of thing he didn't want to do—and it occurred to me that the baby would be born soon. Fleurette thought we should send a gift and embroidered a little gown, but beyond the short note we enclosed with the package, I never once tried to correspond with him. I suspected that we both felt that we'd put our years in law enforcement behind us, and that we'd not only been kicked out of the jail, but out of our old lives, and our old selves. I understood why I hadn't heard from him. He probably understood why he hadn't heard from me.

I took walks around the outer boundaries of our property on fine days, something I hadn't bothered to do in years. Norma kept up the fences and handled the leasing of grazing land to the dairy, so there was no need for me to survey the fifty or so acres that remained of our land. But I found that I liked to walk it, always alone, crunching over the brittle and frozen stubble of our meadows and taking a turn through the scraggly woods at the far end of our holdings. I appreciated the silence, and the silver landscape against a gray sky, and the bare tree branches from which a solitary bird might alight when it heard me coming.

It was on one of those walks that I saw Anna Kayser.

At first I believed her to be an apparition. The snow had draped itself over our farm, obliterating every scrap of meadow grass and hedgerow bramble with its blessed whiteness. The sky was white, too, and when Anna Kayser appeared, she wore a long white coat with her head wrapped in a knitted white scarf. From a distance I could make out only two chips of color for her eyes. She didn't seem to walk toward me so much as float.

I stood and waited for her. She had followed what we called the back lane, an old farm road that traversed our land. When we were almost nose to nose, I said, "Did you come all this way on your own?"

I suspect she took my question to mean something else, because she said, "No. I had some help."

"You're free," I said, "and you look . . . wonderful." She did. Her eyes were bright and her tendency to frown had reversed itself, so the corners of her mouth lifted up even when she didn't mean to smile. Her hair had gone completely white, but it suited her. Strands of it poked out from under her scarf and shone like spun sugar. Even under the weight of her winter coat, she seemed buoyant.

"You can't know what it's like to have your liberty taken away, and then to have it restored," she said.

"I believe I can," I said. "When I was made a deputy, it was just like that. My liberty had been restored. Or . . . granted, I suppose, for the first time."

"And now?"

I shrugged. "Look at me."

"You look the same."

I don't know what compelled me to speak to her so forthrightly. The strangeness of coming across her in the snow, so like a dream, made it seem entirely natural for me to say, "I'm back where I was. Three years ago, I was a spinster living on a farm with her two sisters and no prospects. I'm that woman again, only now I'm forty."

Anna laughed at that. "Forty! What I wouldn't give to go back to forty and live it again! But I'm free now, and that's enough. I have my little house and my daughter. The older ones come to visit and soon one of them will be bringing a grandchild. I do as I please. No one ever asks why I'm taking so long in the bath. Charlotte and I can eat nothing but hothouse cucumbers for dinner and no one complains."

"That's a fine life," I said. I meant it. I envied her such contentment.

"You gave me that life," she said. "But—what are you doing with yours? I read the papers every day and don't see a word about what New Jersey's lady deputy is getting up to next."

All that dazzling whiteness turned to gray around me. "If they print something about it, please tell me. I'd like to know, too."

Anna slipped one gloved hand into mine. Her touch recalled the day, not too long ago, when I'd put her wrists in handcuffs.

"You're free, too," she said. "That's what I came to tell you, because I suspect you don't know it. You're as free as I am."

"But—"

"That new sheriff didn't want you at his jail, did he? But he doesn't decide what you do next. He has nothing to do with the rest of your life. If he did—what a mess you'd have on your hands!"

I had to laugh at that. Imagine: John Courter in charge of my life! He'd ruin everything.

"Don't sit around and suffer on his account," she said. "He won't appreciate it. He won't even know you're doing it. You might as well go off and find something grand to do next."

I felt lighter, all at once, but still I said, "I haven't any idea what that might be."

"You will, once you start to look," she said, and turned to go.

I should've invited her back to the house, or offered her a buggy ride to the train station, but as the whole meeting had seemed a mirage, I just watched her drift away, disappearing into the snowy landscape, treading in the same footprints she'd laid down before.

❧ 41 ❧

I WON'T PRETEND that I rushed right out and found a new occupation for myself, nor, for that matter, did I tell Norma or Fleurette what had occurred, thinking they might not believe me if I informed them that a woman I'd freed from a lunatic asylum appeared mysteriously before me in the snow. But I took Anna's words to heart, and remembered that it was useless to persist in suffering over what John Courter had done to me. For whom had I been carrying that burden? It wasn't any use to me: I might as well cast it off.

So I rose a little earlier each day, and tried to make myself useful, and to keep an eye on the papers in hopes that an opportunity would advertise itself. We were still ice-bound, but the light lasted longer in the evenings and the buds were lifting out of the bare tree branches, all of which suggested to me a renewed sense of purpose, even if I could not yet put a name to it.

And then, all at once, I could. The "something grand" that I might do with my life arrived a few weeks later, just as the snow thawed. It came not from an apparition in white at the end of our lane, but in the far more corporeal form of Norma Kopp.

She marched into my bedroom on a morning in early March and flung open the curtains. Fleurette followed on her heels, still in her nightgown, looking wild-eyed and desperate with her hair down around her shoulders. I thought there might've been a fire in the barn, so terrified was she.

But there was no fire, only Norma issuing orders.

"Get up," Norma said. "Pack your things."

I sank back into bed and squinted at the clock. It was only seven and scarcely daylight outside. "Are you sending me away? Have I been evicted?"

"It's worse than that," Fleurette said, hopping into bed with me and sliding her cold feet under the covers. "Tell her we're not going."

"Going where?"

Norma never wanted to go anywhere. I couldn't help but be intrigued.

Norma stood over us, hands on hips, a letter crumpled in her fist. We had no mail delivery that early, but Carolyn had paid a visit late the night before. She must've brought the letter. The two of them had sat up until midnight in the kitchen, talking of camps and carts and birds and soldiers, but there was nothing unusual about that, so I hadn't thought anything of it.

Norma looked like she'd been up for hours. She was dressed in a traveling suit and coat, and had an air about her of a woman with business to attend to.

"There's to be a Plattsburg camp for women in Chevy Chase. They've agreed to let me show my pigeon cart."

"An Army camp for women? Are you sure?" Suddenly I was wide awake and sitting bolt upright.

Norma snorted. "It's not an official Army camp. They want nothing to do with it, and neither does the Navy, but the officers' wives wouldn't be refused. They organized it themselves, so that women might be prepared to join in the effort. All three of us are going."

"We are?" The notion of women training for war was something I could hardly believe. I pushed a protesting Fleurette away and slid out of bed.

"Of course," Norma said, as if it were the only natural course of action for us. "I applied last month, and they accepted all three of us. We're going for six weeks, to train for war. We leave on Wednesday, and there's a hundred things to do before we go. Fleurette's to make our uniforms."

Fleurette was still quaking under my bed-covers. "I'm not going to camp!" she cried.

Norma turned and glowered at her. She could be quite fierce.

"Of course you are. You may put on one of your little shows if you must, and sew frivolous costumes, but you're going. Our places are paid for, and we're expected by the end of the week."

With that, Norma bustled out. She reminded me of myself, the previous year, when I'd been a woman of purpose. I wrapped a duster around my nightgown and went to follow her.

"But it's still so cold out!" Fleurette cried. "Couldn't we go this summer, when there will be fireflies and parties along the river?"

Norma didn't have to turn around and answer that, because I did.

"We can't wait until summer," I said. "Europe is at war and it's time to do our part. Take my uniforms and see if they can be made over for camp. Did they send Norma a pattern?"

"They did," Fleurette said gloomily. "They want us in the most dull and unflattering costumes imaginable."

"That sounds just right," I said. "Do mine first."

Historical Notes and Sources

CONSTANCE, NORMA, AND FLEURETTE KOPP were real people. I have tried to depict their lives as accurately as possible in these pages. To do that, I've relied on newspaper stories, interviews with family members, and public documents such as census records, birth certificates, property deeds, wills, and so on. To find out more about the real lives of many of these characters, please do visit my website (amystewart.com) and read the historical notes in the previous novels in the series, particularly the first one, *Girl Waits with Gun*.

Tony Hajnacka's story is true, although it actually happened in April, not September, of 1916. Tony really did try to commit suicide with a broken spoon while in jail, and was sentenced the next day to Morris Plains. The events of that evening, including the dive into the river, all happened as I described them. Sheriff Heath really did try to have a medal awarded to Constance for her bravery, but instead was chastised and had the responsibility for transporting inmates taken away from him. He clearly paid a price for standing by Constance, but his support for her was unwavering.

I know less about Anna Kayser's case. Constance was sent to pick her up and take her to Morris Plains along with Tony Hajnacka. The newspaper accounts said only that there was "some difficulty encountered" at the Kayser home that delayed them and forced them to return to the jail that night, but I don't know specifically what those difficulties might have been or what became of Anna Kayser. The names and ages of Mr. and Mrs. Kayser, and their daughter Charlotte, are correct, but everything else about them is fiction.

However, I based the fictional parts of Anna's story on a real-life account of a woman who was sent to institutions around that time so that her husband could be with other women. It's also true that postpartum depression and symptoms of menopause were poorly understood at the time and were common reasons for putting a woman in an institution.

Mrs. Pattengill is fictitious, but her story is also based on a similar crime that took place around the same time. Another minor character, Harry Core, was a real jewel thief who actually did try to break out of the Hackensack Jail with a metal file. The other women in jail and on probation are all based on real women who were arrested around that time for the crimes described. The unionists—and the working conditions they described—are a composite based on several striking workers arrested at the time.

The dynamics of the election, and the outcome, are based on newspaper reports during the campaign season. John Courter did attack Constance and Sheriff Heath with brutal insults, and Constance really was labeled a "demon deputy" and "troublesome lady policeman" in leaflets posted around town. After the election, Constance was fired because Sheriff Courter said that he had no use for a lady deputy. She fought for her job under the civil service rules but lost. Most of the other deputies were allowed to keep their jobs. (And if readers are wondering about the partisanship implicit in this story line, Sheriff Heath was in fact a Democrat, John Courter was a Republican, and all the election results were, in real life, exactly as I described them.)

As in previous books, I know less about what Fleurette and Norma were up to at the time. Fleurette really did perform a concert at the jail with Helen Stewart for Captain Anderson's "Brighter Day League" Salvation Army program. The songs performed, and the oath the inmates took, all come directly from that program. However, I shifted the timeframe around: this concert actually took place in the fall of 1915, not 1916. Another factual bit of Fleurette's story is that May Ward really was making movies at that time, although she might have been in Pennsylvania and not in Fort Lee. However, there was a booming film industry in Fort Lee, and there would have been plenty of work for a seamstress like Fleurette. Another detail that's rooted in fact is that Freeman Bernstein was booking entertainment acts at the Plattsburg camps.

About those Plattsburg camps: First, "Plattsburg" is spelled "Plattsburgh" today, but was more commonly spelled without the "h" at that time. These camps weren't always located in Plattsburgh, New York, but they were generally called "Plattsburg camps" after the location of the first one. These were military-style training camps for men who wanted to be prepared to go to war before the United States was officially involved. My descriptions of camp life and activities are based on newspaper accounts at the time.

Maude Miner, charged with overseeing the girls who hung around the camp, did in real life play a similar role. She founded the New York Girls' Protective League, whose aims were to both protect and police young women. She took on an official role with the War Department as the United States made ready to join the war. I wish I could recommend a good biography of Maude Miner, as she is a fascinating character, but it hasn't been written. I might have to do it myself. Meanwhile, many of her books are in the public domain and easy to find in ebook format.

Norma's interest in pigeons is, as in previous books, entirely fictional. However, it is true that pigeons were used in wartime communications, and American pigeon fanciers were eager to participate in the war effort. The Imperial War Museum in London does, in fact, own a collection of tiny horse-drawn mobile pigeon loft models, made during the lead-up to World War I. My description of Norma's models are based on those.

I quoted directly from these sources:

The *Hackensack Republican*'s gleefully mocking coverage of Constance's dive into the Hackensack River appeared on April 13, 1916, under the headline "Thrilling Movie Stunts by Sheriff Heath's Woman Deputy—Press Agents Tell How She Dived After a Crazy Man, Rescued Him, Fainted, Slept—Will County Buy Her a New Dress?"

The story Fleurette read about Red Cross hospitals in Paris appeared in the *New York Times* on November 13, 1915, under the headline "To Restore Faces Ruined in the War—American Organization Is Being Formed for the Establishment of a Hospital in Paris."

Sheriff Heath's speech at the jail comes from his own speeches, as quoted in the *Bergen County Democrat* on September 22, 1916, under the headline "Hot Shot from Candidate Heath." Some lines also came from a speech he gave to the New Jersey Conference of Charity and Corrections, which took place April 25–27, 1915.

"No Medal for Miss Kopp" ran in the *New York Times* on April 21, 1916.

"Miss Kopp, Ousted by New Sheriff, Just Won't Quit" was the actual headline in the *Evening Telegram* on November 16, 1916. The text quoted is a combination of that story and one the same paper ran two days earlier.